Treasure Built of Sand

Palmyrton Estate Sale Mystery Series, Volume 6

S.W. Hubbard

Published by S.W. Hubbard, 2019.

TREASURE BUILT OF SAND

First edition. May 15, 2019.

Copyright © 2019 S.W. Hubbard.

Written by S.W. Hubbard.

Chapter 1

Nothing is more soothing than a spreadsheet.

Manipulating the rows, controlling the columns, slicing and dicing the data—those activities bring peace to my troubled soul.

But today I'm not feeling the love.

I stare into my computer screen at our third quarter projected income as if the patterns in my Excel spreadsheet can be read like tea leaves.

If I were to get pregnant this month, the baby would be born in late June, the peak season for estate sales. I'd have to hire temporary workers to help Ty and Donna manage the workload while I'm out of commission... for what? Two months? Three months?

Ty has been with me now for three years. Wow—a lot has happened in that time. I'd trust him with my life, but do I trust him with my business? After all, he's only twenty-four with all the impulsiveness of youth.

Hiring Donna has turned out to be an excellent decision. But she still lacks confidence. If I'm not here every day, will she be able to keep Ty in check? But I'd only be out for three months, and they could call me at home every day.

Surely, I could be back at work with the baby in tow by September. I scan our cluttered workspace. The teetering towers of boxes awaiting shipment or removal to the dump, the tangle of wires connecting the computers, the printer, the coffee pot and the mini-fridge. This place would be a snake pit of danger to a toddler. But I suppose it's okay for an immobile infant. I could cram a Pack 'N' Play in that corner beside the supply cabinet, and I could use the folding faux-Japanese screen that didn't sell at the Feeney sale as a breast-feeding retreat.

Breastfeeding! I'm not even pregnant yet. But if I did manage to do it this month....

Our income would fall just at the moment when we need it to rise.

It's true I nurture Another Man's Treasure like the child I don't yet have, but now that Sean and I are trying to get pregnant, I have to be willing to relinquish more duties to my staff. I've been training Ty to manage smaller sales and give estimates, and he's learned so much. But what if we were to land a big job with lots of antiques and artworks right when I'm awake all night rocking a colicky baby? I drop my head into my hands.

This will never work!

My husband tells me I'm being overly controlling. My stepmother, the retired pediatric nurse, tells me there's never a convenient time to have a baby.

Just roll with it.

It'll all work out.

Only my father understands. We Nealons are not believers in puzzles that miraculously solve themselves.

We're chess players. Strategists. Planners.

Now that I've tossed out my birth control pills, I'm all-in on this baby creation project. But I can't relax until I have a plan that ensures my business and my baby will survive the birth.

So far, that plan has eluded me.

I look up from my projections when Ty charges through the office door and collapses into our favorite dilapidated armchair.

"I'm draggin' ass. Made my last trip to the dump."

"You had to haul the Gellner's sofa there?"

Ty arches his back until it cracks and stretches his dark muscular arms above his head. "Couldn't get Sister Alice to take it, not even for that family of Somalian refugees she's helpin'. Even people who just moved outta tents didn't want that ugly-ass couch."

That the burnt orange/mud brown/avocado green monstrosity with knobby wooden arms and a heinous dust ruffle flummoxed our favorite do-gooder nun is saying a lot. At Another Man's Treasure Estate Sales we strive to find homes for items we can't sell, but the Gellner home strained our abilities to the max. "This job has been a soul-crusher," I complain to Ty.

"For a big house in a nice 'hood, it sure didn't have much that brings in the large. Everything was old, but nothing was an antique or collectible."

Given that Mr. and Mrs. Gellner hadn't bought anything new since the Nixon administration, I thought when I accepted the job that we might find some seventies kitsch. But the Gellners seem to have been utterly joyless their entire lives. No Roberto Clemente baseball cards. No Sex Pistols LPs.

No *Love Boat* drinks coasters or Marimekko tablecloths. "Luckily, their son doesn't have unrealistic expectations. But putting on a sale in a five- bedroom colonial is twice as much work as that townhouse we did in Summit, and we'll make half the profit."

"Yeah, it was good luck for us that Summit guy got transferred to Paris and needed to empty his crib of all those leather couches and halogen lamps. That stuff *sold*. We need another big score." Ty stands and touches his toes. "But not a creepy house like the Tate mansion. I'd rather do ten boring houses than another one like that!"

Our last big-dollar sale took a toll on all of us, especially Ty. "Don't worry. I can't think of any other untouched historic homes that might require our services. I'd be happy with another transferred executive."

"You heard anything from Donna yet? Maybe she got us a new project."

As part of my campaign to delegate more tasks to my staff, I let Donna attend the monthly Rotary Club meet-and-greet. No matter how many "how to network effectively" books I read, it never gets any easier. I'd rather scrub toilets than go to that luncheon.

I've asked Ty if he wants to go to these networking events with me, but so far, he's always declined. Like me, Ty is a non-shy introvert. He's perfectly comfortable going out to talk to a potential client to offer an estimate, but he doesn't like the small-talk chit-chat of a networking event any more than I do.

On Saturday, when I was moaning about the Rotary event as we wrapped up the Gellner sale, Donna volunteered to go.

At first, I reacted like a mother whose child has asked to stay at home alone for the first time. "No, you're too young. You won't know what to do if the house catches fire. You'll let a serial killer in the door."

But then I realized Donna is a true extrovert. She could converse with a ficus tree, so why not use that to the company's advantage?

"Do you think you know enough about the business now to give a sales pitch?" I asked her.

"Absolutely!" Donna had danced around the Gellner's dining room, her ever-present spray bottle of white vinegar locked and loaded. "I've been role-playing with my cousin Carmine. He used to sell used cars, so he knows all about overcoming objections. Like, if I say we can clear everything out of your parents' house and sell it in two days, Carmine will say he could do that himself. And then I'll tell him how we can get more money for the stuff. Or how we can help if he gets emotionally overwhelmed. I roll through all our best marketing points."

"It was sweet that she'd been practicing with her cousin," I say to Ty. "I wonder if the overcoming objections role-playing came in handy?"

Ty smiles and shakes his head. "That girl's a talker. If it was me, I'd probably just say, 'Take us or leave us, I ain't beggin.'"

I crack up. "Honestly, that's usually what's going through my head when I make a sales pitch. It's taken me years to learn to repress it."

"That's why sending Donna to this lunch was a genius move. She don't have to fake it. She's honestly nice."

His words cheer me. Ty and Donna get along great. They'll be able to manage Another Man's Treasure if I have to take a few weeks off with a new baby.

As if she could hear us discussing her, Donna charges through the door. "Audrey, Audrey! Guess what? I got us a new customer at the luncheon!"

She dances across the office in the black suit she wears to all her Italian family funerals and the new floppy bow blouse she bought at TJ Maxx. "Except the job isn't in Palmyrton. It's in Sea Chapel."

Ty's brow furrows. "Sea Chapel? Isn't that near Rumson, at the Jersey Shore?"

"Yeah. Is that too far?" Donna spins to face Ty, her face a study in concern. "The lady says it only takes an hour and a half to get there. She has her main house here in Palmyrton, and this is her vacation house."

I don't want to throw water on the flame of her success, but I'm not sure Donna has reeled in the kind of client we're looking for. "It's not one of those beach bungalows that got damaged the last time we had a hurricane is it? I'm not signing on to sell mildewed furniture."

"Bungalow? No way! This house is gorgeous!" Donna whips out her phone. "She shared this picture. Five bedrooms right on the beach."

Ty peers over her shoulder and lets out a low whistle at the picture on the screen.

"So why does she want us to sell the contents? Is she putting the house on the market?"

"Uhm, I don't know. I'm sorry—I guess I should've asked. But she was so nice. I was telling this old fart about Another Man's Treasure when she came up and joined us. We started yakking and the next think I knew, she wanted an estimate. Her name is Brielle Gardner. She owns that gift boutique on South Main. That's why she was at the luncheon—to promote her own business. She seemed excited that she found us as a bonus."

Now I'm intrigued. "Elle's Choices. I've been in there. She sells seventy-dollar scented candles and hand-carved driftwood napkin rings." In other words, nothing I'd ever buy, but she does seem to have good taste and cater to a high-end crowd. I can't recall ever meeting her at previous Rotary Club events. So her beach house might be filled with good stuff. "How did you end the encounter?"

"I told her we were definitely interested...that you'd come and look at the house and give her an estimate. She said you could come tomorrow. I figured it was easier to back out than to stall and tell her you'd call her. Was that too aggressive?"

"Not at all. You handled it just right."

Donna beams. "So you're going to go see the house tomorrow?"

"Not me. We. You landed this job, so you can come with me to do the estimate."

Donna squeals! "Ooo, Audrey—I'm so excited. I like this part of the job even better than cleaning!"

Chapter 2

Late morning on a Wednesday in mid-September is an excellent time to drive to the Jersey Shore. The Garden State Parkway is as wide-open as the Nebraska prairie.

Well, that's an exaggeration, but it's not the bumper-to-bumper, road-rage inducing traffic jam that it is every Friday, Saturday, and Sunday from Memorial Day to Labor Day.

Donna and I cruise along singing to Bruce Springsteen and Bon Jovi. In just over an hour, we take Exit 114 and drive a few miles past lovely homes in Rumson. I navigate a bend in the road, and the GPS begins to chirp, "The destination is on your right."

43 Dune Vista Lane reveals itself.

Donna has her nose pressed against the car window. "Wo-o-ow, Audrey! Brielle's house is the most gorgeous of all these fabulous houses!"

Although I have a soft spot for shingled Victorians with wrap around porches, I have to agree that Brielle Gardner's house is quite spectacular. Pure white stucco in several tiers glows against the bright blue sky. The roof is sharply angled, fanning high and wide at the rear, which faces the ocean. The front door offers the only pop of color—a rich cerulean to match the waves.

I turn my trusty little Honda down the paving stone drive. Although the front yard is sizeable, the houses on either side are quite near. Oceanfront property in New Jersey is at a premium, and even the rich have to squeeze together to allow for as many houses as possible to have that ridge-top view.

We exit the car and stand before the huge double doors. Donna tugs at her slacks, the only ones I've ever seen her wear that aren't fifteen percent spandex. "Do I look okay?"

Before I can utter a word of reassurance, the doors open. "Oh, hello, hello! I'm *so* glad you could make it today!" The tall, slender woman who I assume is Brielle Gardner gives Donna an air-kiss and extends one long, manicured hand to me. "And you must be Audrey! D*elight*ed to meet you."

Brielle Gardner looks like she's been prepped for our visit by the kind of stylist who readies A-List stars for their red carpet walk at the Oscars. No one over the age of ten has natural honey blonde hair streaked with pale gold, but Brielle, at fifty, has a mighty fine imitation. She's wearing perfectly creased white capris and a coral and blue sleeveless blouse, both of which accentuate her light tan. None of that leathery, roasted brown beach skin for her. Her strappy blue sandals coordinate perfectly with the blouse, as does her coral mani/pedi.

"Come on back to the kitchen," Brielle waves us forward. "I was just having some tea and toast. Can I get you anything?"

She was recently eating in that outfit? I'd have jam on my pants and crumbs in my cleavage if I tried to have breakfast after I got so dressed up. To maintain that level of perfection, I'd have to be shrink-wrapped.

"No thank you. We're good." As Donna and I follow Brielle through the open-plan living area, we exchange an awed glance. The far wall is solid glass and we can see big green-blue waves crashing onto the empty beach. The colors of the furniture reflect the scene outside: pale, sky blue sofa, sand beige floors, ocean blue area rug, cloud white chairs.

Brielle passes behind a cream stone wall featuring a fireplace that faces both the dining area and the kitchen. When we enter the kitchen, the view stops us in our tracks.

"Wow!" Donna exhales.

I'm normally not one for revealing that I'm impressed, but a gasp escapes my lips, too.

Dazzling. Literally and figuratively. Everything in the room is white, blue, or stainless steel. Even the cookbooks lined up on a shelf have blue and white spines. The bright morning sunshine pours through the sliding glass doors glinting off the glossy surfaces. The deck on the other side of the sliders cantilevers out over the ridge, so it feels like we're standing in midair and could reach out and touch the waves.

If Brielle has been eating, there's certainly no sign of it. Not even a teaspoon in the sink. The kitchen looks like a model in a very high-end designer showroom. I feel that if I open the cabinet doors, the shelves will all be empty.

Brielle hops up on one of the sleek bar stools surrounding the white granite island. The subtle flecks of blue and gray in the stone are picked up in an intricately hand-painted ceramic bowl that's nearly three feet across. Donna touches it gingerly. "This is so beautiful. Is it from Italy?"

"Yes, we picked it up in a little shop in Sorrento. I used to carry some of their items in my shop in Palmyrton." Brielle rakes her slender fingers through her tawny hair. "I'm so *over* that now. It's too busy. Too ornate. I'm after a calming, Zen vibe. That's why I want to clear out the entire house. I'm starting over with a new decorator."

"You mean, you're not moving?" Donna blinks her well-mascaraed eyes. "But all your things are brand new. You want us to sell *everything*. Even these great stools? Even that perfect sofa?"

Brielle's lips compress ever so slightly. I can see she's a woman who doesn't like her decisions to be challenged. But Donna's oblivious to that subtle tell. She prattles on, twisting in her seat. "What about that gorgeous painting? Surely, you're going to keep that?"

I try to slide my foot over to nudge Donna's leg, but her stool is too far away. If she keeps this up, she'll talk us right out of the job she landed.

Brielle turns her gaze on the stunning expressionist seascape that dominates the wall nearest the dining table. A little shiver passes through her. Is she sad to be letting it go, or horrified she ever acquired such a thing?

"Yes, Hiraku Maki insists on working from a blank slate. I'm very fortunate that he found room for me in his schedule." She drops this name clearly expecting Donna and me to keel off our bar stools. But his hipness far exceeds our humble experience. If it's not on HGTV, we don't know about it. And if he's the kind of decorator who insists I have to purge every remnant of my own personality, I don't want to know about him.

Brielle faces us both with implacable finality. "So you can see it's imperative that the house be entirely empty by October 1."

Worry stabs me in the gut. "That's just two weeks from now," I object. "I need a little more time to do research, so I can get you the best prices." I won't say this to Brielle, but I know more about antiques than contemporary designers. I slide off my stool and peer into the living room. The sleek pale blue linen sofa and striped arm chairs didn't come from Pottery Barn, that's for sure. Even though they're immaculate, I won't get anywhere near what Brielle paid for them. But I know some New York interior decorators who would drool over this stuff. I just need time to catalogue it and get them out here.

Brielle stalks after me and lays a cool, smooth hand on my arm. "I don't care what you earn from the sale. I just want the house cleared."

I don't care what you earn from the sale? That's what clients tell me when they're the executors of their Great-aunt Mabel's paltry estate and they want me to get rid of the old gal's clutter. Brielle may not care if I sell all this at bargain basement prices, but *I* care. I want to wring maximum profits from this sale.

"The set-up won't take long," Donna offers. "We've never done a sale in a house that's so clean and uncluttered."

Brielle looks over her shoulder at Donna. "Clutter makes me anxious." Then she directs her gaze at me, with eyes the same limpid green as the ocean. Her hand has tightened on my arm, and her sharp nails prick my flesh ever so slightly. "I need to know you can unequivocally meet my deadline."

Geez, this is a woman used to getting her way. I try to imagine having so much money that I could afford to toss out all the furnishings in my vacation home without concern for compensation. My head isn't going there. First, I don't see a vacation home in my future any time in the next decade. Sean and I are still scrimping to replace the dog-chewed sofa in our family room.

But I won't profit at all if I don't get the assignment. I'm going to have to bust my hump, especially when I add in the hour commute to get here. "I was only hesitating because I won't be able to drive down here every single day." I take a deep breath. "But we can have the house cleared by October 1. I guarantee it."

Brielle's shoulders relax. I hadn't realized how tense she was. This Japanese designer dude really means a lot to her. I guess she needs to boast about him to her friends.

I step away from her and take out my iPad to snap a few pictures. "Will anyone be using the house in the next two weeks?" I sure hope she's not going to block my access on weekends.

"No. My husband, son, and I will all be in Palmyrton." Brielle brightens. "Would it make your work easier if you stay here?"

Donna's eyes widen. "Live in this great house while we work?"

Brielle pivots. "Why not? I'm getting rid of everything anyway."

I work hard not to laugh. Brielle isn't even aware of how horrible that sounds. It's as if Donna and I are dogs finally permitted up on the furniture now that it's going out to the curb. "That's a generous offer. It would make it easier if we could stay overnight, especially the night before the sale."

"I'll get you the keys and the code for the alarm system." She strides back to the kitchen and returns with a leather covered notebook and a Mont Blanc pen. "Now, tell me what else you require to get this project done on time."

"We need to walk through the entire house so I can take pictures. I can start working on estimates as soon as we get back."

"Easy enough. Follow me."

The only rooms we haven't seen on this level are the powder room, laundry room, and a small study. I take a few pictures and follow Brielle up the wide staircase. One side looks like it's totally open to the living room below, but there's an almost invisible Lucite railing. Nevertheless, I hug the wall as I climb.

Upstairs we follow Brielle into an immense master bedroom suite with a sitting room, dressing room, and the biggest walk-in closet I've ever seen. Who needs this much room for sundresses, sandals and bathing suits? The closet is totally empty. "You've already taken out your clothes. That's good. Are there other personal items you want to pull from the sale?"

Brielle stands in profile to me, her long, narrow nose and pointed chin outlined by the sun. Her nostrils flare. "Nothing. Sell it all."

"What about this nice family photo? You all look so happy." Donna has picked up from a side table a photo of Brielle, her handsome son, and her decidedly homely husband, framed in a white wood picture frame.

Brielle takes it from Donna, flips it over, and attempts to open the back. I guess she wants the photo if not the frame. Brielle's forehead furrows as she pries at the clips, but they refuse to budge. Next, a chunk of perfect coral fingernail sails through the air.

Brielle squawks and the frame crashes to the floor. Wood splinters and glass shards skid across the polished teak.

Did she drop it or throw it down?

Accident or fit of pique that she couldn't immediately get what she wanted?

I've only known Brielle Gardner for half an hour, so I can't tell. But I suspect she's not going to be the most easy-going client I've ever worked with.

"I can sweep that up," Donna offers.

Brielle stoops down to retrieve the photo from the mess, shooing Donna away as she does so. "My cleaning lady will take care of it." Then she leads us out of the master suite to the bedroom across the hall.

Decorated in shades of navy and pearl gray, this bedroom has a distinctly masculine air. "My son uses this room when he's here."

"How old is he?" Donna can't restrain her natural chattiness. "It looks too neat for a teenager's room."

And too impersonal. There's not even a favorite seashell picked up from the beach or a souvenir from the boardwalk.

"Austin is seventeen. He's naturally tidy—maybe it's genetic." Brielle waits while I snap a few pictures and we move on to two luxuriously decorated guest bedrooms. "You can make yourselves comfortable here when you sleep over. And there's another guest bedroom on the lowest level."

So we descend past the kitchen again to the lowest level of the house. The biggest TV I've ever seen hangs on one wall. A cushy half-round sofa faces the screen, and behind it stands a pool table. The windows face a swimming pool.

"Wow, your son and his friends must love hanging out here!" Donna comments.

True, this space could be a paradise for teenage parties, but I can't imagine Brielle allowing bowls of nacho cheese Doritos and red Solo cups full of SunnyD and vodka in this pristine cream and taupe room. Unlike Donna, I feel no need to comment. I keep taking pictures as Donna explores.

"Look, a little kitchenette and another bedroom and bathroom." I follow the sound of her voice and take my last pictures.

I feel a presence right behind me. Then Brielle's smooth low voice speaks in my ear. "Please don't mention to anyone that Mr. Maki will be decorating my home. He's doing it as a personal favor. He usually works on much bigger projects."

I edge away. My ear feels hot from her breath. "No problem. I don't know a soul to tell."

Chapter 3

Once we're outside, I toss Donna the keys. "You drive. I'm going to start my research."

Donna points the Honda toward Palmyrton and immediately starts chattering. "Wow, that's some house, huh? Do you think we'll make a lot of money? We've got to, right?"

"We'll certainly make more than on the Gellner house. The tricky part is getting the right buyers to follow us down here. Brielle's neighbors might show up for the sale to satisfy their curiosity, but I doubt one rich resident of Dune Vista Lane is going to want to buy another's cast-offs."

Donna bites her lower lip. "I hadn't thought of that. Hey, maybe we should promote the sale with some ads in the local newspapers in some of the less ritzy beach towns, like Keansburg and Monmouth."

"You work on that when we get back to the office." My fingers fly over my iPad screen as I Google the names of the designer furniture I took pictures of. Twenty grand for a sofa, five grand for a lamp. Unbelievable that Brielle would toss this furniture the way a college kid jettisons his Target nightstand at the end of senior year.

"Brielle must make a lot of money at her shop in Palmyrton if she can afford to redecorate this beach house from top to bottom," Donna muses as she merges onto the Garden State Parkway.

I snort. "I'm sure that shop is just a hobby—a way for her to satisfy her need to shop once she's already filled up her own houses. Let's just see what her husband does for a living."

A little more Googling and I have my answer. "C. Everett Gardner III, managing director of the Gardner Group, one of the biggest private equity firms on Wall Street. That's where all Brielle's money comes from."

Donna narrows her eyes in determination and floors the gas pedal. The Honda rockets past a lumbering church van in the right lane. "I'm embarrassed I don't know this, but what exactly is a private equity firm?"

"They gather money from rich people and use it to finance start-ups and then the rich people get richer and so does the firm." I let my iPad rest on my lap. "There's a whole 'nother world of wheeling and dealing out there that mere mortals like us know nothing about."

Donna casts me a sidelong glance. "Do you wish you were rich, really rich, and you could do anything you ever wanted?"

I don't answer immediately. When I was in college, many of my fellow math majors chose to become bond traders and stock analysts. I could have followed that path—I had the grades to be recruited by a top firm. If I had, I wouldn't be worrying about how we'll pay for a new furnace if ours dies this winter. But I'd despise getting up for work every morning. And if I'd become a stock analyst, I would never have solved the mystery of my mother's disappearance. Would never have met Ty.

Or Sean.

I have no regrets.

"I know it seems like I'm always worrying about money, but what really matters to me is running my business successfully. I wouldn't want to win a hundred million dollars in the lottery and then spend my days wasting it like Brielle. That would be boring."

"I suppose," Donna sighs. "But I just wish—"

I wait, but Donna doesn't continue. From the depths of her oversize purse in the back seat, her phone begins to trill the opening bars of "Born in the USA".

Donna twists in the driver's seat and looks over her shoulder. "That's Anthony's ring tone."

"Keep your eyes on the road," I command as the Honda drifts out of the left lane. "I'll get it."

When Donna's husband calls, she always answers. I fish her phone out of her purse, accept the call, and hold the phone up to her ear.

Donna opens her mouth to say hello, but before she can form the word, a volley of sound emerges from her phone. I can't make out the words, but they're fast and angry.

"I know. I thought we'd be back by now. But it took longer to get to the house than I thought. And then we had to talk to the lady and then..."

I look out the window in a futile attempt to give Donna some privacy, but I can hear Anthony's angry tirade continue.

"We are on the road. I'm driving, that's why I didn't answer right away."

I steal a glance at my assistant. Donna's hands clench the steering wheel, her knuckles getting whiter by the second.

"Because Audrey asked me to. She had to do some research. But Anth—"

A car lays on its horn as Donna changes lanes without signaling. I want to get home in one piece. "Pull over. I'll drive."

Donna pulls onto the shoulder of the Parkway, and I get out of the car to give her some space. As traffic whizzes past us, I pace on the shoulder. In the six months that Donna has worked for me, I've only met her husband Anthony once when he came to the office to pick her up. He's in his mid-forties, ten years older than Donna. I guess you could say he's good-looking—dark, thick hair, a strong jaw, broad shoulders, perfect teeth. But his muscle is starting to turn to fat and his smile is half sneer. Maybe I'm being ridiculous, but I still hold it against him that he cast his eye over our cozy abode and snorted, "This isn't exactly Trump Tower, is it?"

The insult didn't hurt my feelings, but I can work up a knot of anger every time I recall the emotions that passed over Donna's face that day. First, hurt, that he'd insulted the office she enjoyed working in. Then embarrassment that he'd insulted it in front of her boss. And finally, worst of all, shame that she had once again fallen short in her husband's eyes.

Right then I knew that Anthony is one of those people who makes himself feel bigger by making other people feel small. And I really can't forgive him for that.

At times, Ty and I have noticed bruises on her arms, but she has never missed a day of work or had a mark on her face. But there's no doubt in my mind that Anthony is emotionally abusive even if whatever he does to Donna physically doesn't rise to the level of assault.

The glare of the midday sun on the windshield makes it hard for me to see how Donna is doing. Finally, the driver's side door opens, and she emerges. Her eyes are red and swollen and her tears have left tracks of black mascara down her cheeks. Silently, I hold out my arms and she sinks into them, resting her head on my shoulder.

We stand there and sway in silence as the never-ending tide of New Jerseyans moving from one end of the state to the other surges past us.

What should I say? How can I help her? Sean has warned me not to insert myself into the middle of a domestic abuse situation in my usual bossy-pants way. He thinks Donna will turn on me to protect her husband as he has seen so many women do when he tries to arrest their abusers. He says both Donna and I will be worse off if she feels compelled to leave Another Man's Treasure to shield her husband. So up until now I've tried to be subtle. When we donate items to the Palmyrton Battered Women's Shelter, I talk about what great counseling services they offer. When my best friend Maura and I went away for a girls' weekend, I talked about how important it is for couples to maintain some personal space. But if Donna recognized those messages were directed at her, she didn't let on.

This is different. There's no denying she's in a crisis.

Finally, Donna lifts her head. She rubs her snotty nose against the sleeve of the blouse she was so proud of this morning. I guide her toward the passenger seat. "C'mon, let's get you some tissues and a drink of water."

After we're repositioned in the car, and Donna has done some preliminary clean up, she leans her head against the headrest and speaks while keeping her eyes focused on the roof of the car. "Nothing I do is good enough. Before I had this job, Anthony criticized me for not doing my part, called me a princess who didn't want to work. Now that I have a job I love that pays a decent salary, he criticizes me for neglecting him, not being available when he needs me." She takes a deep, quavery breath. "He called because he can't find his gym membership card. He's mad because I didn't answer right away. Mad that I'm so far away from home. Mad that I don't know where he put his stupid card."

"That's what abusers do, Donna—they make you feel like everything they screw up is actually your fault."

There, I've said it. Called Anthony an abuser.

I wait for Donna to leap to his defense, but she stays silent.

I risk the next move. "Have you thought about leaving him?"

Donna's lip trembles. "God forgive me, I think about it every day. But how would I survive? I have no money of my own."

Her hands clench and unclench. "The house is in his name. Even my car is in his name. I've been so stupid. But when I got married, I thought it would be forever."

I rub her back. "We all think that. There'd be no point in getting married at all if you didn't believe it would last. But people change. And if Anthony's not good for you, you should bail out now while you're young."

Donna bites her lip. "My mother says that's the way marriage is supposed to be. That a man needs to feel like he's the king of his castle."

"Oh, please!" I turn the key in the ignition and swing the Honda back onto the Parkway. "What you need is a good divorce lawyer. I know for a fact that your name doesn't have to be on the title of your house for it to be considered marital property. Sell that house, take half the proceeds, and tell Anthony to go get his own castle without you as his slave."

Chapter 4

Brielle Gardner's offer to let me stay in her house while I catalog the contents has given me a brilliant idea: Sean and I can go down to Sea Chapel for a romantic getaway while I combine business with pleasure. Another Man's Treasure doesn't have a sale this weekend, and Ty has been talking all week about the parties and concerts he plans to go to. Of course, there's no question that Donna would be able to leave Anthony for a weekend away from home. So I'll work solo, with Sean handy for lots of breaks.

I don't ask Donna much about what happened when she got home from our trip on Wednesday, but she shows up for work bright and early on Thursday morning. The day flies by with Donna subdued but energetic in her plans to promote the Sea Chapel sale. When I leave the office on Friday afternoon, Donna and Ty shoo me out the door with reassurances and wishes to have a fun weekend. I swing by the Palmyrton Police Department to pick up my husband, drop off our dog, Ethel, with my dad, and we're off for our spontaneous beach retreat.

"ISN'T THIS GREAT?" I usher Sean into Brielle Gardner's house as if it's a luxury inn I've reserved just for us.

Sean whistles and follows me through the living room to stand at the big windows overlooking the ocean. "Look at that empty beach. September is the nicest time to be at the Jersey Shore. No crowds. No traffic. Just the sea and the sand."

"Yep. Bali in the MidAtlantic." I tug his hand. "The tide is low. Let's go for a walk on the beach before we eat our picnic dinner."

We pull sweatshirts from our suitcases and head right out the back door onto the dunes. Our toes sink in the deep, soft sand as we head toward the water. Once we reach the hard-packed sand where the surf comes in, it's easier to walk. The sand feels cool on our feet, and the fresh salt breeze ruffles our hair. There's not a manmade thing in sight on the horizon, just the vast ocean.

We pause to watch a little boy digging in the sand with his father. The boy fills up a turret-shaped bucket then watches attentively as his dad flips it out of the mold for him.

"You do the next one, Teddy," the father says. "Pack the sand in real tight."

Teddy's little, pink tongue peeks from the side of his mouth as he concentrates on his task. But when he flips the mold, some of the sand stays stuck in the bucket and the turret is missing one of its parapets.

"It didn't work right." His lip trembles.

"No need to cry, buddy," his father says. "It still looks good."

But I can see Teddy is an architectural perfectionist. "You know what I do when that happens to me?" I crouch down beside him and offer him a shell. "I put a little decoration on the broken part and then it looks like I planned it that way."

Teddy takes the shell from me, still dubious about my advice. But when he's placed the shell, his eyes light with satisfaction. "You're right! That looks *better* than the other tower." To complete the effect, he sticks a gull feather flag on top.

The father smiles his thanks, and we continue walking.

"You'll be a great mom," Sean whispers and hugs me close. The only other living creatures we encounter are a flock of tiny plovers pecking for food in the sand and a big ugly horseshoe crab. Most of the dune-top houses we pass are dark.

"Wow, look at that one." The other houses we've passed are relatively new, but this one is a giant shingled Queen Anne with a wrap-around porch painted in cheerful yellow and blue. "That looks like it was built in the late 19th century."

The wind whips a fine salt spray into our faces. "Must cost a bundle to keep that big pile painted and repaired in this climate," Sean says.

We venture a little closer to look up at it. The path leading to the house is marked with a series of stern No Trespassing and Private Property signs.

"Guess they must get a lot of curiosity seekers. People probably think it's a bed and breakfast."

I take Sean's hand as the breeze gets stiffer, and the sunlight slips away. When we reach a long stone jetty, we turn around to come back. My husband pauses and looks out at the horizon. "In just four days, my parents will be on the other side of that ocean for the first time in their lives."

"Did I tell you your mom called me yesterday to ask if she'd be able to fit into the restroom on the plane?"

Sean shakes his head. "She's already asked Colleen and Deirdre that several times."

"I guess she figured her daughter-in-law was more likely to give her the unvarnished truth. I reassured her that she's not even close to being the biggest person to fly coach to Ireland."

"Did you ever travel with your father when you were a kid?" Sean asks.

"Never. He'd go off to math conferences, but he always went alone. Every summer my grandparents would rent the same house on Cape Cod for two weeks, and I'd go up there with them. They didn't like change. The notion that you'd go on vacation to see sights you'd never seen before horrified them. Too stressful."

"Talk about stressful—you shoulda been on our family vacations. Every year we loaded up the station wagon to go camping. Every year, Terry threw up in the car. Every year, it rained, and our sleeping bags got soaked. Every year, we came home early. Brendan says the whole point of those vacations was to make us grateful for our bunkbeds and shared bathroom at home."

Sean eventually made it to Europe on a backpacking trip the summer after college, and I went during a semester abroad program, but we've never taken a long trip together. "Do you want to go to Ireland?"

"Honestly, I'd rather go to Greece. It's sunnier and the food's better." Sean puts his arm around me. "Someday you and I will go to Europe."

"Not if we have a baby."

"We'll drag him with us and make him miserable looking at ancient ruins. Or we'll leave him with my mom. She was just complaining the other day that Brendan's kids are getting too big to need her anymore." Sean pulls me around to face him and tilts up my chin with his index finger. "Stop worrying, Audrey. Life's going to present us with obstacles. But you and I have the resources to overcome them."

I walk the rest of the way back to Brielle's house thinking about what Sean said. He's right: no one's life is devoid of problems. But we're both smart and healthy and we love each other. We have all we need to make our life together successful.

Sean and I share a bottle of wine and the gourmet carry-out feast we brought here from Palmyrton. Then we make love in Brielle's luxurious guest room. The rhythmic sound of the waves crashing against the shore plays constantly in the background.

"Isn't that relaxing? How could anyone be tense here with that sound lulling you, sleeping or waking?"

"Mmmm." I stretch my naked legs against the cool, satiny sheets and in minutes, we're both asleep.

———————◈———————

IN THE MIDDLE OF THE night, I jolt awake. An unfamiliar hulk at the end of the bed stimulates my heart into overdrive.

Where am I?

Then I remember. Sean and I are at Brielle Gardner's house. That shape across the room is a tall chest of drawers. My heart quiets.

But what woke me?

I hear Sean's steady breathing beside me. Through the open window, I hear the sound that surrounds this house: the distant whoosh of the waves hitting the shore.

And then I hear voices. Shouting.

That's what woke me. Someone is down on the beach.

I slip from underneath the covers and pad to the open window.

The moon illuminates the whitecaps of the ocean. Where the waves stop, I see the beams from several flashlights crisscrossing. Borne on the ocean breeze, men's voices float up to me.

"We shouldn't move him."

"We have to. The tide will carry him away."

The tide will carry who away? "Sean, come here. Something's happening down on the beach."

A light sleeper, Sean is at my side before the words are out of my mouth. "I think they found someone hurt on the beach." I shiver in the fresh breeze. "They're worried the tide will sweep him out to sea."

Sean peers over my shoulder. "I'd better go out there and see if I can help."

I grab his strong forearm. "Wait. You don't know who they are. Maybe the guys with flashlights are the ones who hurt the other person."

Sean slips away from me and heads into the bathroom attached to our room. The window there faces the house next door. He pulls up the shade. "There are three police cars parked on the road. Those guys on the beach are cops."

Now I know Sean won't be left out of this action. I pull on some clothes and follow him downstairs, determined to watch from the deck. The clock on the oven reads 3:35 AM.

A few minutes after Sean disappears through the dunes, an ambulance pulls up on the street. Two men carry a stretcher down the path between Brielle's house and the neighbor's.

I see lights come on in that house as they are awakened too. With the balmy days and cool nights, every house that's occupied has its windows open. Out on the deck, I can hear the neighbors' voices.

"What's going on? Why are there cop cars here?" The female voice sounds young, a little whiny—maybe a teenager.

"How should I know?" Another female voice, but lower-pitched. "My god, I have an important conference call at nine. I'll never get back to sleep now."

Their back door opens and a girl in droopy flannel pants and a ratty t-shirt comes out onto the deck. Her hair stands up in tufts. In the moonlight, it appears to be pink. She pads over to the deck railing and cranes to see what's happening on the beach below. "They're putting someone on a stretcher," she calls out to her mother. "I'm going down there."

The door flies open and bangs against the house. A heavy-set woman in a clingy nightgown charges out. "Sophia, don't you dare leave this house!"

But the girl is already halfway down the tall deck staircase. I see her plowing recklessly through the deep sand.

"Sophia!" The mother shouts from the deck, hugging herself in the cool breeze. But she may as well save her breath. Sophia is on her way, and the mother clearly has no intention of running after her.

I feel like an eavesdropper, but I'm certainly not hiding standing here on Brielle's deck not fifty feet away. The woman turns back to the house with an exasperated shrug and lets out a shriek when she notices me. "Who are you?"

"Hi. My name's Audrey Nealon. My husband and I are staying here for the weekend."

She squints her eyes suspiciously. "Brielle never rents out her house."

I don't owe her an explanation, but I don't want any trouble. "I'm getting Brielle's house ready for a contents sale. She's redecorating. Brielle's letting me stay here while I organize the sale."

The neighbor crosses to the side railing of her deck to get a closer look at me. Her arms are crossed over large, pendulous breasts, and her shoulder length hair whips in the breeze. "Oh, you're the one. Brielle did mention you'd be coming. I'm Jane Peterman and that was my daughter, Sophia. We live here full-time."

As soon as she introduces herself, a scream pierces the night. Then we hear Sophia's high-pitched voice. "Oh. My. Ga-a-a-wd! It's Trevor!"

Jane's attention swivels toward the dark beach. "Sophia? Sophia! Come back here now."

A cop appears out of the darkness supporting a weeping girl who keeps looking over her shoulder.

They are followed by the EMT workers making the return trip toward their ambulance.

The form on the stretcher is covered from head to toe.

Chapter 5

"Late night dog walker found the body. It was pretty badly decomposed. Fish got to it."

The horizon is beginning to brighten when Sean takes a seat across from me in Brielle's pristine kitchen. Contrary to my belief, she does actually keep food products in the house, and I've made us both a mug of coffee as Sean tells me about the scene on the beach. "But the local police think from the clothing that it's this teenager who's been missing for a week. Trevor Finlayson. Apparently, he left a suicide note. And the pants on the body had rocks in the pockets."

I put my hand over my mouth. "How horrible! So he just walked into the ocean and waited to sink? That's an awful way to die."

Sean stares into his coffee cup. "Sure wouldn't be my top choice."

"What about our neighbor, Sophia—she knew the boy?"

"Yeah, that was a bad scene. The girl came charging up. I grabbed her arm, but not before she got an eyeful of that corpse. The local cops were already speculating that the body was Trevor since that was the only missing person they had, but Sophia recognized his sweatshirt. Bumford-Stanley School Lacrosse."

I clunk my coffee mug down. "Bumford-Stanley is in Palmyrton."

"Yeah, according to the local cops, the family has a vacation home here in Sea Chapel, and this is where Trevor was last seen, but Trevor is from Palmyrton, and that's where he went to school."

I tilt my head toward Jane and Sophia Peterman's house. "The neighbors live here full time, so Sophia must go to the local high school, but she and Trevor were friends."

"The town of Sea Chapel is less than two miles long. The cops told me there are fewer than one hundred houses that front the ocean, and a thousand more inland. The off-season population is about two thousand people. That swells to ten thousand in the summer. So I'm sure all the rich regulars know each other."

Sean gets up and paces around the kitchen. "What could possibly be so bad in a seventeen-year-old's life to make him do that? The cops said he's from one of these wealthy families with the big houses." Sean shakes his head. "Probably thought his life was ruined because he didn't get into Harvard or something."

"I read that suicide is one of the leading causes of death among people ten to twenty-five." I didn't have a sunny childhood, but I sure don't recall feeling that kind of despair.

Sean stares out the window at the beach. "Seventeen years ago, the Finlaysons were posing their son for adorable baby pictures. Today they're planning his funeral, and they don't even have an intact body to bury."

<hr />

THE BODY ON THE BEACH has cast a pall over our romantic getaway. Sean has gone into the small study to read in a space where he doesn't have to see the waving yellow crime scene tape. I go upstairs to do some pricing. After all, this weekend wasn't meant to be all play and no work.

In the upstairs hallway, I hesitate. What shall I tackle first, the master suite or Brielle's son's room? Perhaps if I start with the smaller room, I'll get my mojo back and feel more energy to tackle the huge master bedroom.

As I enter Austin Gardner's room, I'm struck again by its impersonality. No teenage boy would have chosen that soft watercolor seascape or that shelf filled with model antique cars. Does his mother impose her formidable taste on his room in Palmyrton, too? Or is the kid allowed to have a few tacky posters of sports heroes and music icons there?

I open a dresser drawer, and I'm surprised to find clothes inside. A few well-worn sweat shirts and pairs of basketball shorts—the kind of basic clothes you'd leave at a vacation house so you don't have to pack them every time you come. I make a note to ask Brielle if she wants them returned or if, like everything else, they should go into the sale. As I take a quick picture to send to her, I notice the sweatshirts are emblazoned with a school name: the Bumford-Stanley Academy, Palmyrton's premier private school. No surprise that Austin would go there. So he too must know Trevor Finlayson.

The closet and other drawers are empty. I guess Brielle just overlooked this one.

I know that all the sheets and towels in the linen closets are to be sold. I check Austin's bed to see if it's been stripped. No, there are blue striped sheets under the duvet that will have to come off. I pull the pillowcases off the fluffy pillows, then pull the fitted sheet off the mattress. Naturally, Brielle has the highest thread count, deepest pocket sheets, so I really have to tug to get the far fitted corner out from under the mattress. It resists my efforts, so I slide the mattress slightly off the box spring. When I do, a folded 9 x 12 business envelope falls to the floor.

I pick it up and scan the front: it's addressed to Austin Gardner at a post office box in Palmyrton. The company name printed in the return address is AG Solutions, Boulder CO. On the back of the envelope is a list of seven names written in extremely precise block printing:

Brenna

Mason

Graydon

Ava

Trevor

Clark

Sienna

Prep school teenager names, for sure. Kids Austin wanted to invite to his next party? Kids he had a grudge against? Kids in the running to be valedictorian?

None of my business.

I put the envelope in the drawer with the forgotten clothes and continue with my work.

Half an hour later, Sean appears in the doorway to the bedroom with a sly smile on his face. "Our sleep was interrupted last night. Can I interest you in a nap?"

I grin and drop my iPad.

No doubt about it: sex is more interesting in a new setting. The fresh sea breeze, the call of the gulls, the steady rhythm of the waves all contribute to a very enjoyable romp. Still, I have a hard time staying totally focused on the matter at hand. Is this the encounter when we'll finally achieve our goal?

Sean pauses. "What's wrong?"

"Nothing. Everything's great."

His eyes narrow suspiciously, but I pull him into a tighter embrace and push images of madly swimming sperm out of my mind.

Afterwards, Sean dozes off, but I remain awake. I raise my knees on the off chance that this old wives' tale really might help the swimmers find their mark. I feel so powerless. The more I read medical articles about conception, the more extraordinary it seems that anyone ever gets pregnant. So many challenges to overcome to create a new life. And the whole battle plays out deep inside me.

It's a fight on my turf, yet there's nothing I can do to affect the outcome.

Oh I know—eat healthy, get plenty of rest, blah, blah, blah. I'm talking about a true intervention. I don't like being a passive bystander, sitting back and waiting for the magic to happen.

Why haven't I gotten pregnant yet? I've never had any of the diseases or conditions that can limit fertility. My sisters-in-law all conceived in two months. Hell, Deirdre got pregnant the fourth time when she was using an IUD!

The only strike against me is my age. Thirty-six.

I think about my lady parts shriveling up inside of me, and a tiny hiccup of a sob escapes my mouth. Sean's eyes flip open.

It never ceases to amaze me how he can move from asleep to totally alert in a blink.

"There *is* something wrong. You're crying." He smooths back my hair and brushes a tear off my lashes.

I bury my head in his shoulder, so he doesn't watch me when I say the words. "I'm letting you down because I can't get pregnant. You should have married someone younger. I'm probably all dried up."

"Audrey, Audrey. What would I do with a young girl?" Sean nuzzles my ear. "She wouldn't know who Monica Lewinsky is. She wouldn't remember episodes of Third *Rock from the Sun*. She wouldn't want to listen to Weezer."

"What if I'm too old to get pregnant? What will we do?"

"We'll adopt. But it's too early to consider that. We haven't even been trying for a year yet."

"But if there's something wrong with me, we should find out sooner, not later. I want to go to a fertility specialist and have some tests done."

"I think you're worrying needlessly."

"It would make me feel better...make me feel like I'm in control. This cycle of trying, then waiting two weeks to see if it worked, is killing me."

"You always have to be driving the bus, don't you?"

I sit up. "And *you're* content to be a passenger? Right!"

Sean laughs and pulls me back into the covers. "You do realize that once we have kids, neither one of us will be driving the bus. For the next twenty-one years, we'll be careening madly through traffic in a driverless vehicle."

Chapter 6

By the time we wake up, the sun has moved westward, and the tide has erased all signs of the tragedy on the beach. The stretch of sand behind the houses on Dune Vista Lane looks the same as it would have in 1491. Sean and I decide to walk along the beach to Elmo's, the little seafood restaurant near the marina with an ocean view in what passes for downtown Sea Chapel. As soon as we get to the water's edge, we encounter a small white dog, maybe a Bichon. I bend down to pet him. "Hey, cutie—where's your owner?"

The dog scampers off, chasing a receding wave and barking as if he's the tough guy scaring it away. As soon as the next wave comes in, the dog turns tail and charges up to the dry sand.

Chase. Bark. Flee. He does it over and over again as we stand laughing at him.

"Ya gotta hand it to dogs—once they find a game they enjoy, they'll play it 'til they drop."

We've been watching him for a good five minutes, and there's still no sign of another human on the beach. "Do you think he's lost?"

"Nah—he's clearly done this a million times before," Sean reassures me. "He probably lives in the house next to Brielle's."

We look up at the Petermans' house. It's not quite as grand as the Gardner house, but it's plenty big. As we stare up at the deck, a teenage girl in droopy sweats and bare feet comes out on the deck. "Paco, get in here!"

Sean squints. "Is that Sophia?"

The late afternoon sun emerges from behind a cloud and illuminates the deck. "Yep, there's the hot pink hair."

Paco cocks his head to listen to the girl's voice, then returns to his game.

"Paco, you are such a brat," Sophia yells. "If I have to come down there and get you, you're going into your crate."

I have yet to meet a dog who comes in response to a threat. But Sophia's had a pretty rotten day, so I try to help. "Paco! Here, boy—come get a treat."

I hold out my hand, and Paco comes running on the off chance that I might be holding a chunk of steak. The little dog dances at my feet, and I scoop him into my arms and carry him up the beach toward his house.

Sophia comes halfway down the deck stairs to meet me. Up close, I can see her eyes are red and swollen.

She takes the dog from me and starts walking back up the stairs. A few steps up she turns her head. "Thanks."

⸺⸺⸺◉⸺⸺⸺

ONCE WE GET TO ELMO'S, I realize all the exercise I've gotten today, both horizontal and vertical, has made me ravenous. I study the menu the way I used to peruse my differential equations text during exam week. Blackened grouper, sautéed sea scallops, grilled bluefish—they all sound fabulous.

Sean has already closed his menu and turned his attention to the TV screen above the bar.

"Authorities have confirmed via dental records that the body found this morning on the beach in Sea Chapel is that of seventeen-year-old Trevor Finlayson. The teen has been missing for ten days and was feared to have been a suicide."

I turn in time to see a school photo of a gangly but sweet teenage boy flash on the TV screen. He smiles broadly, his cheeks rosy with good health. Sean looks away and gazes out the window at the crashing waves. I wish the story hadn't come on now. We had just about succeeded in pushing this morning's tragedy out of our minds, and now Sean has to recall that the decomposed corpse he saw this morning was once a good-looking kid brimming with life.

I reach across the table and squeeze his hand. The waitress shows up at that moment and begins to quiz us on our choices: grilled or fried, chowder or bisque, balsamic or ranch. She hustles toward the kitchen.

"Man, you could hire her to interrogate suspects."

Sean chuckles and the sad moment surrounding the news story passes. We talk about the sale and our latest remodeling project and the future of Donna's marriage and the prospect of Sean's parents reconnecting with distant Coughlins and O'Sheas in Ireland. The food arrives and we chat some more, passing bites of shrimp and grilled bluefish back and forth. The restaurant has slowly been filling up around us.

The crowd at the bar has grown bigger, too. They're a rougher group than the dining patrons—two men in New Jersey Transit uniforms, a woman with the deep, vertical mouth wrinkles of a heavy smoker, another guy with a full sleeve of tattoos and a doo-rag. The buzz of conversation envelops us.

The loud slap of a palm on the bar hushes the crowd. "Dammit, Reg—that's a lousy thing to say. He was just a kid, no matter what you think of his grandparents."

Sean and I turn our heads toward the bar, as do several other diners. The two men keep arguing, oblivious to our stares.

The man with the tattoos prods the NJ transit worker with his index finger. "You would defend those people after what they done to me?"

"That's ancient history. Let it go."

"It's a helluva thing for Trevor's mother—knowing that her boy was so depressed," the woman sitting with the men says. "As a little boy, he used to play with my sister's kids on the beach. So sweet, friendly to everyone—not like the old man."

The other conversations in the restaurant have begun to pick up again, and we can no longer hear exactly what's being said at the bar. But the man with the tattoos is clearly still disgruntled.

"Wonder what that's all about," Sean murmurs. "Seems like Trevor's family is not too popular with the locals."

I use a wave to our waitress as a means to look at the crowd at the bar without staring. The tattooed man and the New Jersey Transit guy are getting heated again, and the bartender scowls and makes a "pipe-down" gesture. Then the tattooed guy throws some cash on the bar and storms out.

When our waitress brings our check, she tells us to pay at the bar. Sean reaches for his wallet and heads to the far end near the cash register. I watch as he and the bartender exchange a few pleasantries. Then as Sean signs his credit card receipt, their conversation becomes more involved. I smile. Sean really knows how to use that Irish gift of gab to get whatever information he's after.

Eventually, he turns to the table and raises his eyebrows at me. That's the code for, let's leave and I'll tell you all about it when we're outside.

As we walk down the beach toward Brielle's house, Sean lights our way with a bright penlight he's had the foresight to bring. I hold his other arm, a little unsteady with wine and exhaustion. "So, what did the bartender have to say?"

"The Finlayson family has had a big house down here for generations—it's that old yellow and blue one you liked. Everyone in the extended family uses it. The grandfather has a reputation for being a prick, trying to restrict access to the beach in front of his house even though there's no such thing as a private beach in New Jersey. After Hurricane Sandy, there was a big movement to build up the dunes to protect houses in low areas from flooding. But Finlayson used his political influence to prevent any dune construction in Sea Chapel because it blocked his view. The guy with the tatts lost everything in Hurricane Sandy, and he's terrified his house will get washed away in the next big storm. Of course, Finlayson's house is on the ridge, so he doesn't have to worry. I guess the debate divided the town: rich against working class. So the guy at the bar said the old man deserved to have his only grandson die."

"That's harsh. Would someone really have killed Trevor as an act of revenge?"

Sean squeezes my hand. "When your house is your biggest asset and someone else is threatening it through their actions, it's a plausible motive. I've seen people killed for less. The bartender says the old man has pumped a lot of money into the town, so no one wants to cross him. But he agreed old man Finlayson is a jerk. Trevor's father was the old man's only son, and he died a few years ago. After that, the old man didn't want Trevor's mother and her new husband to use the house. Only Trevor was welcome."

"So the night Trevor killed himself, he was down here with his grandparents?"

"I guess so. The local cops didn't go into that with me."

By this time, we've almost reached the Finlayson house. We gaze up at the many windows glinting in the moonlight. "I bet the mother's blaming the grandparents," I speculate. " 'If I'd been there, this never would have happened', would be a normal response, especially if the old man specifically refused to let her come."

"The grandparents are probably blaming themselves. With a suicide, there's plenty of guilt to go around."

Chapter 7

Sunday is an uneventful mix of work and play, and Sean departs very early on Monday morning. I look forward to a full day of steady work cataloguing the kitchen. Today the room is not flooded with brilliant light. Instead, the huge windows reveal gray storm clouds rolling in over the waves. The kitchen is so dim that I have to turn on the tiny recessed spotlights and the stunning blue glass orb that hangs over the island.

Brielle really does have a great eye for contemporary furnishings. Everything she has chosen for this home is striking yet subtle. No cheesy nautical themed tchotchkes, no predictable sea shell lamps or cutesy star fish platters. The woman has impeccable taste. Why does she feel the need to ignore her own discernment and replace everything with some Japanese man's choices, even if he is famous?

This isn't the first time I've been baffled by my clients' decisions, and it won't be the last. I know there are lots of people who will be very happy to acquire some of Brielle's vision.

I start with the cabinets above the sink. The woman has enough glassware to entertain the entire Royal Family. As I count and price, the wind rattles the furniture on the deck. This is going to be some storm.

A clap of thunder makes the fine glass bowl in my hands vibrate. A bolt of lightning splits the sky.

Then I hear a smaller, quieter noise.

Right behind me.

I spin around, and there's little Paco the dog scratching at the sliding door. With his white fur plastered against his body, he looks half the size he did yesterday. I rush to open the door, and he shoots into the kitchen. Paco shakes himself vigorously, sending sprays of water across Brielle's pristine floor.

"Hey, buddy—did you get shut outside by accident?" I peer over at the neighbor's house, but I don't see any signs of activity in the windows that face Brielle's house. A torrent of rain flings against the windows and lightning strikes the ocean again. "Well, Paco—looks like you'll be keeping me company for a little while. I'm not venturing next door in this storm."

Paco cocks his head and wags his tail. He snuffles around the kitchen but shows no impulse to explore the house, preferring to stick close to me.

It's nice to have some canine company. I miss Ethel. But soon he's jumping up on my legs wanting more interaction. "Let's see if we can find you something to play with." I open the lower cabinets hoping to find an old margarine tub or deli container to use in a game of fetch.

Nothing. In fact, Brielle doesn't even have a set of perfectly color coordinated Tupperware. On the rare occasions that she eats in this room, I suppose she must toss out any leftovers. They do tend to clutter up a refrigerator.

I open some drawers and confirm my suspicion: this house does not have a junk drawer! That's gotta be a first. Everyone has random odds and ends that need to live somewhere.

Not Brielle.

Every drawer and cabinet is sparsely populated with the highest caliber kitchen tools: German knives, gleaming stainless steel All-Clad pots, matching Oxo spatulas and spoons. Nothing that's not part of a curated collection.

Sean is meticulous, but as a serious cook, he possesses a mish-mash of essential tools. Even our good knives don't match because he feels one brand makes the best chef's knife while another makes the best paring knife. He wouldn't last ten minutes married to Brielle.

Finally, in the cabinet above the stovetop, I find an almost empty container of pink Himalayan sea salt.

Designer salt! Frankly, I'm shocked that Brielle would allow pink salt into her blue and white kitchen. I dump out the remains and roll the empty container across the floor. Paco chases it in delight.

I go back to work, occasionally doing my part to keep Paco's salt soccer game going. An hour passes, and the rain finally lets up. A beam of sunshine breaks through the gray clouds. "Time for you to go home, Paco. Although I must say, your owners don't seem particularly worried about you. Maybe they thought you were sleeping upstairs in your own house all this time."

I scoop the little fluff ball up and make the hike over to the Peterman house.

When I'm on the deck, I can see Jane sitting at her kitchen island stirring a mug of coffee in front of her. She appears to be having an animated conversation although no one else is in the room. Then I see the white wireless earpods and the cellphone lying next to the mug.

I tap on the glass to get her attention, then move to slide open the door and drop off the dog. When she sees me, Jane starts gesturing me into the house. I dump the dog off and wave since she's obviously busy with her call, but her gestures become more emphatic. She wants to talk to me.

So I follow Paco into the kitchen.

Could there be a room more different from Brielle's?

The pale birch cabinets are modern and top quality, the counters are speckled beige granite, and the floor is a coordinating color of Italian tile. It would be a lovely kitchen if it weren't for the towering stack of unwashed dishes in the sink, the crumbs and coffee rings on the island, the sandy footprints across the floor, the jumble of unopened mail on the table, and the crowning glory, a pile of hardened dog poop next to the sliders. Paco looks at me sheepishly as if to say, "I tried to tell them I had to go out, but they wouldn't listen."

"The key performance indicators should be more challenging," Jane shouts. She listens for a brief moment then resumes yelling. "Deliverables! We need to see deliverables!"

Jane jabs at her phone and directs her attention to me. "Idiot!"

"Excuse me?" Is she angry that I rescued her dog from the storm?

"Not you, my client. Why do they hire me if they want to keep plodding along on the same path to nowhere?" She gets up from the high barstool and I see she's still wearing the flowered nightgown she wore in the middle of the night last time I saw her. Except now it's nearly lunchtime. "You want some coffee?" She looks around the kitchen and tries to pick up a mug, but it's stuck to the counter.

"No thanks. I'm good." There's an awkward silence that I feel compelled to fill even though Jane is the one who called me in. "Paco was scratching at my door during the storm, so I brought him inside Brielle's house until the rain let up."

"Sweet Jesus, don't let Brielle know!" Jane peers down at the dog. "What were you doing outside? You weren't out all night, were you?" Jane laughs and tosses her teaspoon in the sink, where it lands with a clatter. "Our Paco is quite the man about town."

She doesn't seem to notice I'm not smiling. What kind of pet owner doesn't even check to see if her dog is in for the night?

"So tell me about your business, Annie." Jane stands confidently before me as if she's wearing a Ralph Lauren business suit instead of a semi-transparent, coffee-stained nightgown.

"Audrey," I correct. "I own a small business called Another Man's Treasure Estate Sales. I'm based in Palmyrton."

"Oh, Palmyrton! Sophia and I used to live there until we moved down here full-time last April. Sophia needed a change of scenery. Her school environment was toxic. Just toxic."

"Oh? She didn't like Palmyrton High School?"

"Good Lord, she didn't go *there*." Jane tosses her unbrushed hair. "She went to Bumford-Stanley. But it wasn't a good fit for her. Sophia is a nonlinear learner. She needs space and a student-directed learning environment."

I choose to ignore the slam against my alma mater. "Oh, so Bumford-Stanley is how she knew Trevor?"

"Mmmm. The Finlaysons are part of our circle." Jane's gaze drifts to the window facing Brielle's house although it's so coated with salt spray she can barely see out. The windowsill is lined with orange prescription pill bottles. "When is this big sale Brielle is holding?"

"The first weekend in October. I have a lot of work to do, so I need to get back." I edge toward the door.

Jane blocks my path. "That's what I want to talk to you about. I'd like Sophia to have an internship with you."

"Internship? Doing what?"

"Whatever." Jane waves her hand. "I mean, you don't have to pay her or anything. Surely, she can help you with something."

I could use some help, but the little I've seen of Sophia doesn't give me the confidence that she'll be a hard worker. And I'm pretty sure I give linear instructions to my staff. Besides, I thought prep school kids require internships in finance or cancer research to prepare them to be masters of the universe. "Working with me wouldn't be particularly educational."

Jane snorts. "That doesn't matter. She's supposed to have an internship. It's part of her homeschooling plan."

I take a closer look at the clutter of papers and books on the kitchen table. Mixed in with the Pottery Barn catalogs and sewer bills are a tattered paperback copy of *The Scarlet Letter* and *Everyday Physics*, a tome that looks like it's never been cracked open. A tumble of half-completed worksheets surrounds them. Palmyrton High School has its shortcomings, but I'm pretty sure the teachers there know more about the laws of thermodynamics than Jane here. "You're homeschooling your daughter? That must be a lot of work."

Jane grimaces. The entire time we've been talking her phone and laptop have been chirping and buzzing. "Let me take this." She jabs the screen of her phone and launches into more corporate babble. "Let's take a deep dive into the numbers to look for synergies."

I'm getting restless. I have a lot to do, but it seems rude to simply walk out. Of course, I wouldn't be any ruder than Jane herself. While I'm debating my options, Sophia wanders into the kitchen. She shuffles toward the fridge, then stops in her tracks when she notices me.

Jane pauses in mid-synergy and nods at her daughter. "I was just talking to Annie about your internship."

"What would I have to do?" Sophia takes a carton of organic milk out of the fridge and sniffs it. Her face contorts with disgust. She closes the carton and puts it back on the shelf.

Clearly, Sophia is no substitute for Donna on the cleanliness front.

"...globally incentivize the value-added potentialities..." Jane natters behind us.

Before I can open my mouth to say there will be no internship, Sophia pivots toward the back door. "Never mind. I'll do it. Let's go."

Jane waves good-bye while continuing to shout "it's the deliverables" into thin air like an angry drunk on a late-night subway. Sophia is already out the door. I have no choice but to follow.

I catch her by the arm out on the deck. "Listen, Sophia—I don't have any interesting work for you to do."

For a split second, the mask of sullen teenage boredom slips, and I get a glimpse of true despair. "It doesn't matter. I just need to get out of my house. Please."

Somehow, I've acquired an intern.

Chapter 8

Although I'm angry at myself for getting sucked into this internship arrangement, my irritation dissipates as I get to know Sophia. A bowl of Cheerios with fresh milk has perked her up, and she turns out to be a willing worker.

Since she doesn't go to high school, I know better than to ask the usual dumb adult questions about classes and activities. Instead, I tell her about estate sales and how Brielle's sale will be different since everything is so new and in such pristine condition. Then I set her to work pricing kitchen tools and other small items while focusing my attention on the more valuable pieces. I worried she might be the timid type who would need constant reassurance. "Is it okay to make this a dollar? Or should it be fifty cents?" But Sophia seems to have confidence in her own judgement, a quality I appreciate.

We work in silence for a while, and I steal glances at her from the corner of my eye. Sophia doesn't conform to twenty-first century beauty conventions—her face is a little too round, her body a little too curvy—but she's not unattractive. I suspect the pink hair and the nose ring and the shapeless Badflower T-shirt are her effort to thumb her nose at expectations. If she can't attract attention by being cheerleader-pretty, she'll attract it by being outrageous.

Soon Sophia opens a new drawer and gazes at the perfectly arrayed contents in wonder. "This house is so freakin' clean. Sometimes Austin comes over to our house just so he can eat chips on the sofa. But then he gets grossed out by how dirty our house is, and he has to leave."

I smile at her brutal honesty, and at the thought that Austin both rebels against and embraces his mother's standards. "How long have you and Austin been friends?"

Sophia hesitates before answering. "We've always known each other. Our mothers were in a play group in Palmyrton together when we were little kids."

I register the distinction between knowing each other and being friends.

Sophia shuffles over to the next drawer, talking to me without looking at me. "When Brielle and Mr. Gardner bought this beach house, my mom decided we should have a beach house, too. And she got one, right next to her bestie."

Way to keep up with the Joneses!

I note that Brielle is "Brielle" to Sophia, but her husband is "Mr. Gardner." Is there a Mr. Peterman? It doesn't sound like it. If Sophia's parents are divorced, I don't want to ask prying questions that could be painful. "But now you live down here full time?"

"Yeah. We sold our house in Palmyrton. My mom is a business consultant, so she can work from anywhere. Besides, she can't keep one house from falling apart, let alone two."

Another spot-on observation from this teenager.

"Do you like living down here full time?" I busy myself taking a photo of a ceramic pitcher. Seems to me Sea Chapel in the dead of winter would be mighty quiet for a teenager.

"My friends were here all summer. I just have to get through this winter. After that, I can go away to college. Assuming I come up with a high school diploma."

"How's the homeschooling?"

"A joke. Obviously."

Sophia seems pretty cleared-eyed for a seventeen-year-old. I feel a stab of concern for her. Being upper middle class is not guaranteed protection against parental neglect. What if she can't get accepted to college because of this haphazard homeschooling plan? "Do you have a tutor to help you with math and science? You have to take the SAT."

Sophia executes a dismissive wave remarkably similar to her mother's. "The college I want to go to—Bowdoin—doesn't require any of those tests. It's very nontraditional. Perfect for a freak like me."

Is freak a compliment these days? Or is Sophia simply embracing the label that the kids at Bumford-Stanley hung on her? "What do you want to study?"

"Art and creative writing. I want to write graphic novels. I have a portfolio. Being out of regular school gives me plenty of time to add new drawings to it."

I don't want to point out that she won't be living in a four-bedroom beachfront home on a graphic novelist's pay. It's not my job to destroy the kid's dreams; that's what parents are for. "I'd love to see your portfolio sometime."

Her face lights up. "Do you like graphic novels?"

"I do. I've read *Fun Home* and *Maus*. And I like everything by Phoebe Gloeckner."

"*Diary of a Teenage Girl* is amazing! If you like her work, you have to read *Gast* by Carol Swain"

Finding this common interest has elevated me in Sophia's estimation. Now she starts chatting like an African Gray parrot. She covers her passion for Manga and *The Handmaid's Tale* without even pausing for me to answer.

"What do you like to watch on Netflix?" I'm enjoying her review of popular culture and want to keep it rolling. "I like *The OA* and *Stranger Things*."

Sophia quiets as if I had pulled her plug. "Trevor loved *Stranger Things*," she says softly. "We used to watch it together."

Oh, crap—I've been so careful to tip-toe around her friend's suicide, and now I've stepped right into it. "I'm sorry you lost a friend in such an awful way." I want to reach out and stroke her arm, but I'm not sure if she would welcome that. I keep my distance.

"He had a lot of issues. He always did." Sophia traces the pattern in a cloth napkin she'd been pricing. "I hope—"

She seems to want to keep talking about Trevor but doesn't know how to continue. I try to help with a question. "Have you known him as long as Austin?"

Sophia shakes her head. "Trev and I met in middle school, when he first came to Bumford-Stanley. He hated the school even more than I did, but his parents wouldn't let him leave."

"Why not?"

"Because BSS is one of the most highly rated prep schools in the country." Sophia says this in a prissy, mock guidance counselor voice. "It's a superhighway to the Ivy League." Sophia's eyes well with tears. "Trev took the only off-ramp he could find."

My throat feels dry as I swallow. Is this why the poor kid killed himself—because his parents insisted he go to a high-pressure prep school and shoot for the Ivy League? Suddenly, neglectful Jane looks like a lot better mother to me. "Did he struggle to keep up?"

"No, Trevor was smart. He went to public grade school, and he wanted to go back to that—to transfer to Palmyrton High where his real friends were. But Mr. Gardner pulled strings to get Trevor into Bumford-Stanley, and Trev's parents said he couldn't turn around and quit after Mr. Gardner had done them that favor."

So the Gardners are friends with Trevor's parents, too. What a tight little circle these people travel in. I wonder how Trevor's parents feel about their decision to put friendship with the Gardners over their child's happiness? But maybe I'm being too harsh. Kids whine and complain all the time, and maybe Trevor's parents thought he'd be sacrificing a great education for the sake of hanging out with friends they might not have cared for.

"Do Trevor's parents have a house down here, too?"

"No, his grandparents do. Trev didn't really like his grandfather, but he loved the shore, so he put up with the old man so he could come down here. That was another thing Trev and I had in common—mean grandparents."

"What's wrong with yours?"

"My mother's parents got divorced when she was little, and they pushed her back and forth because neither one of them really wanted her. That's why she's so messed up." Sophia says this as matter-of-factly as if she were explaining why petunias won't bloom in the shade. "Both of them got remarried. My grandfather and his new wife retired to Costa Rica, and no one's seen or heard from them in years. My grandmother married some rich guy from Boston and she's, like, totally involved with his kids and grandkids." Sophia keeps her head down and concentrates on arranging the glassware in a precise, geometric pattern. "We spent Thanksgiving with them once, and they treated us like we were homeless people who wandered in off the street. No lie! So we don't see my mom's mother anymore, either."

Sophia steps back from the table and admires her handiwork. "But that's okay. We don't need them."

I sense it's time to leave the topic of Sophia's family. But I'm definitely curious about the elusive Mr. Gardner who pulled strings to get Trevor into prep school. "Does Mr. Gardner spend much time here in Sea Chapel?"

"No. He's always in the city working. They have an apartment there, too."

Three homes within a 60-mile radius—talk about excess!

"I'd love to spend the weekend in the city in that apartment," Sophia plunges into Brielle's collection of modern stainless-steel serving utensils. "Go to all the galleries in Soho. Not that Soho is where the really kickass art is anymore. We'd have to take the ferry over to Red Hook for that." Sophia chatters on about her ideal New York weekend.

"Austin shares your enthusiasm for art?"

"Nooo. He shares my enthusiasm for partying." Sophia cackles. "That's probably why Mr. Gardner won't let us come. He's not clueless like my mother."

Now that we've become buddies, I feel like I can satisfy my curiosity with a question. "What about your dad?"

"I don't have a dad. No one wanted to marry my mother. She's got an MBA from Wharton, ya know, but she's way too crazy for most men. So she let herself get knocked up by some actor guy and had me on her own."

There can be no polite response to that conversation-stopper, so I switch gears by asking Sophia to help me move a tall ceramic vase. I study Sophia's face as we half-carry, half drag the thing out of the corner. Like Jane, the girl has a soft, round face and full lips. But her eyes are an extraordinary gold-flecked green with long, dark lashes. Did those come from the unknown man Jane recruited to help her make a baby? Was he someone she'd dated or a stranger she picked up in a bar? Did Sophia's artistic talent come from him?

I can't help thinking about the baby Sean and I are trying to make. Will it be a mathematical introvert or an athletic extrovert? Will it have the best of both of us—a sociable, point guard, math genius? Or the worst of both of us—a shy, clumsy kid stymied by quadratic equations? Will we have patience and love for this child no matter how he or she turns out?

The ringing of my phone jolts me out of my daydream.

When I see it's Ty, my heart skips a beat. He never calls, always texts.

"Hi. What's wrong?"

"I'm in the emergency room with Donna. She's bein' x-rayed. Anthony broke her arm."

"What!"

Sophia stops working at the tone of my screech and stares at me with open curiosity.

"He went crazy when he found out she was goin' to be working alone with me today." Ty's voice pounds through the phone hard and fast. "When I get outta here, Imma find him and kick his ass. He'll be sorry he ever laid a hand on her."

"No! Call the police."

"Donna won't let me. She says that'll only make things worse."

"Worse? Next time he'll kill her." I pace circles in Brielle's kitchen as Sophia continues to stare. "She needs an order of protection."

"She made me promise I wouldn't call the cops." Ty pauses. "She didn't say nuthin' about tellin' you."

"Fine. I'll call Sean. Tell me all you know."

Ty takes a deep breath and goes into story-telling mode. "They've been fighting all week about her working for Another Man's Treasure. Anthony wants her to quit. Says the job is puttin' ideas in her head."

"He's right. Ideas that she's smart and competent and doesn't need him."

Ty grunts at my commentary and keeps talking. "So this morning when he found out Donna would be workin' all alone with me because you were down the shore, he told her she wasn't allowed to go to work. Seems he don't care for my black ass too much."

"Not *allowed* to go to work? What century is this?" I'd throw the phone across the room if I didn't need to hear all the details of this crazy story.

"So Donna told him she had to go to work and headed for the door, and Anthony grabbed her and twisted her arm and threw her down."

I wince, feeling the pain in my own right arm.

"He left her at home and went to work himself. Figured she wouldn't be able to go anywhere hurt like that. But when Donna didn't show up at our office, I knew something was up. She wouldn't answer my texts, so I went over there. Found her rolled up in a ball, arm hangin' all limp like a rag doll's."

"Bastard!" This argument sounds like a continuation of the one Donna and Anthony were having when she was driving us back from Sea Chapel last week. She wasn't ready to leave him then. Will this attack be the motivation she needs?

"Did she say anything about leaving Anthony?"

"She didn't say a word the whole way to the hospital. I think she was in shock. But once we were in the examination room waiting for the doctor, I told her she hadda leave him, and she said, 'I know.' Then the doctor came in."

"What did she tell him about how it happened?"

Ty heaves a sigh. "Donna told the doctor she fell down the steps. He gave me the side eye, like I was the one who hurt her."

"Did you get a photo of her arm? Does she have other bruises? We need evidence to get Anthony locked up."

"I knew you were going to say that. I took pictures of her at the house. But sittin' here alone at the hospital, I'm feelin' nervous. That's why I figured I better call you."

"You did the right thing. Send me the pictures, and I'll call Sean. And let me know what the doctor says when Donna gets out of x-ray."

After I hang up with Ty, my whole body trembles with rage. How can a man break his wife's arm because she wants to go to work? But I know there's no logic to domestic abuse. Anthony does these things because he can. It's all about power. Well, we'll just see how powerful he is when he's locked up in Rahway State Prison! Then he'll get to see what it's like to be knocked around by people who are tougher than he is.

Before I can call Sean, I need to get rid of my new intern. "Sophia, you've been a huge help this morning. But I have an emergency to deal with back in Palmyrton, so you can go home now."

Sophia looks crestfallen. "Can I come back after lunch?"

I pat her on the back. "Sure. I'd appreciate that."

As soon as she's gone, I steady myself enough to call Sean. Donna's terrible story pours out of me at twice the clip it came from Ty.

"Whoa, Audrey—slow down. Do you know where Anthony works?"

Somehow, I manage to pull the name of Anthony's uncle's business from the depths of my memory.

"Good. I'll send two officers over there. With these pictures as evidence, we can arrest him even if Donna doesn't cooperate. But if he doesn't have any priors, he'll probably be released until he's arraigned."

"Released? He'll kill her for turning him in!"

"That's why she needs a restraining order. I'll help her file it."

"They won't keep Donna at the hospital for long. Where can Ty take her? Her family doesn't support her. Her own mother tells her marriage has its ups and downs, and she needs to stick it out. They make her feel like his abuse is her fault. I think she should come and live with us for a while."

"No, Audrey." Sean's voice is quiet, but firm. "Our house is the first place he'd look. This is the most dangerous part of the process. Donna needs to be at the Palmyrton Battered Women's Shelter. The location isn't published anywhere, and even if Anthony managed to figure out where she is, they have a security protocol in place to protect all the women. She'll be safest there. And she'll get the counseling she needs."

"A shelter! Donna can't stay in a shelter. You know what a clean freak she is."

"I've heard it's quite nice. All the women have their own rooms."

"But Sean...."

"No buts. Do you want me to send you the stats on abusers who've killed their victims' friends and family and then killed themselves? You're playing with fire, Audrey."

I hear the seriousness in Sean's voice, and I know this isn't bluster. The situation between Anthony and Donna is dangerous. And here I am, having to manage the crisis from two hours away.

"All right. Let me know when you have Anthony in custody. Then I'll call Donna."

Chapter 9

When I get through to Donna, I brace myself for an onslaught of tears. What I get is much worse.

Her voice is wooden, her tone robotic. She sounds like she's on another planet, not just forty miles up the highway in Palmyrton. She tells me she's fine; she apologizes for being a bother.

I patiently explain the benefits of the battered women's shelter: the undisclosed location, the security system, the counseling. "And Sean says it's very nice. You'll have your own room. They can pick you up from the hospital and take you right there. Please say you'll go."

Donna launches back into her litany of apology and deflection. "I can't take a spot from a woman who really needs it. I'm fine. My arm's not actually broken. It's just dislocated. The doctor popped it back in the socket. No cast, I only have to wear a sling for a while. I can come back to work tomorrow."

"I'm not worried about you missing work. I'm worried about your life! Donna, listen to yourself. Are you saying that because the bone isn't broken, Anthony's not an abuser? He intentionally hurt you. Hurt you badly enough that you needed to go to the hospital. Hurt you because he's trying to control you and keep you from working at a job that gives you independence."

There's a long pause when I can only hear her breathing. I want to plunge into that silence with more logical reasons why she has to go to the shelter. Something—the hand of God, maybe?—holds me back.

Finally, Donna speaks.

"Okay. I'll go to the shelter."

THE CRISIS BACK IN Palmyrton takes a chunk out of my work day, so I'm glad when Sophia returns in the afternoon. I let her finish the cataloging work on the main floor while I settle down to email photos of interesting pieces to some of my regular clients who might be interested. The key to making this sale successful is going to be matching the right buyers to the right items.

I start by sending photos of the paintings to a gallery owner in East Hampton, Long Island. The impressionist seascapes are lovely, but they're not by artists well known enough to sell at an auction house like Sotheby's. Seems to me a gallery in an even more high-end beach community than Sea Chapel is my best bet for a good price. Then I send photos of the furniture to an interior designer I know who does staging for high-end real estate agents. Surely Brielle's barely used sofa and chairs could improve the looks of some shabbily furnished co-op in a prime location in Manhattan. Finally, I send photos of Brielle's kitchenware to my friend who owns a high-end resale shop in Summit.

Soon replies start pinging into my inbox. The most interesting one comes from Tim Ruane, the interior designer who does real estate staging.

Did I understand you correctly? You're at the house of Everett Gardner...THE Everett Gardner, CEO of The Gardner Group?!? Is his company on the ropes? Is that why he's selling off all his assets?

Good grief! I'm going to start a rumor that will cause the stock market to crash. I quickly answer.

No! His wife Brielle simply wants to redecorate this house. She apparently got a chance to work with some famous Japanese designer, so she's getting rid of everything to give him a clean canvas to work on. Rich people problems ☺

Seconds later, Tim responds. *Hiraku Maki? That's strange. I can't imagine he'd accept a gig at the Jersey Shore, even if it is for Everett Gardner. He prefers high profile architecture.*

What a snob Tim is! I can practically hear the drawl of contempt coming from the words on my laptop screen. And I might have realized he's the one person I know who's actually heard of this guy that I'm not supposed to mention. *I don't think that's the one.* I quickly type a face-saving lie. *Anyway, I still have to sell what's here. Are you interested in the sofa and chairs, or not?*

Tim says he's interested, and we negotiate the price and a pick-up time.

His last email of the night ends with a warning. *You'd better do good work on this sale, Audrey. I hear Everett Gardner is a real bastard. He'd be a bad enemy to make.*

After I finish the transaction, a nagging uneasiness mixes with my satisfaction in closing a deal. Tim is one of those annoying people who really does know everything about everyone. Has Brielle lied to me about why she wants her house emptied? Why would she bother cooking up this tale about the Japanese designer when I'm not even sophisticated enough to know who she's talking about?

Shrugging off the question, I head out to the kitchen to check on Sophia's progress. To keep herself company as she works, she's turned on the TV mounted behind a sliding panel in the kitchen. I didn't even know it was there, but of course, Sophia has been in this house many times before. She clicks through the channels. I'm not sure if she's looking for something specific or simply bored by all 300 choices the Gardners' satellite dish offers. Game shows and soap operas and ads for ambulance-chasing lawyers spin across the screen in dizzying array. I'm searching for a snack in the fridge when an earnest news reporter's face catches Sophia's attention, and she stops clicking.

"Ocean County authorities have completed the autopsy on Trevor Finlayson, the teenager found on Dune Vista beach on Saturday. According to the medical examiner, no sea water was found in the young man's lungs. He did not drown. Police say this was not a suicide. They are now classifying the death as a homicide."

Chapter 10

Before I can even reach the kitchen table, Sophia has charged out through the deck door. I see her pink head bobbing against the beige sand as she runs headlong down the beach toward town. I'm left standing in the kitchen with the TV news droning on about car accidents and tax protests, Paco snuffling at my feet.

Trevor was murdered? Why? And what about the suicide note he supposedly left?

Should I pursue Sophia? She's got quite a head start on me, and I have no idea where she's headed. Perhaps some friend who can offer comfort lives down the beach from here. I don't even have Jane's phone number, and I don't relish going next door to barge into her teleconference.

I reach for my phone to call Sean. He befriended some of those local cops on the night the body was discovered. Maybe he'll know something or can offer some advice.

Unfortunately, my call rolls over to voicemail. He must be busy, so I leave a quick message. No sooner do I hang up and uneasily return to work than I hear footsteps on the deck. Has Sophia returned?

No, it's her mother.

I wave Jane into the kitchen. She looks totally different today. For one thing, her hair is combed. She's applied some make-up. And she's not wearing PJs. In fact, she looks quite nice in a casual navy dress and flats.

She glances around the kitchen. "Hi, Audrey. Where's Sophia?"

"I don't know if you've heard...." I gesture toward the TV ".... But the news just announced that Trevor's death was a murder, not a suicide. Sophia ran down the beach toward town as soon as she heard it."

I stop myself from apologizing for not following or notifying Jane. After all, I didn't sign on to be the kid's babysitter.

Jane scratches her head as if she's contemplating some thorny problem she must solve for one of her consulting clients. "Ye-e-es—I was worried she'd...overreact... when she heard the news." She peers out Brielle's windows—considerably cleaner than her own—but Sophia is now out of sight. "I suppose I'll have to drive down to Elmo's. I really don't need this today."

Jane sounds like a mom annoyed to have to drop off her daughter's forgotten soccer cleats. The poor kid's distraught that her friend was murdered. Surely that deserves a little maternal comfort. "How do you know she went to Elmo's?" I ask.

"She's befriended some local kid who works in the kitchen there." Jane pulls out her phone and presses a speed-dial. After a few moments of listening, she drops it on the table. "Rolled to voicemail. She never picks up when I call." Jane massages her temples. "I have a splitting headache after that video-conference. I had to explain my market saturation strategy to the client ten times before he could see the wisdom. All I want to do is crawl into bed."

Did Jane come over here to manipulate me into going after her daughter? No way! But, of course, I do feel sorry for Sophia. "You don't think Sophia will do anything, er, reckless because of this, do you?"

"You mean like tattoo Trevor's name across her forehead? That's entirely possible. Sophia loves a grand gesture." Jane plops onto one of Brielle's exquisite chairs and kicks off her shoes. "She was finally settled down after his suicide, and now this! I don't know how our local-yokel police can possibly say Trevor was murdered. Everyone knew he was depressed. He'd been seeing a therapist for years."

As the wife of a cop, I know a thing or two about autopsy results, and I take it upon myself to clarify the situation for Jane. "If there was no sea water in his lungs, that means he didn't drown. He was dead before he went into the water. So if he did commit suicide, someone disposed of his body by tossing it in the ocean. Why would anyone do that?"

Jane's brow furrows. She clearly doesn't like being contradicted. "Humpf. Trevor's mother has been crying every day since he disappeared, and she read the note he left at his grandfather's house. It said 'I can't take this anymore. I hate my life. I'm sorry.' What else could that mean, but that he planned to kill himself?"

"Why was he so unhappy? Why did he need therapy?" I continue pricing items from the dining area buffet. Despite the house's uncluttered appearance, Brielle possesses an incredible volume of stuff. Two sets of twenty napkin rings, wine carafes, sangria pitchers, iced-tea glasses, champagne flutes, beer steins. Is there a beverage she doesn't have a specialized container for?

"Well, his family was complicated—a yours, mine and ours situation, you know. Trev was Jeanine's son from her first marriage, and Ken's got two from his first marriage, and then they had little Roxie together. Trevor used to tell Sophia that he felt like a stranger in his own family. And it didn't help that Ken was the father of all the other kids, but Trev never knew his own father. He died when Trev was a toddler."

"Trevor was staying with his grandparents the night he disappeared?" I nod in the direction of the huge Finlayson house.

"Yes, Jeanine and Ken and their kids were personae non grata there. But who knows what Trevor was up to that night? The old folks probably go to bed at eight."

Jane picks up one of Brielle's champagne flutes and pings it to hear the crystal ring. "And Ken *is* a prick—there's that. I was always willing to let Trevor hang out at our house when things got too hairy at home, but Ken didn't approve. Said I didn't supervise the kids enough. I'm sure he thinks Sophia is a bad influence." She mimes the action of smoking a joint.

If you ask me, Trevor's stepfather had legitimate concerns about Jane. But Trevor's problems sound like standard teenage angst to me. "But would the family drama be enough to make Trevor want to kill himself? Maybe the note meant something else?"

"Possibly." Abruptly, Jane swivels on her stool to face the dining area. "How are you going to sell that painting? You're not going to put one of these sticky price tags on it and sell it to some gawker from Seaside, are you?"

Nothing makes me bristle more than someone assuming I don't know how to do my job. "I've already found a buyer for it. A gallery in East Hampton."

"Hmmmm." Jane stands up and stretches. "I've *got* to take a nap. If Sophia shows up here, tell her we're due at the Levoniak's house at seven."

"I thought you were going to look for her at Elmo's."

Jane yawns so wide I can see her fillings. "Well, I've spent so much time sitting here talking to you, there's hardly time for that now, is there?"

And she sashays off, Paco at her heels.

Jane's not winning any Mom-Of-The-Year awards, that's for sure. While I debate going to Elmo's to look for Sophia, Sean calls. He's gotten some information from the Sea Chapel police.

"It turns out Trevor has a huge trust fund from his dead father. So there actually is a motive for killing him. All the money goes to his baby half-sister, who is his only blood relative. The parents would control it."

"The Sea Chapel police think Trevor was murdered by his own *mother*?"

"They've turned the case over to the Ocean County Sheriff's Department. It's too big for them to handle. I think it's the stepfather the county detectives are looking at. He's got some financial problems. If his wife controlled Trevor's money, he could get a bailout."

"But what about the suicide note?"

"The way the note was worded, the family was holding out hope that Trevor simply ran away. The stepfather came down here to look for Trevor after the grandmother found the note and called them in Palmyrton. So maybe the kid did start off running away and his stepfather decided to make sure he never came back. And conveniently used the note as cover."

"He probably thought the body would never be found."

"Yeah, your average nonprofessional killer doesn't realize how deep you have to sink a body for it not to wash ashore."

I shiver. I'll never get used to the fact that my husband knows these things. "So if Trevor didn't drown, does the coroner know what killed him?"

"His trachea was crushed. Trevor was strangled."

"Are they going to arrest his stepfather?"

"I don't think they have enough evidence yet. Motive alone isn't enough. The Ocean County Sherriff's Department will have to keep digging for some forensic evidence or witnesses."

A brief silence falls between us. Sean breaks it. "Are you all right down there? Why don't you head home right now and go back down when you can take Ty with you."

"I'm fine, "I assure my husband. "That poor kid's murder has nothing to do with me. And nothing to do with this house. The tide just happened to wash the body up here."

"Don't be so offhand about murder, Audrey. Seems to me everyone in Sea Chapel is connected to this case somehow."

I spent thirty years of my life feeling like no one was ever worried about my well-being. I'm intensely grateful to now have so many who care. Still, my natural impulse is to pull against any reins that try to slow my forward movement. "The house has an alarm system," I remind Sean. "I'll lock myself in while I work. I'll see you tomorrow."

When I hang up, it's five-thirty. Early for dinner, but there's nothing in the house for a snack or a meal, so I may as well break now. I can get a little more done before bedtime when I return. Should I drive to Rumson to try a new restaurant or just walk down to Elmo's?

The rational part of my mind tells me to get in the car and drive far in the opposite direction. But I keep imagining Sophia bereft in the kitchen of the little seafood restaurant waiting for her friend to be done scouring a mountain of pots. And after my long conversation with Sean, my phone is nearly out of juice. If I walk down the beach to Elmo's, I won't need it.

So I plug in my phone to charge and set off for Elmo's.

The wind has kicked up and the surf is rough. I carry my sandals as I walk through the sand. At the jetty, waves crash against the black seaweed-covered rocks, sending up a dramatic white spray each time they hit.

The sand castle little Teddy built so lovingly yesterday is now a crushed heap of sand, sticks, and shells. All that remains of his masterpiece is one tower flying a jaunty sea gull feather flag.

When I get to the restaurant, there's only one table of early-bird old folks in the dining room. All the action is at the bar.

I hop up on a stool between a burly guy wearing a Perillo's Home Remodeling shirt and a skinny guy with two shots lined up in front of him, order a beer, and ask for a menu.

"Get the oysters," the shot guy next to me commands.

"Oysters are the one seafood I don't like."

"They're fantastic," he insists.

Just what I need—a belligerent drunk making my menu choices. "I'm sure they are; I just don't care for any oysters. I don't like the texture."

"Get her half a dozen blue points," the drunk hollers at the bartender.

I make eye contact with the server and shake my head.

"Calm down, Donnie. The lady doesn't want oysters." He leans in closer to me. "What can I get ya, hon?"

"I'll have the Cajun grouper and a salad." Before he turns away, I grab his arm. "Have you seen Sophia Peterman down here today?"

"Yeah, she came in a while ago lookin' for one of our dishwashers, but he's not working today."

"Did she go to his house?"

The bartender shakes his head. "The kid lives a few miles inland. Sophia couldn't walk there. She didn't even have shoes on."

Now that he mentions it, I can picture Sophia's ratty flip-flops on Brielle's deck, where she kicked them off before entering the house. Maybe while I was on the phone with Sean, she came back up the beach and went home. Good. I can eat my dinner without performing psychotherapy.

The Perillo's contractor guy on my other side strikes up a conversation with me. "You're working at the Gardner's house?"

I explain my task, and he nods. "I've worked for Mrs. Gardner. She's a real piece of work."

I don't want to disparage my client, especially in this neighborhood hang-out. But I'm curious about what the contractor has to say. I give a noncommittal response. "I've only met her once."

"She hired me to build an outdoor shower next to her pool. People warned me not to take the job, but I didn't listen." He shakes his head and whistles. "She made me tear the thing out three times and redo my work until she was finally satisfied. I lost money on that job."

That's concerning. I hope Brielle isn't going to find some way to screw me. "She strikes me as a perfectionist."

"That's for sure. You know, my boss has worked for all those people on Dune Vista Drive. They're always having parties at each other's houses. The Gardners have the fanciest house of all, but the parties are never there." He shakes his head. "Everything's for show, but no one ever gets a chance to see it. Like that shower. The only person I've ever seen use it is her son."

"Have you done any work for Jane Peterman?"

"Oh, yeah—ol' Janey's a hoot. Nuthin' like her best friend." He says this with a leer. "I hafta go meet her later this week. She wants me to refinish the deck on her little sail boat. I do boat repair as a side gig."

"How does she pay you?" the skinny drunk cackles.

Luckily, my food arrives, and so does the contractor's, so we don't have to delve into Jane's sex life any further.

I eat without much more conversation among the crowd at the bar, pay my check, and leave. Outside, the wind has turned sharply colder, and I wish I'd worn a heavier fleece. I walk briskly up the beach, keeping my head down as I stride into the wind. After five minutes, I glance up to see how close I am to the jetty, which is the halfway point between Elmo's and Brielle's house. I'm almost parallel to it.

Then I see a figure out there on the rocks. A huge wave strikes the jetty, and the figure reels.

Surely, that's not safe! Why would anyone go out on those sharp, slippery rocks at dusk?

I approach the point where the jetty meets the beach and squint at the figure. My heart sinks. Soaked, yellow flannel pants stick to her legs. Pink hair ruffles in the wind.

"Sophia, come back here!" The wind carries my words away like a discarded plastic bag.

I jump up and down and wave, but she looks out to the horizon. She doesn't notice me.

I look up and down the beach for assistance, but the sand is empty for as far as I can see. Every house I've passed on my walk has been dark. Going back to Elmo's or running ahead to Jane's house will take equally long.

Too long.

I reach for my phone. My pocket is empty. Damn—I can picture the phone charging on the counter.

I haul myself up onto the first rock. If I can get a little closer to Sophia, maybe she will hear me, and I can coax her in.

Gingerly, I stand and put my bare foot onto the next rock. The sharp surface scrapes my sole, but this rock is fairly flat, so it's not so hard to stand on it. Below me, the water is only a few inches deep. Still, a fall would be painful.

The next rock is tall and jagged and only has a narrow foothold. I reach out with my hands to hold onto the top of it while searching for the foothold with my toes. A wave splashes against the rock, drenching me with cold spray.

I drag myself onto the second rock and look ahead. Sophia is still out on the tip of the jetty, allowing the waves to crash over her as if she deserves the punishment. Another one hits, and she staggers under the impact.

It's a matter of time before she's knocked off the jetty and flung against these unforgiving rocks.

"Sophia!"

If she hears me, she doesn't react.

I edge around the tall rock, and scoot across a flat one while the waves are out.

The next obstacle terrifies me. Two tall rocks touch on my left side, but there are no handholds or foot holds. The rock I stand on slopes downward slightly. About four feet away, another flat rock stretches invitingly. Between my rock and the other is a small inlet where the ocean churns like a washing machine on the "football uniforms" setting. The distance is too far to step across. I would have to jump.

Maybe at low tide on a calm day, daredevil teenagers would enjoy this challenge. Maybe the possibility of skidding off the landing rock into the heaving sea would add to the thrill. But honestly, I'd find it scary any time. When people describe skydiving or skiing a double black diamond trail as "a rush," I can't get my head around what they're saying.

Apparently, they like feeling out of control.

I hate it.

I stand trembling before my challenge. I imagine how it will feel to slip and be smashed against the jagged rocks. How I will thrash before being sucked under by the tide's pull.

Sophia must have made the leap.

But I'm not doing it.

I'm not that brave.

Or stupid.

Damn it, I want to be home in my own bed. With Sean. And Ethel.

I wait for the interlude between two waves. Then I take a deep breath and bellow. "So-phee-a!"

She turns, and I sense rather than see her gaze lock with mine.

I hold out my hands like I'll catch her, the way I used to do when Ty's nephew, Lo, was learning to walk.

Slowly, as if she's sleepwalking, Sophia moves toward me.

The rocks she has to cross on her side of the divide are relatively flat. She slips once and my heart lurches, but she regains her footing.

Now she stands on the other side of the chasm.

She will have to jump again from her side to mine.

But sticking the landing will be harder on the return trip. The rock I stand on slants slightly toward the tumultuous inlet five feet below us. Sophia must launch herself with enough force to make it across, but then retain her balance on the slick, uneven surface so she doesn't pitch into the sea.

Her eyes widen beneath that mop of pink hair as she realizes what she must do. I step to one side and point with my toe to a spot in the middle my rock. "Try to land there and I'll grab you."

She gazes at me, seeking reassurance. She may be a high school senior, but she looks like a five-year-old who doubts her father's sanity when he removes her training wheels and urges her to pedal down the driveway.

For a moment, I reconsider our position. Maybe now that I've coaxed her back from the edge, I should go back to shore and run to Elmo's for help. But the tide is getting higher, the surf rougher, by the minute. By the time I get to Elmo's and back, the rocks we're standing on will only be a few inches above the water.

Sophia must jump now.

She must launch the second after a wave hits, so she lands when the surf is out, and we have time to brace ourselves for the next wave.

"When I yell, 'now', I want you to jump. Don't hesitate, okay?"

A wave hits. I give the command. Sophia's knees flex, but she stays rooted to the spot, terrified.

She pushes her soaked hair off her face. "I'm sorry. Let me try again. I'll do it this time."

I watch the waves for the next opportunity. "Now!"

Sophia sails through the air and lands next to me with a scream and a thud. Her feet aren't under her body and she slides down the rock. Desperately, I grab her t-shirt and hear it begin to rip.

We both are sliding—me standing and her flat on her chest, her feet out over the inlet.

I get a grip on her arm. The kid is heavy.

The next wave hits.

Chapter 11

When the saltwater stops burning my eyes and the shock of the cold water passes, I realize my hands are empty. My heart pounds so hard, I can't make a sound.

Then I feel a hand on my shoulder. "Get back on this rock, Audrey. Here comes another wave."

Sophia has scrambled to our next perch, and I follow.

We make our way back to the beach in silence. I can't talk. I can't think. I just want to be inside the house.

Silently, we trudge through the sand, the sharp wind slicing through our wet clothes.

I've left the light on in Brielle's kitchen, and it shines like a beacon, guiding us home.

The Peterman house is dark. Jane must've gone off to her dinner engagement, unconcerned with her daughter's whereabouts.

Nice.

Sophia follows me up the deck stairs to Brielle's house. We leave our sodden clothes on the kitchen floor and head off to separate bathrooms for long, hot showers.

When I get back to the kitchen, Sophia sits wrapped in one of the luxurious terrycloth robes from Brielle's guest bathroom. She's nuked two mugs of tea and pushes one toward me.

I gulp the steaming liquid trying to dissolve the frozen cube of terror still lodged behind my ribcage.

Finally, I find my voice. "What the hell was that about, Sophia?"

She stares at me for a long moment. Is she going to dare offer me the standard teen BS: *Nothing... I don't know... Leave me alone.*

Then her eyes well with tears. She hangs her head, and a tear plonks into her tea. "Thank you for saving me," Sophia whispers.

I squeeze her hand. "Sure, kiddo. But you're lucky I saw you out there."

Sophia spoons sugar into her tea and begins to talk. "I totally freaked when I heard the news that Trev was murdered. I went down to Elmo's to talk to Dante, but when he wasn't there, I just got...crazy... in my head." Sophia takes a big gulp of tea. "He *told* me this could happen."

"Dante?"

She raises her voice. "No, *Trevor*. He told me he could be killed. I didn't believe him."

My body stiffens. "Trevor said someone wanted to kill him? Who?"

"He acted all mysterious. I thought he was being paranoid." Sophia gets up and paces around the kitchen. "I loved Trev. When he was up, there was nobody funnier or more creative. But then he'd get in these moods." Sophia shivers. "He'd talk and talk and half of it made no sense. His parents took him to so many different shrinks, and they'd all give him pills, so many pills, and sometimes he'd take them and sometimes he wouldn't."

So it wasn't just average teenage angst. Trevor had true mental illness problems. And he didn't take his meds. "So you thought it was his illness talking?"

Sophia looks grateful that I understand. "The last time he had one of his episodes was at the end of the summer. He started talking about how he didn't agree with them and they were after him and they would kill him, and—" Sophia cradles her head in her hands.

I put my arms around her and pull her head onto my shoulder. "What?"

"And he seemed scared. Really scared." She murmurs softly into my sweatshirt.

"Who was the 'they' he talked about?"

"I don't kn-o-o-w," Sophia wails. "Because sometimes Trevor mixed up movies and TV shows and video games with reality. And then if I looked at him like 'wha—??', he'd laugh like what he said was a joke."

"So at the end of the summer, you thought his complaints weren't real. But now you think they were valid." I want to ask about Trevor's stepfather, but I don't want to plant ideas in Sophia's fertile imagination. "Do you think it's possible the person he was afraid of could be an adult?"

"He doesn't know any adults down here except his grandparents."

I watch her intently.

Sophia cocks her head and rolls her eyes, the kind of eye roll that causes mothers everywhere to say, "your eyes are going to get stuck like that." "You mean Ken? Ken's just an asshole, he's not dangerous."

Sophia doesn't think much of the prevailing police theory, I guess. "Do you have any idea who could have killed him?"

Sophia looks down at the mosaic tile floor as if the answer is spelled out in the beautiful blue and white tiles. After a long moment, she whispers, "It had to be kids from Bumford-Stanley."

"Bumford-Stanley? But the murder definitely happened here in Sea Chapel."

"All the kids at Bumford-Stanley have some kind of vacation home." Sophia waves her arms like a professor carried away by his lecture topic. "Some at the Jersey Shore. Some in the Hudson Valley. Some in Vermont. The really rich kids have ski houses in Vail and beach houses in Palm Beach, but that's actually not ideal. 'Cause once kids are old enough to drive, the thing to do is have parties at the vacation houses when the parents aren't there. You tell your mom you're at a sleepover in Palmyrton when you're really down here at the shore or up in Vermont with ten or fifteen kids from BSS."

"So there could've been kids from BSS down here the weekend Trevor disappeared, and his parents wouldn't necessarily have known that."

Sophia nods.

"Do you know if there was a house party that weekend?"

Sophia gives her head a quick shake. "I hardly ever got invited to those parties. There could've been one that weekend, but I wasn't there."

"But wouldn't kids have been talking about it on social media? You could find out about it even if you weren't invited, couldn't you?"

Sophia refuses to meet my eye.

I reach out and touch her hand. "This could be important, Sophia. It could help the police figure out what happened to Trevor."

"I don't know! And even if I could, I don't want to rat on them! They already hate me. I don't need for people to be hating on me even more. And I could be wrong." She jerks away from my touch. "Besides, Trevor is dead. Nothing's going to bring him back."

Of course. What am I thinking? Trevor's death being ruled a murder has put Sophia in a terrible position. What seems like a simple action of cooperation to an adult is much more complicated for a teenager. I decide to back away from urging her to talk to the police and just get her to talk to me a little more. Clearly, she still has a lot on her mind.

"The other day you told me Trevor wanted to transfer back to Palmyrton High School where his real friends were. Would he have told one of them about who was scaring him?"

"I don't know his friends there—I've never hung out with them or anything. But there was this kid named Fly who Trev always talked about."

"Fly? Fly is a nickname—do you know his real name?"

Sophia shakes her head. But I know Sean can use this. An unusual nickname is probably easier to track down than a common name like Connor or Scot or Luke.

Sean. I've been married to a cop for just over a year, and already I think like him. Trevor's murder isn't Sean's case, but if I can draw out some useful information from Sophia, Sean can pass it along. It's not like I've been doing unauthorized digging; she's been gushing. And she's not done.

Sophia continues pacing laps around the kitchen. "Trevor said he hated all the kids from Bumford-Stanley, but he hung out with them all the time. He'd complain about having to go to a party and I'd say, 'so, don't go,' but he always went. Always."

I hear some resentment there. Trevor was Sophia's friend. He got invited to the parties she was excluded from. He complained about them, but he went, leaving Sophia behind. "You never tagged along with him?"

Sophia gazes at me, her eyes full of anguish. "The last time I saw him, we argued. I told him I was tired of listening to him complain about those kids when he kept going and hanging out with him. And the next week, he was dead."

"What went on at those parties? Was it more than just the usual smoking and drinking and making out?"

Sophia looks at me like she's stunned I know what kids do to have fun. Geez, it's not like I was a teenager with Jane Austin and went to harpsichord concerts for a good time.

"There was a special group. Not just anyone could go—that's why he couldn't bring me. There was something they wanted him to do."

"Like a fraternity initiation, only for high-schoolers?" I feel queasy at the thought that Trevor's death was the result of some stupid hazing incident, otherwise decent kids egging each other on to do something dangerous. But Trevor was strangled. How could that be an initiation rite gone too far?

Sophia shakes her head. "It wasn't a dare—like drink ten shots in a row or something stupid like that. He said there were things they had to decide. That he had to pick a side."

"A side for what?"

"I don't *know*!"

"So why did you go out on the jetty?

Sophia flings her head back. The bathrobe begins to slip, and she gives the belt a vicious yank. "I know it doesn't make sense. But I wanted to be out there near where he died. I wanted to be scared like he was scared. I wanted him to talk to me. Tell me again what was scaring him. Tell him this time I'd listen to him." Tears stream down her face. "Really listen."

Chapter 12

All cried out, Sophia collapses on the family room sofa and falls asleep almost instantaneously. I can't believe her mother hasn't called looking for her in all this time. Then I see the pile of our soaked clothes on the kitchen floor. Sophia's phone must be ruined by saltwater. I look out the window, but the Peterman house is all dark. Jane must still be at the dinner party she and Sophia were invited to tonight.

How much Sophia reminds me of my own teenage self! Only one parent, and that parent distant and preoccupied. Wanting to fit into mainstream teenage life, but always on the fringe because of interests other kids don't share. Just a few close friends.

But none of my few friends was murdered.

Sophia's phone makes me recall my own phone, which I left charging on the counter hours ago. When I pick it up, I see I've missed two calls and two texts from Sean. The last reads, "You OK? Should I be worried?"

Sean and I have a policy of giving each other a lot of space. As a cop, he's often not in a position to respond immediately to my texts. And when I'm running a sale, I'm too busy for idle chit-chat. But I'm sure he expected I'd be home alone here at Brielle's house tonight with plenty of time to talk, not out on the jetty rescuing a crazy teenager.

I call him back, aiming to get advice on the information I've gleaned from Sophia while glossing over the riskier parts of my rescue operation. I'm also eager to hear if Sean managed to arrest Anthony and get Donna into the battered women's shelter. I haven't heard a thing from Donna. I've been afraid to text or call her in case Anthony is monitoring her phone. But when I call, I get Sean's voicemail. So I text, *Busy night. I'm fine. Call when you have time.*

Soon he answers: *Dealing with family chaos. See you tomorrow. Drive safe.*

Hmmm. That could mean anything from one of his nieces or nephews needing stitches to one of his siblings getting arrested—Sean's family turns to him for help no matter the situation. However, I have to assume chaos doesn't extend all the way to death, so I decide to go to bed.

What to do about Sophia?

She's sleeping so peacefully—I hate to wake her. I decide to make a big note informing Jane of her daughter's whereabouts and tape it to Jane's deck door. Hopefully she'll see it when she comes home.

With that task done, I turn out the lights, lock the doors, set the alarm system, and tumble into the guestroom bed. It's only ten p.m., but I feel like I've worked an all-night shift in a Bronx ER.

———— ◉ ————

A NOISE DRAGS ME FROM the depths of sleep and sets my heart pounding.

My phone says 2:05. I listen closely.

Footsteps downstairs.

Sophia must've awakened to go to the bathroom or search for food. I hold my breath and tune my ears. A bang and a murmur—maybe she bumped into something in the torn apart kitchen. I prepare to roll over and go back to sleep when it dawns on me. If Sophia should decide to open the kitchen door and go back home right now, there will be a very short grace period before the security alarm goes off. The last thing I need is a crew of Sea Chapel police here in the middle of the night.

I jump out of bed and trot down the hallway. I hear a low murmur of voices. Who is she talking to?

Now I'm halfway down the stairs. "Sophia?"

A light in the kitchen casts a dim glow into the living room. The stairs, with their clear, Lucite railing, are even more disorienting now than in the daytime. I hug the wall as I see a tall, wiry person move across the vast living room.

Certainly not Sophia.

A man.

My heart kicks into overdrive.

Who is he and how did he get in here? I know I set the alarm.

In the shadowy light he looks vaguely familiar. Yet he's not any of the few men I've met at Elmo's. What other men do I know down here?

He looks up and sees me trying to melt into the wall.

A scream escapes me.

"Hey." He raises his right hand in a casual salute. His voice is young.

Hey? What kind of home invader is this? And where is Sophia?

"Who are you?"

"Austin Gardner. I live here."

I creep all the way down the stairs and flick on the bright overhead light. Both of us reel away from the glare. Yes, this is the young man in the family photo that fell and broke when Donna and I were touring the house with Brielle. That's why he looks familiar. Why did he arrive in the middle of the night?

I look around, befuddled. "Is your mom here, too?"

"No." He studies me through narrowed eyes, daring me to question him. It is his house—I can hardly demand an explanation from him. He must have been talking to Sophia.

Moving into the living room, I notice that the blanket I had laid over Sophia is now on the floor beside the family room couch. I keep walking toward the kitchen, talking to Austin over my shoulder. "Well, you startled me. Where's Sophia?" As the words leave my mouth, I notice that the mound of wet clothes by the deck door is gone.

For the first time since I encountered him, Austin appears flustered. "Sophia.... Uh, yeah. She left."

Austin follows me. He's wearing khaki pants, a crisp white Oxford shirt, and topsiders. I'm not sure what I consider appropriate garb for a middle of the night visit to one's shore home, but this seems rather formal.

"What was Sophia doing here, anyway?" His gaze darts to the tumbled blanket on the floor. Surely, he's never seen such a sight when his mother is here.

"She's been helping me with sorting and pricing." I can be as cagey with my answers as he is.

"She talks a lot of trash. Don't take her too seriously." He speaks with the same imperious tone as his mother, but he hasn't learned to cloak it with an air of civility as she has.

"I set the security system before I went to bed. Was it on when you came in?"

"No. But Jane knows the code, so maybe Sophia does too."

I look over at the Peterman house. All dark. The sliding doors are unlocked, so I lock them again as Austin watches. "I'm driving back to Palmyrton in the morning. I need to get back to sleep."

Austin perches on a stool at the kitchen counter. "Sure. Sorry I woke you."

I walk back toward the stairs, feeling his eyes bore into my spine. He had been heading upstairs when I encountered him. Clearly, he's waiting for me to go back to bed before he makes a move. But if he just wants to go to his bedroom, why wait? What's he up to?

I get back to my room and lock the door behind me. The kid makes me feel uneasy. I'm sure his mother doesn't know he's here. Is he planning one last blow-out party before his mother redecorates? But I'm due to return next weekend, and I'll have Ty with me. Would prep school kids come down to the shore for a party in the middle of the week?

I lie down in the big luxurious bed, but sleep eludes me—too much adrenaline still surges through my bloodstream after that scare. As I stare silently at the ceiling, I hear Austin's footsteps on the stairs. He walks past my bedroom door with barely a sound and opens the door to his bedroom, right next to my room.

It dawns on me that I forgot to tell him I'd already stripped the sheets from his bed. Oh, well—he'll find out soon enough.

I realize I'm holding my breath as I tune my ears to his movements. The floorboards creak as he moves around the room. A little grunt of frustration escapes him.

Now he's rustling through drawers, drawers that I know contain only some old T-shirts and sweats. Certainly, he didn't drive down here for that.

He's looking for something.

"Shit," I hear him mutter.

And I guess he can't find it.

Then a dresser drawer closes, and I hear Austin stride back down the hallway, no longer attempting to be quiet. I get up and look out my bathroom window, which faces the road. Soon, I see Austin, empty-handed, hop into a Jeep parked in the driveway and zoom away.

I check the time: four-thirty in the morning. There will be no traffic. The kid will be home before his parents rise.

Naturally, I have to go into his bedroom.

It's as spotless as it was when I left it. I open the top dresser drawer—the sweatshirts, tees, and shorts are tumbled but seem to all be there.

But one thing is missing.

The envelope with names written on it. I found it under the mattress but put it in here.

That's what the "shit" meant. Not that he hadn't found what he was looking for, but that I had clearly found it too.

Chapter 13

There's no point in trying to get back to sleep now. I shower and make myself a cup of coffee. The sky is just beginning to brighten; I can be on the road long before rush hour.

Only one concern nags at me.

What to do about Sophia. Is she home safely in her bed? How can I reassure her, so she cooperates with the police? How can I even get in touch with her—I don't have a cell number for either Sophia or Jane, and they don't have a landline.

I really don't want to bang on their door before daybreak.

Reluctantly, I decide to leave. Once I'm back in Palmyrton, I can get Jane's number from Brielle.

Leaving Sea Chapel behind, I cruise north on the Garden State Parkway thinking about Austin and Sophia and their parents. Why did Austin sneak down to Sea Chapel in the middle of the night for that envelope? What did he say to Sophia? Why did he warn me about her? Most of all, what is my obligation to talk to their parents about this?

My friend Tim's warning echoes in my mind. Don't cross Everett Gardner. He'd be a dangerous enemy to have. I just want to run this sale, make a tidy profit, and be on my way.

I don't need these complications.

The longer I drive, the more I convince myself to take a step back from the drama of these Sea Chapel families and keep my eyes on the prize of the sale.

I arrive home just as Sean is stumbling into the kitchen.

After we embrace, I pull away and look into his bloodshot eyes. "Don't take this wrong, but you look like crap."

"My grandfather fell and broke his hip last night. My parents spent the night with him at the hospital. Now they say they have to cancel their trip to Ireland."

"Oh, no!" Sean and his siblings have spent months planning this trip to Ireland as a fortieth wedding anniversary present to their parents. Touring the Emerald Isle with a bus full of elderly Royal Hibernians isn't my idea of a fun time, but his parents have been as excited about this vacation as two kids at a Chuck E. Cheese birthday party. They've had their bags packed for weeks, Mary has bought gifts for every Coughlin and O'Shea in all of County Cork, and Joe has their priest saying weekly novenas that their plane doesn't crash. They can't not go now.

"What are you going to do?" I ask as Sean paces the kitchen.

"I'm organizing a schedule with all my siblings so we can care for Granda twenty-four hours a day while Mom and Dad are away. They're all coming here this morning to work out the details."

I put on a pot of coffee, and the Coughlin sibling summit soon convenes at our house. Brendan stands at the kitchen counter picking at the corners of an Entenmann's coffee cake that Deirdre, who never goes anywhere without food, has supplied.

"We have eggs and bacon, Brendan." I place a mug of coffee in my brother-in-law's hand. "Sit down and I'll fix you a plate."

"Nah, I'm good. This is nervous eating." He swallows a big slug of coffee. "Can you believe that spiteful old man? He probably threw himself down just to ruin this vacation for our mother."

"Oh, Brendan—stop." Sean's older sister Deirdre wrings her hands. "This is simply an accident with terrible timing. We have to pull together to take care of Granda so that Mom and Dad will agree to still take their trip."

"Look, we'll put him in a rehab place—not a nursing home." Brendan knocks back the dregs of his coffee and bangs the mug on the counter. "I'll pay whatever it costs."

"Mom will never allow that." Sean and Colleen speak in unison.

In the Coughlin family, putting elderly relatives into assisted living is tantamount to placing them on an iceberg and floating them out to sea.

Brendan scowls. He's not used to being crossed. "It's temporary, for God's sake. We'll spring him as soon as they get back."

The siblings continue to discuss their options. Granda lives in a tiny two-story house in Kearney. The traffic, the parking, the steep stairs, the bathroom on the second floor all make it a nightmare for a recovering invalid and his caretakers.

"No way we're leaving him alone with a home health aide," Deirdre says. "Look what happened to that old woman in that big house where Audrey was working last year."

"But it wasn't—" I protest, trying to explain that the aide had provided good care, but I'm shouted over so completely that I retreat to a corner.

"Can we reschedule the trip? Send them with a different tour group?" Terry asks.

This suggestion falls in a volley of protest. They'll lose thousands of dollars at this late date. And Sean's dad refuses to travel with anyone but the Royal Hibernians. "Besides," Colleen adds, "I've spent hours on genealogy websites tracking down all those Coughlin and O'Shea cousins and great aunts and uncles. Mom and Dad have plans to meet up with scores of them. They can't reschedule that."

"The only way Mom and Dad will agree to go on the trip is if we promise to take care of Granda in his own home." Deirdre speaks with her hands on her hips.

"We'll have to set up a rotation and stay with him," Terry agrees.

"I have a job, Terry—unlike you." Brendan glares at his perpetually disheveled brother, who's currently freelancing as a website designer.

Bringing Terry's sporadic employment history into the discussion seems totally unproductive to me, but what do I know? I'm an only child.

"They're stabilizing him now, but Mom says they'll release him by Tuesday." Sean grabs the note pad we keep by the fridge. "He can go back to his house if we get the right equipment. We'll need to rent a hospital bed, a wheelchair, and one of those potty chairs."

"I am *not* wiping his ass," Brendan shouts. "I'm hiring a home health aide for my shifts."

Sean steps up to his brother. "You will cover your shifts until that plane takes off on Wednesday. Once they're in the air, I don't care who you hire."

"If the spouses help, then each person would only have to work one eight hour shift every..." Colleen stumbles through the math on her phone's calculator.

"They're gone for two weeks. That's 336 hours, divided by ten of us, that's four eight-hour shifts a piece, give or take a few hours," I offer.

"Thanks for the speedy calculation, Audrey, but there aren't ten of us." Brendan tosses his mug into the sink with a crash. "I'm separated, remember?"

Brendan and Adrienne are still trying to decide if their marriage can be patched together or not. Now is definitely not the time to ask her to pitch in with elder care. Although, honestly, even if those two were happy as cooing doves, I can't imagine the stylish and high maintenance Adrienne doing the messy work of caring for Granda.

In fact, I can't quite imagine myself doing it, either. I'm not known for my nursing skills, but I do get a kick out of Sean's crusty old grandfather. He swears like the sailor he once was, and he's full of hilarious stories. He also goes out of his way to offend every member of the family in the way that will bother that person the most. He insults the Pope in front of Sean's mother, tells raunchy jokes to Deirdre's kids, and insists Colleen isn't a real lawyer because she's a girl. He hasn't figured out a way to bug me yet, but Sean says it's just a matter of time.

And I did marry Sean for better or worse.

"We'll each work one shift until the plane takes off," Sean declares. "Then we'll reconvene to see if we should hire outside help."

With some grumbling, the siblings accept the plan.

When everyone finally leaves, Sean catches sight of the oven clock. "My God, look at the time! I've gotta get to work." Heading to the door, he pauses as he passes me. "By the way, Anthony's uncle sent him to South Carolina on business." Sean makes air quotes to indicate the business was keeping his nephew out of jail. "I got Donna set up at the shelter, and the restraining order is in place."

"Thank you, honey. I really appreciate it." Still, I'm not quite satisfied. "But can't the police arrest Anthony down there and, like, extradite him or something?"

Sean offers a rueful smile and rubs his thumb and index finger together. "Not for a simple assault charge. Too expensive. Besides, Donna will be safer with five hundred miles between her and her husband."

"But what if he doesn't stay down there?"

"I met the uncle. He's not the kinda guy you'd want to cross." Sean grins. "I'm betting Anthony will stay put until Uncle Nunzio says he can come back. But Donna should hire a lawyer and get the divorce process underway."

I put my arms around his neck. "You're a good man, you know that, right?"

He kisses the top of my head. "You bring out the best in me." Then he pulls away and looks down into my face, his brows drawn together in concern "Was there something else you needed to talk to me about last night?"

The story of Trevor and Sophia is so long and complicated. I can't saddle him with that when he's already late for work and preoccupied with Granda. "It can wait."

After Sean leaves, I send Brielle a text with an update on my progress. I don't mention her son's visit, and I close with a request for Jane's cell number.

She replies with a brusque *Excellent!* and forwards Jane's contact info. After pondering my approach, I send Jane a simple request: *It's Audrey. Have Sophia contact me. I can use her help next weekend.*

Let's hope she doesn't respond that she has no idea where her daughter is.

Chapter 14

When I get to the office, Ty is already there. His face lights up when he sees me. "Yo, Audge—how'd it go down the shore?"

"Pretty well, but there's still a lot to do." I fill him in on the details. "You're still on to come down there with me this coming weekend, right?"

"Yeah, I'm all in. Not so sure 'bout Donna being able to handle the Freidrich sale all alone, though."

"How is she?"

"Better. She's been callin' me from the shelter. At first, she'd just cry the whole time. But as soon as she got there, she had all these counseling sessions and shit, and she's startin' to get her game back. It helps that Anthony's clear down in South Carolina. But Donna's mother doesn't want her to get divorced. She keeps tellin' her to forgive and forget."

"What! What kind of mother wants her daughter to stay with an abuser? Wait 'til I talk to Donna. I'll tell her—"

Ty raises his hand for silence. "We're not supposed to boss her around. We gotta just listen and say, "uh-huh, what do you want to do?" Ty pulls a crumpled pamphlet from his back pocket and passes it to me. "Sean gave me this."

How to Help a Victim of Domestic Abuse

Number One on the list is don't offer advice.

I guess it makes sense that a woman who's been repressed by a domineering husband doesn't need to be bossed around by her friends and family. Holding my tongue will be a challenge, but I'll give it a shot if that's what Donna needs.

"Is she allowed to leave the shelter?"

"Of course—she's not in jail. She says she'll be here today around ten-thirty—right after her morning counseling session."

"What about the Freidrich sale?" I hate to bring it up given all the emotional trauma Ty has had to deal with in my absence, but the whole point of my going to Sea Chapel without my staff was so that we could work on setting up two sales at the same time.

"It's a-l-l good. I got a little behind with Donna gettin' hurt, but I had my friend Zeke helpin' me yesterday and we all caught up." Ty holds out his hands. "And don't worry—you don't hafta pay him. He owes me."

I figure I'm better off not knowing what that favor is all about. "Thank you, Ty." I squeeze his hand. "I appreciate all you do."

"You know I always got your back, Audge. Donna says she has to do some work with the ads and the signs for the Freidrich sale today. Then tomorrow, the two of us will do the final pricing, and Donna can make the little shit look pretty like she always does. I think we'll be all set by the time I have to leave with you on Friday. And maybe Zeke can help Donna on Saturday."

"So you don't need me at all?"

Ty slaps his leg. "You look like Grams when she comes home and sees I went and made dinner for Kyle and Lo and me without her."

I laugh along with him. This is exactly what I'm going to need Ty and Donna to do if I take time off with a new baby, but it doesn't make it any easier to accept that I'm no longer essential to every aspect of my own business. Maybe now is the time to tell Ty that Sean and I are trying to get pregnant. I take a deep breath, but before I can speak, the office door rattles and Donna walks in.

She stands in the doorway offering us a shaky smile. Her arm is in a sling and there's something different about her eyes, but otherwise, she looks pretty good. Before I can say a word in greeting, Donna's eyes well up and she uses the back of her good hand to head off the tears' path down her cheek. Then the words tumble out faster than the tears. "I'm so glad to be here! Don't look at my eyes! I had to give up wearing mascara 'cause I've been crying so much. And don't worry about the sling. I'm allowed to take it off. I'm just supposed to rest my arm when I can. I'm ready to work."

I move to hug her, but Donna marches past me to her desk. "Sean was a big help to me, Audrey. And Ty, well—" Her voice trembles. "I gotta stop talkin' about it, okay? I just gotta *work*. Last night I scrubbed the oven at the shelter and that helped me more than all the counseling sessions. But the other ladies there are nice. They really are."

There's nothing like being surrounded by people worse off than you to make you feel better about yourself. Even with one hand literally tied to her side, Donna can outclean three able-bodied women.

Donna rips the sling off her arm. "Wouldja look at my desk! Oh my God—I gotta get this mess cleared up fast."

Donna sits down and begins sorting and stacking. In truth, all that's on her desk is Saturday's mail and a FedEx envelope. Ty and I exchange a glance and a grin.

Donna's back and on the road to recovery.

Ty heads back to the Freidrich house. Once he's gone, I expect Donna to open up to me about what's been going on with Anthony and her family and life at the shelter, but she keeps her face buried in her computer screen and works silently. Occasionally, her phone chirps, but she doesn't even glance at it.

Messages from Anthony?

Pleas from her mother?

It's hard for me to resist inquiring, but I do as the shelter brochure instructs, and butt out.

Soon, my own phone chirps. Good—a message from Sophia: *When are you coming back? I have to talk to you!!*

I'll be back on Friday evening. What's the matter?

I'll tell you when I see you.

Call me now.

I wait.

Silence.

Teenagers—so much drama! I should know a teenager would never use her phone to initiate a conversation. I'll have to call her.

Sophia's phone rings endlessly and rolls to voicemail.

A second later, another text arrives. *I CAN'T TALK NOW!!! I'LL TELL YOU ON FRIDAY.*

Fine. At least I know the kid's alive. Once I talk to Sean about what I've learned about Trevor, I'll decide how to handle Sophia. Right now, I have work to do.

The morning passes peacefully as I continue to track down potential buyers for Brielle's high-end furnishings. At 11:45, I glance up to find Donna standing in front of my desk. "I updated our website, placed ads for both sales, posted pictures on Facebook and Twitter. I'm going to grab some lunch and then go help Ty at the Freidrich house."

I study Donna's face. Despite this burst of efficiency, she seems edgier than when she first arrived in the office. "Is everything okay?"

"Yeah.... sure...I'm good." She hitches her big purse up onto her good shoulder. "Did you need me to do something else before I go out?"

"No—have a good lunch." Still uneasy, I watch through the window as she walks toward her car. Maybe I'm being overly protective. It's true I've never, ever seen Donna without eye makeup, even when she's scrubbing floors. Maybe that's why she looks forlorn and nervous to me.

I find some not-too-old yogurt in the office fridge and some not-too-stale almonds in my desk drawer and keep working. By late afternoon, Sean calls with an update. "Deirdre and I have everything set up at Granda's house. I'm working on the care schedule. You get first choice."

Hmmm—sooner, when he's all drugged up and more dependent, or later when he's less fragile but more ornery? "How about Wednesday evening."

"THERE'S NOTHING AT our house for dinner tonight," Sean confesses.

"I'll pick up a pizza and some beer on my way home. But first, I have to get Ethel. See you in an hour."

I leave the office for the day, double-locking the door behind me. As I walk along the tree-lined street, a low rumble vibrates the cool fall air. Glancing over my shoulder, I see a large, low black sports car idling by the curb. Two plumes of noxious fumes rise from the twin chrome exhaust pipes. A muscle car! He can't do much drag racing on a suburban street lined with parked cars.

As I prepare to tootle off in my Honda, the car peels out and speeds away.

Chapter 15

When I reach Dad and Natalie's apartment, there's a post-it note stuck to the door:

Audrey, come in.

I test the doorknob and it turns. Good thing Sean's not with me or the first fifteen minutes of the visit would be a lecture on why two people in their late sixties should not sit around with their door unlocked and a note inviting thieves and murderers to enter. I walk in calling, "Hi, I'm here."

Ethel races down the hall and hits my solar plexus at about thirty miles per hour. We dance in joyful reunion until it dawns on me that no humans have greeted me. I walk further into the apartment and discover Dad and Natalie sitting in their living room staring at their Alexa speaker. Dad points to a chair. "Shh. We're listening to Gregory."

Ah, their favorite podcast, Gregory Halpern's *The World in a Week*. Sean and I like it too, but we're not fanatics like Dad and Natalie. They tune in as soon as a new episode is released. I listen to the mellow voice emanating from the speaker.

"And that's how the world looks this week from Sri Lanka."

The closing music begins. "The World in a Week with Gregory Halpern has been brought to you by our sponsors..."

"Alexa, off," Dad commands. Then he gets up to kiss me on the forehead. "Sorry to make you wait. This episode was positively gripping."

"Mesmerizing," Natalie adds.

"Do you two ever miss an installment? Sean and I liked the episodes on Peru, but I gotta tell you, the Shetland Islands was a little slow."

Natalie jumps up to fix us some tea. "Some episodes are better than others, I suppose, but we just love Gregory himself. Listening to him is like having a conversation with an old friend. We feel like he's right here in the room with us."

"And now we're going to get to meet him," Dad says. "I hope that doesn't destroy the magic."

"Meet him where?"

"He's giving a lecture at Drew University on Thursday. We've had our tickets for months. And this week, we got invited to the reception after the lecture. Gregory's mother, Lorraine, worked at the hospital for many years. She and I are old friends, and she invited us."

"Oh, so that's how you two discovered the podcast. You knew Gregory before he was famous."

"Knew of him. His mother would share her worries about him with me. Gregory was a real free spirit, and when he dropped out of Columbia Law School, his father cut off all financial support." Natalie pours hot water over my Yogi green tea bag. "Lorraine was beside herself with worry when Gregory said he was going to the Mideast to work as a freelance reporter. He knocked around over there for years, looking for adventure in war zones, earning just enough as a stringer for the *Times* to hold body and soul together."

"And then he hit upon this idea for the podcast," Dad dunks a Lorna Doone in his tea, "and in two years he has five million subscribers and makes a bundle."

"I always knew he'd turn out just fine," Natalie says. "Of course, now his parents are just as proud of him as can be."

We sit and sip tea as I tell Dad and Natalie about my sales and Sean's grandfather and Donna's husband. When my father leaves the room to collect Ethel's toys and dog blanket, I lean across the table and whisper to Natalie. "Another month and I'm still not pregnant. I'm worried, Natalie. Do you think I should go to a specialist and get checked out?"

My stepmother purses her lips and thinks for a moment. She's not one for hasty responses or reassuring platitudes. "There's no harm in running a few tests and finding out early whether you have a problem or not. The best fertility doctor in Palmyrton is Dr. Karl Stein. He has a long waiting list, but I can get you in. I know his scheduler. But you'll have to take someone's cancellation. Are you flexible?"

"Sure. I can go any time, as long as it's not during a sale."

Natalie scrolls through the contacts on her phone and has a quick conversation, finishing just as Dad comes back into the room. "Tomorrow at three? Wow, that's quick." She looks at me with raised eyebrows.

"Sure, that's great."

I asked for this. I got it.

———————◈———————

NEXT, ETHEL AND I HEAD to Rocco's to pick up the pizza. The dog rides shotgun with her head out the window and her ears rippling in the breeze. Her nose twitches as we pull into Rocco's parking lot, where the kitchen exhaust fan blasts a hot wind of deliciousness even my lame human nose can detect. Ethel scrambles to exit the Honda.

I pull her back and raise the window until it's only open a crack. "You have to wait in the car."

Ethel's big brown eyes convey a level of shock and disbelief usually only seen in stunned tornado survivors.

"I won't be long." I look back at her when I reach the sidewalk. She has one paw pressed against the passenger window. "I'll bring you a meatball," I shout and hurry inside.

When I open the door, I'm clobbered by a wave of aromas that would send Ethel into sensory overload: garlic, basil, tomato sauce, and molten mozzarella. As always, there's a long line at the counter where the pick-up order line and the place order line intertwine in front of the display of pies and strombolis. To my left, every booth is filled: frazzled parents feeding their kids while on the run to some activity, early-dining old folks, and most notably, rowdy teenagers. As I wait to give my name to the counter person, I notice one booth crammed with boys in familiar maroon clothing—it seems to be the starting line-up of the Bumford-Stanley lacrosse team.

"Yo, Wells—how come you didn't catch that pass?"

"'Cause you throw like a girl, douche."

"Oooo."

"We coulda kicked their asses if—"

"Hey!" Rocco himself sticks his head out into the dining area. "You punks watch your mouths in my store. You wanna talk trash, go somewhere else."

A kid at the end of the booth stands up. "I'm sorry, sir. My friend here doesn't know how to behave in a fine dining establishment."

The rest of the gang collapses in laughter, and Rocco scowls and returns to the kitchen. When a tall man in front of me steps away with his order, I have a clearer view of all the boys. One of them is Austin Gardner. I watch him for a second then look away. He seems to be comfortably in the mix with his friends, and no worse for wear for being up half the night driving around New Jersey. He sits with an arm extended along the back of the booth, and occasionally he nudges the head of the kid sitting next to him. The other kid shoots him an annoyed look and squirms to get away, but he's packed in too tightly to avoid Austin.

Friendly horseplay or harassment, who can tell?

Finally, I make it to the counter. "Pick-up for Nealon."

The counterman scans the stack of pizza boxes staying warm on top of the oven. "I don't see nuthin for Neil."

"Neal-*on*," I shout over the hub-bub around me. "Audrey Nealon. Mushroom pie, Caesar salad, and an order of meatballs."

"Aw-right—ya don't hafta yell."

I take my order, pay, and escape. Out in the parking lot, I struggle to hold my pizza level while opening my trunk. There's no way I can trust Ethel with this in the back seat.

"I'll hold that for you," a male voice behind me says. Two hands relieve me of the box while Ethel barks and scratches inside my Honda.

I spin around and find myself face-to-face with Austin Gardner.

"We meet again." The kid is tall. I'm forced to look up at him.

"Yeah. Small world."

There's an awkward silence. He clearly followed me out here. What does he want?

Austin shifts his stance. "Hey, listen—about last night...uh, like, there was this envelope that was under my mattress. Were you the one who...like..."

"Moved it to the drawer. Yes. I stripped the sheets off the bed because your mother said she wanted all the bedding sold. I found the envelope and put it in the drawer with your clothes. I figured you might want that and the clothes."

"Yeah...uh... but did you open it and read it or anything?"

"Of course not! I don't read private mail that I find in my clients' houses. I alert the owners that they might have left something important behind."

Austin's eyes widen. "You told my mother?"

"I texted her that there were some clothes and mail left behind, but I don't think she ever responded." I reach for my phone to look over the thread of messages between Brielle and me.

But Austin isn't interested. He thrusts the pizza box back at me and takes off like he's chasing a lacrosse ball down the field.

Chapter 16

Ethel bounds into our house and races around sniffing every corner. As much as she loves my dad, she's clearly glad to be back on duty guarding our house. Once she's assured herself that no squirrels or other terrorists have gained access in her absence, she settles under the kitchen table and waits for the action to begin.

Sean arrives as I'm setting the table. While we eat our Italian feast, I tell my husband about everything that's happened to me since he kissed me good-bye at Brielle's house: the jetty rescue, Sophia's suspicions about Trevor's death, Austin's visit, and the encounter at the pizza parlor.

Sean listens without interruption.

I'm careful to tone down the danger of what happened on the jetty. I make it sound like we both skipped easily over those rocks. The fear I felt at the time has receded, and now I'm more freaked out by the business with Austin.

"So what do you think I should do?" I ask after I lay out all the details. "How can I make sure the police get Sophia's information? And should I tell Brielle about her son's visit?"

"I wouldn't worry about Austin," Sean says. "The kid probably had a stash of coke or pills in that envelope that he'd forgotten about. The names were probably kids that he sells to. Raced down to get his product and discovered you'd moved it. Believe me, his mother won't thank you for opening her eyes to what her precious boy is up to."

"It's so handy being married to you." I give my husband a second beer. "You always know the most plausible criminal activity any given person could be engaged in."

"Thanks. I try." He takes a swig from the bottle. "I'm not sure I can be so helpful regarding Sophia."

"Can't you call those Sea Chapel cops you met on the beach and tell them to talk to Sophia? If they come to her, she won't feel like's she ratting. I hope."

"Those guys weren't detectives. The Sea Chapel police force is five patrolmen in the off-season. In the summer they hire a few cadets from the police academy to break up bar fights and keep the house parties from getting too rowdy. They haven't had a murder since 1986, and that was an open and shut case because the killer was still holding the knife when the cops drove up. Trevor Finlayson's murder is way more than they can handle. The chief is sixty-four-and a half and just putting in his hours until retirement. I told you, they turned this whole case over to the Ocean County Sherriff's department. And those guys really don't want any interference from the likes of me."

"Not even if it's important evidence? I've never known you to advocate withholding information from the police, even if there's a turf war going on."

"Not withholding. Believe me, the sheriff's department will interview all Trevor's friends soon. And when they do, your girl Sophia better be prepared."

"Prepared for what?"

Sean chews his pizza with his eyes half shut. Is he luxuriating in its greasy, cheesy goodness or contemplating what I've told him?

He swallows, takes another swig of beer, and speaks. "Sounds to me like Sophia could be involved in her friend's murder."

A wad of mozzarella catches in my throat. Gasping, I finally find the breath to reply. "No way! She loved him, and she's devastated by his death. She says it's those other kids and their secret club or society or whatever. She wasn't a part of that."

Sean contemplates me with the unblinking intensity of a hawk studying a clueless mouse. "So she says. Maybe the cool kids did invite her to join, and she couldn't resist."

I keep babbling in Sophia's defense. "You didn't see how anguished she was on the night I rescued her from the jetty. She feels guilty that she let Trevor down."

Sean's sandy eyebrows arch. His eyes look bluer than normal. "Oh, I agree that guilt drove her out to the end of that jetty."

The dry crust of my slice slips from my fingers. "You think she was considering killing herself because she participated in Trevor's murder?"

"Murder-suicide. Happens all the time. Most common when a man kills his wife or girlfriend, then turns the gun on himself. But remember that lawyer in Chatham a couple years back? He killed his longtime partner over some business disagreement, then jumped off the Route 24 overpass during rush hour. Helluva traffic jam."

"Okay, I get it. But I'm sure that's not what happened here. Sophia's a good kid. I've gotten to know her these last few days and—"

Sean starts to chuckle. And the chuckle escalates to a full-throated laugh.

I dive into the pizza box for another slice. "All right, Mr. Ace Detective. I know I don't have a stellar track record in separating good guys from bad guys, but come on—" I straighten up and go into defensive mode. "Sophia is a teenager, not a life-long politician. I don't think she's clever enough to double-cross me. She could've just clammed up and gone home without telling me a thing. Instead, she poured out her heart to me. And now I've got important information I don't know what to do with."

Sean leans across the table and traces my cheekbone with his thumb. "I don't think she set out to deceive you. And I'm not saying Sophia's the one who strangled Trevor. But I've interviewed a lot of teenagers in my time. Kids in a group get caught up in bad acts that they'd never do on their own. Sophia may be trying to convince herself that these other kids were to blame. But if she was there—"

My mushroom slice heaves in my stomach. "—she could be held responsible, too. So she'd better have a lawyer before she talks to the police, right?"

Sean sighs. "You didn't hear that from me, but yeah, she needs to lawyer up. How old is she, anyway? If she's already turned eighteen, she could be in a world of trouble."

"I'm not sure if she's seventeen or eighteen. Should I call her mother and warn her about what's going on?" To my own ears, my voice sounds uncertain and querulous.

"I take it you're not keen on that?"

"Jane's not easy to talk to. Very unfocused. Very self-absorbed." I toss my pizza crust to Ethel. "And I doubt she'll take Sophia seriously."

"Yet you take her seriously. You've known her for two days—why do you care so much?"

Yeah, why do I? I pick at the cheese stuck to the pizza box. "Good question. She reminds me of me at that age, I guess."

Sean grimaces. "You had pink hair and a nose ring?"

"No, I wasn't brave enough to be so nonconformist. And I was a straight-A student. But...."

"But what?"

"I was a lost soul, like Sophia. Only one parent, and that parent disinterested. I acted like I didn't need guidance, but I was dying for some adult to see me, really see *me,* not just my good grades and my math and chess skills." I slap the empty pizza box shut. "But no one ever did."

Sean reaches out for my hand. "Yet you turned out all right."

"I'm all right now." I entwine my fingers with his. "As you will recall, I was a bit of a mess when you first met me.

"I wish I'd gone to Palmyrton High School instead of St. Benedict's. I could've fallen for you at eighteen and saved us both a lot of heartache."

I snort and start to clear the table. "Right. Like a Catholic school basketball jock would ever have looked at the public-school chess nerd."

Sean comes up behind me and nuzzles my neck. "Rumor among the St. Ben's guys was that you public school girls were fast."

"Want me to prove the rumor true?"

"Leave the dishes. I'll close the windows and turn out the lights. You let the dog out."

I stand at the back door while Ethel runs a few laps around the yard and pees on her favorite tree. The cool autumn air carries the first scent of falling leaves. I never did resolve whether I should call Jane. I'll deal with that decision tomorrow.

Ethel shoots back into the house.

The last thing I hear before locking the door is a sports car roaring down our street.

WHAT A DAY! EVEN THOUGH Brielle's guest room had 700 thread count Egyptian cotton sheets, it feels so good to be back in my own best-of-Target bed. After demonstrating to my husband that I really am a fast public school girl, I welcome Ethel into the bed for a cuddle while Sean brushes his teeth.

Sean returns and slips under the covers. "I was lonely here last night. I've already forgotten what it's like to sleep alone."

"You're going to be alone Friday and Saturday when I go back down to Sea Chapel."

"I'm doing my overnight with Granda on Friday. I hope your parents can watch Ethel again. How did it go when you picked her up today?"

"They had fun with her—they won't mind having her again." I curl along Sean's body. Now is the time to mention that Natalie got me an appointment with Dr. Stein. But the words won't come. I know he won't approve, and I don't want to argue. Instead, I tell him about their plans to see Gregory Halpern's lecture.

Sean yawns. "Better them than me."

"I thought you liked his podcast."

"I don't mind listening when I'm driving or cooking, but I don't think I'd want to sit in a theater and stare at him on a stage for two hours."

"He's supposed to put on a great show."

I reach to turn off the bedside lamp and check my phone one last time. There's a text from Natalie. *Do you want to go with us to see Gregory Halpern? I'm sorry, but Lorraine only has one extra ticket.*

I chuckle and text back. *Love to!*

"What's so funny?" Sean asks.

I peck him on the cheek. "I'm going to see Gregory without you. I'm sure you won't mind."

Chapter 17

I sleep through my alarm and awake at eight to find Sean already off to work, Ethel pacing in front of the hook where her leash hangs, and my phone chirping the arrival of a text from Sophia.

Driving up right now 2 Trevor's funeral at 1. Will stop @ ur office when I get 2 P'town.

My thumbs flash across my phone. *Wait! Call me first. I need to talk to you.*

Driving now. Can't talk.

Oh, the girl who walked to the end of the jetty in her bare feet at dusk during a rising tide is now Miss Safety First. *I won't be in my office all day*, I warn.

But I know I'll be there in the window when she's arriving.

Before I eat breakfast, I take Ethel out for a walk in our neighborhood. We see the young moms' group powerwalking behind their strollers, get a Milk-Bone from our favorite UPS driver, and wave to the landscapers who turn off their leaf blowers to let us pass. Before the roar of the blowers begins again, I hear a different, lower rumble.

There's that black muscle car again! It roars down the street as Ethel lunges at the end of her leash, barking furiously. I only catch the first three letters of the license plate: EZT.

This can't be a coincidence. Someone's watching me. Who do I know who would drive a car like that?

Flashy. Loud. Macho.

Anthony!

Maybe he's back from South Carolina. This can't be good.

I take Ethel home, eat my breakfast and drive to the office, all the while worrying about an encounter with Anthony.

Donna is already behind her desk when I walk in. "What kind of car does Anthony drive?"

"A cream Cadillac El Dorado. Why?"

"Oh, good." I toss my tote bag on my desk, glad that my paranoia is unfounded, and stand on a chair to retrieve a box of price labels on a high shelf. "I got nervous because I keep seeing this black muscle car, and I worried Anthony might have sneaked back from South Carolina."

I hop down from the chair with the box in my hands. "I'm just paranoi—"

Donna's eyes are as wide as a kid's on Christmas morning. But it's not delight I see there.

"What's the matter? You know the car?"

"Was it a Camaro ZR1?"

"You're asking *me* about cars? It's black and low to the ground and loud. And it has twin exhaust pipes. License begins with EZT."

Donna's face crumples. "Oh my Ga-w-wd—it's Ray-Ray. He works for Anthony's uncle. Anthony must've told him to keep an eye on me. And you."

"Have you noticed the car following you? Has he followed you to the shelter?"

"No. Ray-Ray would know that I'd recognize his car."

I face her with my hands on my hips. "Yeah, so why is he conducting surveillance in such a distinctive car? Doesn't seem too bright to me."

"Anthony wants me to know that he's watching without going so far as to put a tail on me. That would be a violation of the restraining order. But he knew you'd notice the car and tell me soon enough."

"Intimidation. Well, if I see Ray-Ray—what a ridiculous name—I'll tell him to get lost."

Donna lunges at me. "No, Audrey—don't! You don't know who you're messin' with. Ray-Ray's a nut-job. He likes hurting people."

"Ray-Ray doesn't realize what it's like to mess with me." I thump my chest. "I'll get Sean to put the Palmyrton police on him and just wait for him to go one mile over the speed limit. I'll, I'll—" I don't know what I'll do, but I won't stand by helplessly and let this thug intimidate Donna. "Call your divorce lawyer and tell him about this."

Donna doesn't move.

"Seriously." I wag my index finger at her. "This is the kind of stuff he needs to know about so he can negotiate a good settlement for you."

Donna rakes her hands through her hair. "I'm not sure.... It's, it's not easy ending a marriage, Audrey. We've been together for ten years. Our families are all intertwined. You're acting like I'm just quittin' a job or droppin' out of the gym."

A wave of remorse smacks me. I'm bossing Donna around, exactly what I'm not supposed to be doing. "Oh, honey—I'm so sorry. Of course, I understand it's hard. I'm going to butt out. You let me know if you need my help with anything, I mean anything, and I'll be here for you, okay?"

Donna swallows hard and nods. "Thanks, Audrey. I'm sorry about Ray-Ray. Just ignore him."

I make a gesture that Donna can interpret as compliance if she wishes. But how I handle a thug outside my own house is my business, not hers.

Donna spends an hour working on emails and social media promoting our upcoming sales. Then she heads out to the Friedrich house to help Ty. Our plan is for Ty and Donna to get the sale perfectly set up so that Donna can run it solo on Saturday with help from a temporary worker while Ty comes to Sea Chapel with me for the weekend to manage the much larger Gardner sale. I've second-guessed every conceivable problem she might have running the sale, but haven't accounted for interference from thugs like Ray-Ray. I make a note to ask Sean to have a patrol car swing by the Freidrich house periodically on Saturday. I'm nervous, but I can do this.

I can let go.

I can.

At twelve-thirty I hear a timid tapping at the door.

When I open it, there stands Sophia. Her pink hair is neatly combed, and she's wearing a long black skirt and a fringe-y T-shirt. A little funky, but funereal enough.

"You look nice. Come on in."

Sophia enters and looks around at the cheerful clutter that is Another Man's Treasure. I rarely meet clients here, so I make no apologies for the mismatched chairs and the hit parade of unsold kitsch that decorates the walls.

Sophia approaches a framed Velvet Underground album cover. "Awesome! I've always wanted one of these."

"You can have it if you agree to sit down and listen to me for a minute." I pat the seat of the overstuffed easy chair covered in butterfly chintz and pull up the faux Chippendale throne chair beside her. "I talked to my husband about your concerns about Trevor. He says the Ocean County Sherriff's Department has taken over the investigation of Trevor's death."

"Murder," Sophia corrects.

"Right. He says the cops will definitely interview all Trevor's friends. You need to be prepared for that. You need to tell the truth. But also..."

Sophia tips her head and squints her eyes. "Also what?"

"You need to be cautious. That special group that the Bumford-Stanley kids invited Trevor into. You need—"

"I was wrong about that. Just forget I ever mentioned it."

Oh, lord—Sean was right. Maybe Sophia was involved. "Forget about it? After we came back from the jetty, you seemed pretty positive that the kids who go to those special BSS parties had something to do with Trevor's death. What's happened to change your mind?"

Sophia twists in the chair, throwing one leg over the arm and ruching up her skirt. "I, I just talked to someone and realized I might have gotten the wrong impression."

"Talked to whom?" I press.

Sophia flounces into an upright position. "It doesn't matter. I was just wrong, okay? Haven't you ever been wrong about someone?"

Have I ever! But this isn't the time for sharing my life story. I purse my lips and study her.

"On Monday night when you fell asleep on Brielle's sofa—did you talk to Austin?"

"Austin? What are you talking about? I haven't seen Austin since Labor Day weekend."

Is she lying? I'm sure I heard Austin talking to someone that night. Had Sophia returned to her own house before Austin got there? If so, whom was he talking to?

Before I can ask another question, Sophia begins chattering. "I'll know what to do about the police after I go to this funeral." Sophia picks at the fringe on her blouse. Then she looks up at me. "I've never been to a funeral before. Not even for an old person. And my mom and I never go to church. I don't know what to do there. Will you go with me?"

Go with her? I've got a million things to do today. But her eyes are so big and sad. One minute she's a defiant young woman, the next she's a scared toddler unwilling to enter an unfamiliar room. And what does she mean that she'll know what to do regarding the police once she goes to the funeral? "I'll consider it. The church is only a few blocks from here. But you have to tell me what you meant by knowing what to do after you've been to the funeral."

"The whole church will be full of people who knew Trev. I'll be able to tell when I see them all." Sophia looks at the cuckoo clock. "C'mon—it's quarter to one."

Chapter 18

First Presbyterian is the largest Protestant church in Palmyrton. Outside its gray stone walls, the balmy autumn sunshine beams down on the well-manicured grounds and a sign that cheerfully proclaims "All Are Welcome Here." A steady stream of black-clad people marches up the walk to the heavy wood doors. Every parking spot for blocks is filled, and a cop directs late arrivers to the municipal garage. Sophia and I have walked over from the AMT office. As we draw closer, Sophia walks slower. The cop stops traffic and waves us across the intersection. Sophia grabs my arm. "I can't do it. I can't go in there."

I tug her forward. "You've come this far. You'll regret it if you don't pay your last respects."

Sophia searches my face for reassurance. Apparently, she finds it because she gives a brisk nod and heads into the crosswalk.

I hope I've done the right thing.

She keeps her eyes focused on her feet as we walk into the church. If she knows any of the other mourners, she doesn't let on. Inside the cool dim interior, the deep tones of the organ drown out any brief whispered conversations of the people in the pews.

An usher hands us each a program. When Sophia reads the words on the cover, Memorial Service to celebrate the life of Trevor Finlayson, 2001-2019, her hand clenches the thick, cream paper and she sways.

I grab her elbow and propel her up the aisle. Virtually every pew is fully occupied, and Sophia and I must move toward the front to get a seat. We end up just a few rows back from the pews reserved for the family. On the right side of the aisle sits a woman in her forties, her face a frozen mask of grief. A handsome man sits next to her and three kids sit next to him. This must be Trevor's mother, stepfather, and the half and step siblings. Occasionally, the man leans toward the woman, but she sits stiffly erect and holds herself apart from any comfort he tries to offer. On the left side of the aisle sits a dignified elderly couple who keep their eyes focused straight ahead on the empty choir stalls behind the pulpit. They must be Trevor's grandparents. The old lady looks fragile and lost. But the old man sits ram-rod straight, his mouth pressed in a hard line. Years ago they lost their son, and now they've lost their only grandson. Behind them is a sparse row of extended family.

The Bumford-Stanley community is well represented in the next ten pews. I recognize the headmaster, Grayson Peale, whose aristocratic visage I've seen pictured in the local news many times. He's surrounded by men and women who must be staff, and behind them sit several rows of students, all wholesome and clean cut, the girls in modest dresses, the boys in blue blazers, white shirts, striped ties, and khakis. I twist and stare, not caring if anyone notices. Austin Gardner is there among the teens. Is the boy he was pestering at Rocco's also there? Honestly, I can't tell. They all look the same: fair skin, short hair, straight teeth.

On the far side of the church, I spot Brielle's distinctive honey blonde hair. I stand up to take off my long cardigan, using the move as a way to get a better view. Yes, there next to Brielle is a short, bald, homely man. Looks like Everett Gardner has taken the day off from making megabucks to come to this funeral. While I'm standing, I notice another young man sitting apart from the Bumford-Stanley crowd. His long dark hair scrapes the shoulders of his denim jacket, and the silver ring in his eyebrow glistens when he turns into the beam of light coming through the stained-glass window depicting the Resurrection. Maybe this is Trevor's public-school friend that Sophia mentioned.

Now that Sophia has gotten over the initial shock of seeing her friend's name on the funeral program, she's looking around with as much interest as I have. She scans the family members, but she really stares at the pews full of BSS kids. Most of them seem to ignore her, but Austin raises his hand in tentative greeting and a tall, slender girl seems to smile in Sophia's direction.

Silence descends on the crowd when the minister approaches the pulpit. The organist kicks into high gear, and we all stand and sing, "For All the Saints." After a welcoming prayer and a reading of Psalm 23, the minister begins his homily. He's got a smooth, reassuring voice, but his words seem generic, like he's got a standard spiel for the tragic passing of a young person. He's tip-toeing around the elephant in the room: the cause of Trevor's death.

Next, we sing "My Shepherd Will Supply My Need," then reach the portion of the service marked, "Sharing of Personal Reflections." Three people are scheduled to share: Trevor's great aunt, his art teacher, and his soccer teammate. The poor aunt, who seems to be Grandpa's sister, can barely make it through her remarks on Trevor's childhood, she is sobbing so much. The art teacher, more composed, comments on Trevor's talent and discerning eye. The soccer teammate reads awkwardly from a prepared text, relying heavily on "awesome," "amazing" and "super" to define Trevor's skills on the field. As the eulogies continue, I find myself growing more morose. Is this all the poor kid's life amounts to? A few soccer goals, a few entries in the Art Fair? Of course, no one mentions his struggles with mental illness. But neither do they mention his imagination, his love of *Stranger Things*, his friendships. This wan tribute doesn't sound like the boy Sophia misses so much.

While the reflections have been going on, Sophia continues to squirm in the pew, frequently glancing back at the BSS students. Many of them are gazing down at their laps. I assume they're texting, not praying.

"Is there anyone else who'd like to share a tribute to Trevor?" the pastor asks when the soccer teammate leaves the mic.

The pastor looks ready to cue the organist for the final hymn when Sophia jolts to her feet. Before I can grab her arm, she's out of the pew and heading for the pulpit. A cold sweat breaks out on my chest. Dear Lord, don't let her do anything crazy.

Behind me, I hear a restless murmur from the Bumford-Stanley contingent. The minister smiles encouragingly at Sophia.

He may live to regret that.

Sophia grips the sides of the pulpit for support and gazes out into the congregation. "Trevor was my friend, my good friend. We shared a lot about things we liked and things we thought were messed up. Trevor loved *Stranger Things*, and K-Pop and Keith Haring, and guacamole. He hated Beyoncé, and chemistry, and *Lord of the Rings* and brussels sprouts."

I relax in the pew. Sophia's doing a great job—she's giving her friend the kind of heartfelt, spontaneous send-off he deserves.

Sophia holds her head high and gazes directly at the prep school crowd. "But most of all, Trevor hated hypocrisy."

Uh-oh.

"Trevor hated having to pretend he was a certain kind of person just so he could avoid constant criticism. He hated living a lie. He hated being pressured. And in the last days of his life, he was afraid. Really scared."

Trevor's mother leans forward, her hands gripping the back of the pew in front of her.

Sophia's head droops. "I let him down. I didn't offer to help him the way I should have. Maybe now Trevor's in a place where there is no fear," Sophia casts a sidelong glance at the minister, "or maybe he's just in a cold, dark, nothing." She takes a deep breath. "But the people who scared him are right here in this church."

Trevor's mother emits a choked wail.

Trevor's grandfather looks like fire could come shooting from his eyes to ignite the pew cushions.

The kids elbow one another.

Brielle's skinny arm extends, her hand gripping the pew back in front of her.

Sophia lifts her gaze to the church's magnificent vaulted ceiling. "And now they're going to know what it feels like to be afraid."

Chapter 19

While the stunned minister steps forward to try to regain control of this service, Sophia darts down the center aisle. Every head in the house is turned to watch her. I'm not brave enough to follow in her wake. Instead, I clamber over the knees of the people to my right and duck out down the side aisle. Across the large church, I see that the long-haired boy in the denim jacket is also headed out.

And right behind him are two burly men wearing suits that definitely didn't cost a thousand bucks and shoes built for comfort.

Cops.

Clearly, detectives from the Ocean County Sherriff's Department made it their business to attend this funeral. And Sophia's speech makes them confident their effort has paid off in spades. What did she see here in the church that prompted her to say that?

I make it to the door just as the organ begins to play, and the mourners launch into a shaky rendition of "Amazing Grace." Ahead of me, I see Sophia on the church sidewalk facing the long-haired boy. They both have their phones out—trading numbers, I guess.

The cops stride toward them, and the boy sprints across the street just as the light changes. One cop moves to follow, but a lumbering bus blocks the intersection, and by the time it moves, the boy is out of sight.

I arrive at Sophia's side in time to hear the bigger of the two cops say, "We'd like to talk to you," as he flashes his badge.

I grab her arm. "Sophia, wait. You should have a lawyer with you when you talk to the police."

The cop glares at me. "And who are you? Her mother?"

"No, just a friend. Sophia, listen—"

She shakes free of my grasp. "It's okay, Audrey. I want to talk to them. And I don't need a lawyer. I didn't do anything wrong."

Famous last words. "Let's call your mother. She should be with you."

"Puh-leeze. What good would she do? Besides, I'm eighteen." Sophia tosses her mop of pink hair. "I don't need her permission to do anything."

The taller cop trades a glance with his young partner. This is exactly what they want: a chance to talk to a vulnerable, overconfident teenager all alone. I feel queasy.

"My car is parked near her office," Sophia tells the cops.

"Come with us to the Palmyrton police station, and we'll give you a ride back when we're finished." The younger cop smiles, friendly as a car salesman. They're not Palmyrton cops, but I guess they can count on the local police to help them out.

Mourners begin to trickle out of the church. Sophia notices and starts walking. "C'mon," she calls over her shoulder at the cops. "Let's go."

My head throbs as I watch Sophia walk between the cops to their un-marked car. What could have possessed her to make that dramatic threat in front of hundreds of people? If Trevor's murderers really were in the church today, does Sophia have enough information to give the cops to ensure the perpetrators are arrested? Because if she was just staging a dramatic scene and only has her feelings and resentments to share with the police, Sophia herself might be in danger after the cops let her go.

If they let her go.

If she doesn't manage to implicate herself in some way.

Should I text Jane and let her know her daughter could use some parental support? While I'm waffling in the middle of the sidewalk, the funeral atten-dees dodge around me, and I overhear snippets of conversation. "Tragic..." "Jeanine looked ghastly..." "Who *was* that girl?" "They should have known better than to have a public funeral."

This last remark catches my attention. The woman who said it is wearing black stilettos that would cripple me and a black sheath dress that exposes her long, sinewy arms. Her make-up, although artistic, doesn't do much to im-prove her gaunt, frowning face. Maybe she's simply the kind of person who spreads negativity wherever she goes. Or maybe she knows a real reason why this funeral shouldn't have been open to everyone acquainted with Trevor and his family.

She's walking in the direction I need to go, so I keep an eye on her from a few steps back. A shorter, more conventionally maternal woman walks beside her, while three teenage girls trail behind.

Just before we reach the corner, I hear the rapid clack of high heels on pavement. A woman puts on a burst of speed, overtaking me and catching up to the group ahead. She catches the tall, skinny woman's elbow and they all stop.

The running woman is Brielle.

The serene self-confidence that usually radiates from her face has vanished, replaced by concerned urgency. She speaks too quietly for me to overhear, but I notice she never loosens her grip on the tall woman's skinny arm.

The woman shakes her head.

Brielle raises her voice. "Are you sure? It's important!"

That I hear loud and clear.

The skinny woman twists her arm away. Her face, sour even in repose, now looks venomous. She says something, the light changes, and she and her group cross the street. Brielle stands watching them go as if her entire family has set sail for the New World without her.

In a moment, my client is going to turn around and see me standing right behind her. My presence at this funeral will be hard to explain, especially since I'm no longer willing to say I came with Sophia, the pariah of the event.

There's a flower garden and a historical plaque at the corner of the church property. I make a beeline down the garden path and show intense interest in some shaggy yellow flowers. From the corner of my eye, I see Brielle rejoin her husband, who's tapping his wing-tipped foot and scowling at his phone as he waits for her.

Whew! I read the historical plaque until I'm sure they're gone then head out of the garden. At the end of the path, a slouching figure waits for me.

I stride up to him with a smile and an outstretched hand. "Hi, my name is Audrey. Are you Trevor's friend, Fly?"

"Yeah." He studies me, uncertain whether to be relieved or suspicious that he doesn't need to introduce himself. "How do you know Sophia?"

"She's worked for me a bit. How do you know her?"

"I don't, really. Trev talked about her and showed me her picture." He kicks at a rock on the garden path. "Why did Sophia go off with the cops?"

"She seems to think she knows who scared Trevor. I'm not sure if she actually knows something about his murder, or if she just doesn't like those kids from Bumford-Stanley and Trevor's family and knows they made Trevor unhappy."

Fly nods. "Those BSS kids are douches." He gazes out at the traffic zipping around the Palmyrton square. "I wish she hadn't gone off with the cops before she talked to me."

You and me both. "Sophia's a little impulsive. Do *you* have information to share with the police?"

Fly takes a step backward. "I don't wanna mess with the cops. I'm already on probation for selling weed...and stuff."

Hmm. "And stuff" sounds more serious. So Fly has had a brush with the law and doesn't relish another close encounter. Unlike Sophia, whose mother could well afford to hire a lawyer to accompany her to the police interview, this kid, with his frayed jacket and down-at-the-heels sneakers, looks a little strapped. And of course, he should be in school right now. "Do your parents know you came to the funeral?"

Fly waves his hand. "My mom's at work. My dad ran off a long time ago. That's why me and Trev were friends. He didn't know his dad, either."

"Because he didn't have any memories from before his dad died?"

"That's what I used to think he meant. But the last few weeks, shit started gettin' strange."

"Strange, how?"

Fly looks up at the sky while keeping his hands jammed in his jacket pockets. "Trev kept saying that no one in his family had ever been straight with him. That they were keeping stuff from him."

"What kind of stuff?"

Fly gives a contorted teenage shrug that makes him look like he's trying to take off a heavy jacket of responsibility without unbuttoning it first. "Trev started acting all paranoid and stuff. I didn't know what to, to...."

Stuff, stuff—this kid has one all-purpose word to cover everything he can't or won't discuss. I'm about to press him harder when Fly's face crumples. The poor kid is going to cry right here on the sidewalk. I reach out awkwardly to comfort him. "Sophia told me something similar. She wasn't sure if Trevor was sick or rational, whether she should take him seriously or not."

Fly's eyes light up. "Yeah, exactly. So tell that to the cops."

"Me?"

He flips his shaggy bangs off his forehead. "I get a good vibe from you. Do the right thing, okay?"

And he lopes off.

Chapter 20

I stand on the corner and watch Fly diminish into a speck among the bustling pedestrians on Palmyrton's sidewalks.

Donna...Sophia...Granda...and now this. How many more people can possibly be counting on me to do the right thing today?

My phone chimes a reminder: appointment with Dr. Stein at 3:00.

Geez, I nearly forgot all about that. Well, this is something I'm doing for myself, even if it's not particularly pleasant. The doctor's office isn't far from here, so I might as well walk. The exercise might help me put my tumbling thoughts in order.

Sophia said she'd know what to tell the cops once she went to the funeral. What did she see there? To me, nothing seemed out of the ordinary until Sophia made her dramatic speech. What did she notice that I didn't? And why was Brielle so agitated? Does she think Sophia's threat was directed at Austin? I wish now that I'd pressed Sophia harder on this person she said she'd been mistaken about.

With so much on my mind, I walk right past Dr. Stein's office and have to double back. Before I enter the office, I text Sean. *The Ocean County cops are talking to Sophia at the Palmyrton police station. Have you seen them?*

I wait for a response, but when it doesn't come immediately, I enter the doctor's waiting room and look around. The place is packed, every seat occupied by anxious women in their thirties and forties. I take the forms from the receptionist and sit down among my fellow sufferers. A door on the far side of the room opens, and a man in a suit and tie emerges, flushed and flustered. Hanging his head, he slides a plastic cup across the reception counter and scurries out the door.

The woman next to me glances up from a weeks old copy of *People* magazine. "Another potential daddy does his duty. I hope for his sake the magazines in there are better than the ones out here."

The implication of her words takes a minute to sink in. "What? Wait... you mean... No!"

The woman smirks as she flips past pages of celebrity tragedies. "You're new here, eh? Your husband will have to do that, too. Better start preparing him."

"Why? There's nothing wrong with Sean."

She drops her magazine and faces me with raised eyebrows. "You can't be sure until he's tested. My husband and I both had a problem."

That possibility had never occurred to me. This woman sounds like a real expert. "How long have you been seeing Dr. Stein?"

"Six months, this time." She points with her head. "Dinah over there has been at it for three years." She scans the room. "Rachel's not here today. She's been at it the longest. Dr. Stein owes his Ferrari to her persistence."

The knot in my stomach tightens. Are visits to this office going to be a regular part of my routine for years? Is trying to have a baby going to impoverish us? "What did you mean 'this time'?" My voice sounds squeaky with dread of the answer I anticipate.

"I have a son who's two years old. Dr. Stein got me pregnant then, so I'm giving him another shot for Number Two. But I'm not trying past Thanksgiving." She tosses the magazine onto the end table and snorts. "Who am I kidding? I'll probably be here at Christmas, and Valentine's Day, and Easter. This place is like crack for mommies. Once you get started, you can't give it up."

"Mrs. Killian," the receptionist calls.

My new friend jumps up. "Finally." She starts across the waiting room, then pivots and gives me a thumbs-up. "Good luck, kiddo!"

With my chatty companion gone, I find my gaze drawn inexorably to the unmarked door where the poor husband went to do his duty. Apparently, anxious couples are required to give up all privacy and dignity in their quest to have a baby. As if he can read my thoughts, a text arrives from Sean.

I'm at a crime scene. Will ask about Sophia when I get back to the station. Where r u?

Went to Trevor's funeral with Sophia today. Big scene. Running errands now. Leaving for Granda's at 4.

I'll call u there or catch up at home.

Running errands—does that qualify as a lie? I squirm in my seat and search for something to distract me from what's going on behind that closed door. I paw through the magazines on the side table.

Car and Driver, Sailing Today, Modern Bow Hunter—-what kind of selection is that for a room full of anxious women? Nestled among the tattered copies is a cardboard stand holding a thick bundle of brochures. Let Us Help You Build Your Family declares a headline over a picture of a smiling blond mother, a grinning blond father, and an adorable, chubby baby. Fertility Solutions of Palmer County is printed in smaller type along the bottom.

I thought Dr. Stein was helping us build our families. What's this for? I open the brochure. Inside is another beaming family, this one Asian.

"Mrs. Coughlin."

Mrs. Coughlin? I glance around for Sean's mother before I realize the receptionist means me. Flustered at almost missing my turn, I leap up and the brochure falls to the ground. The lady next to me picks it up and thrusts it at me. I jam it in my tote bag and scurry after the nurse to meet my fate.

Ten minutes after being weighed and quizzed by the nurse, I sit shivering in a paper gown waiting for Dr. Stein to appear.

He bounds in, trailed by a nurse. Short, with Harry Potter-ish glasses and a ridiculous comb-over, Dr. Stein is hard to picture behind the wheel of a Ferrari. He shakes my hand without making eye contact as he scans my chart. Then he gestures me to lie down and begins my physical exam, his brow furrowed in concentration.

After all that waiting, the exam is over in minutes. He snaps off his latex gloves and stares at a point over my left shoulder. "Do you have a partner?"

"Yes, of course—my husband, Sean."

"We'll need to see him at the next appointment." He washes his hands at the sink while rattling on. "In thirty-five percent of cases, the failure to conceive is the male's problem, and in an additional twenty percent, both partners have a problem. So we'll need to check him out."

"Can he bring his... er...sample from home?"

"Nope. Has to be fresh!" The doctor smiles brightly and bounces out.

Chapter 21

After the doctor's appointment, I walk back to my office to get my car. I don't know what I was expecting from the fertility doctor, but it wasn't this. So many anxious women...so many automated steps. I feel like I've stepped onto a factory conveyor belt. Will I emerge at the other end with a baby? Or will I be plucked off the line by a quality control technician and tossed into the rejects pile?

I quicken my walking pace. Round One with Dr. Stein took so long that I have just enough time to drive to Kearney to report for nurse duty at Granda's house. When I arrive at the office, Sophia's car is gone from its parking spot on the street. I hope that means the police released her. The "two-hour parking strictly enforced" sign looms over me. Maybe her car was towed because she hasn't fed the meter since noon. I don't have time for this, but I text her anyway.

How did it go with the police? Are you ok?

No answer. Does that mean she's been arrested, and her phone confiscated? Or is she just being a typical teenager—when Sophia wants me, I have to drop everything and listen. But when I want her, she ignores me. Hopefully, Sean will have some information for me later.

I hop in my car and drive east toward the more congested part of New Jersey where Sean's grandparents raised his mother and her three siblings. In those days, four kids was considered a small family. Sean's mother often talks about her best childhood friend, who was one of twelve.

And I can't produce even one.

I hope Granda won't quiz me on the topic of when I'm going to start producing more great-grandchildren for him. I'm nervous enough about this stint as a caregiver.

I'm no Florence Nightingale. But he's been home a few days now. I think he's through the worst part of his recovery. All I have to do is keep him company, make him tea, and prevent him from getting up without help. Even I can do that.

I hope. What if Granda tries to get up while I'm in the kitchen or the bathroom? What if he gets re-injured during my watch? Or what if his heart chooses my eight hours of guardian angel duty to stop beating? The man is eighty-nine—the end could come at any moment. But if it comes while I'm on watch, I'll be forever blamed.

As I drive toward Kearney, the houses get smaller and closer together. I leave behind the coffee bars that serve latte and mochaccino and enter the land of diners with bottomless cups of joe and eggs over easy with greasy hash browns. Kearney has gradually gone from being one hundred percent Irish and Italian Catholic to being fifty percent with the balance made up of more recent Chinese, Indian and Spanish immigrants.

There's still a bar and a church on every block of the tightly packed business district. Granda's house is within walking distance of both St. Malachi's and Jimmy's Roscommon Bar and Grill. Location, location, location. No wonder Granda refuses to move.

I park on the street in front of the tiny two-up, two-down house where my mother-in-law was raised. Only two bedrooms and one bath with four kids and two parents. I've never enquired about the logistics of her childhood, but the modest three-bedroom, two bath split level in Palmyrton in which she raised Sean and his four siblings must have seemed like a palace.

I mount the tiny stoop and ring the bell at precisely 5:55. I'm taking over for Terry, and I know I'll never hear the end of it if he has to work even five minutes past his allotted shift.

I hear a series of locks turning, and the door opens. "There you are! Finally!"

I step into a close atmosphere of cooked cabbage and Pine-Sol, scents that indicate a recent visit from Deirdre.

"Who is it?" I hear a disembodied voice shout from above. "Is it that old bag from next door? Send her away. Tell her I don't want nunna her Dago food."

Terry rolls his eyes. "The neighbor brought us the most delicious escarole soup. I highly recommend it. Just don't let Granda catch you enjoying it."

"How's he doing?"

"Full of piss and vinegar, so I guess he's on the mend." Terry leads me down a narrow hall to the kitchen. An array of orange pill bottles lines the Formica counter next to the electric tea kettle. "He spent the afternoon telling me how worthless I am for not being able to repair his broken TV antenna if I know all about computers. Go figure. Then he said he didn't trust me to cook him a proper meal, and he'd wait for one of his grand-daughters to do it right." Terry opens the fridge, which Deirdre has stocked with enough food to feed a platoon of infantrymen. "You have to take it up on a tray. He stays upstairs to be near the bathroom. His chair has an alarm that goes off if he tries—"

A faint beeping commences above. Terry pivots and takes the steep stairs to the second floor two at a time. "—to get up. Granda! Stay still! Here I come!"

I follow, worried about what awaits me. What special hell will Sean's grandfather devise for me?

Granda sits in the sunny front bedroom. Although it's the larger of the two, there's barely room for the hospital bed, chair with a lift seat, and a second caretaker's chair.

"Who's this, then? Not our Colleen."

Terry has arrived in time to grab his grandfather's elbow and support him as he wavers next to his chair. The old man peers at me through watery blue eyes.

I move forward to give him a peck on his grizzled cheek. "Hi, Granda. It's Audrey, Sean's wife."

He pulls away from my embrace. "Harlot! You're not married."

Terry pats his arm. "Now, Granda—you were at the wedding, remember?"

"Sean never got his first marriage annulled. That's why they got married out in that field, with no priest in sight. Bah!"

He points a gnarled finger at me. "Yer not a Catholic."

I smile. "That's right. I'm not." If this is the best he can do, bring it on.

"All right, Granda. I'll take you to the bathroom, then I'm leaving. Audrey will make your supper and keep you company."

"Ay, ye better help me. I'll piss my pants before I let that harlot take me to the loo."

"I'll go down and start making the meal."

"I want a bacon butty," he shouts after me. "And a glass o' Glenfiddich. Right alongside o' my tea. And may the devil make a ladder of your spine if you try bringing me those foul veg."

Terry returns as I'm loading the tray with Granda's request. "Deirdre says he's not supposed to have so much bacon because of the salt. And no booze when he's taking pills. And give him some steamed broccoli for the fiber."

I make no comment, just keep prepping. As far as I'm concerned, when you're eighty-nine, you can eat whatever the hell you want, whenever the hell you want it. "Where are the tea bags?"

"Oh, sweet Jesus—don't try to give him bag tea. You've gotta brew the leaves in this pot." Terry pulls out a chipped brown teapot and launches into instructions as complex as one of Sean's Food Network recipes, concluding with, "and he gets two of those blue pills at six o'clock. Good luck, Audrey."

He heads for the door.

"Bye, Granda," Terry shouts up the stairs. "Be nice, ya hear?"

"Don't let the door hit ya in the arse, ya worthless gobshite. Ya never worked a day in yer life."

Terry shudders and makes his escape. I carry the tea tray up into the lion's den.

I walk in haloed in the scent of bacon, and the old coot can't help but show some interest. He lifts the bread and examines the bacon. "Aw, and why is it burnt to cinders? Do you not know how to cook streaky bacon proper? And surely you could grill the tomatoes. Did yer ma teach you nothing but how to drop yer knickers fer a man?"

"You're right. I'm a lousy cook. I never set foot in the kitchen at our house. Sean does it all. And yeah, I wasn't a virgin when we got married. Anything else you need to get off your chest?"

"This tea is bitter. Did you let the water come off the boil before you poured it in the pot?"

I reach for the teapot. "I'll just pop down and make a mug of Lipton's in the microwave, shall I?"

He stares at me, then breaks into a brown-toothed grin. "Saucy, you are. Remind me of my wife. Except she was a good Catholic." He reaches for the bacon sandwich.

Hmm. That seems to be a compliment. I sit down in the chair beside him. "Where did you meet?"

That's all it takes. Granda is off on a long trip down memory lane. I learn about his village in County Cork and his constant struggle to wrest a few scraps of food at the table he shared with his thirteen brothers and sisters. I learn about his decision to leave Ireland for America and the gut-churning, foul-smelling trip on the boat, and the moment, on the next-to-last day aboard, that his eyes fell on red-haired, green-eyed Moira, still lovely and laughing even after the horrors of their journey. As he talks, he eats every crumb of the bacon sandwich, ungrilled tomatoes and all.

Granda takes a deep breath and leans toward me. "And after the boat landed in New York, you know what happened next?"

"No, tell me."

He takes a jolt of the Glenfiddich and continues.

"I got off to be processed at Ellis Island. Thousands and thousands and thousands of micks pourin' offa them boats. More red hair and freckles and green eyes than ye ever seen in one place in yer whole life. And my oldest brother's been in New York already for five years, and he's supposed to meet me on the docks. And mind ye, I had not seen the boy since I was this high." Granda holds out a trembling hand at waist height. "Paddy left home to find his own way when I was just a bairn. But I got outside on the docks, the crowds were pushin' me this way and that. And no one had those foul contraptions in those days"—he points to my cell phone—"so how was I going to find me brother? How would I even know him? And I felt the tears in my eyes, I did, because I had only five dollars to my name and no clue where I would sleep or how I'd set about finding work." Granda stabs one of the slippery canned peaches I subbed for the broccoli and sits back to let me ponder his long-ago dilemma.

It's quite a story. I find I'm on the edge of my seat dying to know how Granda survived his first day in New York. "Did you find him?"

Granda downs the last swallow of whiskey and raises his right hand like some ancient oracle. "And out of that crowd came a voice. 'Declan,' he cried. And I turned around and there stood me brother. I'd 'a known him anywhere."

"But how did he find you? How did you know it was your brother? There must've been hundreds of Declans on the dock."

"Blood! Blood speaks louder than words. Blood will tell."

After Granda makes this pronouncement, his eyelids flutter. In seconds, he's sound asleep in his chair. I slide a pillow under his head and tip-toe out of the room.

Maybe all a nurse needs is good ears.

Chapter 22

"How did it go?"

Sean's voice emerges from the darkness as I slip into bed at midnight. Deirdre's husband had arrived at Granda's house at eleven to take over, but I hadn't heard from Sean at all during the time I kept a vigil over the snoozing old man.

Nor had I heard from Sophia.

"No problems whatsoever." I don't mention that I totally ignored Deirdre's dietary restrictions. "You must've been busy at work."

"Swamped. Sorry I didn't call." Sean props himself on his elbow. "You honestly had no problems with Granda? He didn't complain and insult you and curse you?"

"Well, sure—but I expected that. What I didn't expect was how much I'd enjoy listening to the old man's stories. He told me about how he met your grandmother and what it was like to arrive—"

"—on Ellis Island." Sean turns on his best Old World brogue. "Ay, there were more red-headed lads than ye could shake a stick at. And how was I to find me brudder in all that crowd?"

I laugh. "I take it you've heard that one before. It is pretty amazing, though—you and I can't find each other at ShopRite without our cell phones. Granda claims he and his brother were drawn to each other by their shared blood."

"Ah, yes—the O'Shea blood is like a divining rod to find other members of the clan. Did Granda mention he also had a large sign pinned to his shirt that spelled out his complete name and address and his brother's name? That may have aided Uncle Paddy in finding him."

I slap his arm. "You're destroying the magic. I like his version better."

"Thank you for being such a good sport about Granda." Sean pulls me into his embrace. "Once I work my shift this weekend, this branch of the Coughlin family is off-duty. Mom and Dad have arrived in Ireland, and nothing can go wrong now. How was the rest of your day?"

"Trevor's funeral...Sophia talking to the cops—remember?"

"Shit. I totally forgot. By the time I got back to the station, no one was there but a few night shift guys. I'll ask around tomorrow, first thing. I promise."

"Oh, and one other issue—there's some thug named Ray-Ray following me in a black Camaro."

Sean bolts upright in bed.

"He hasn't approached me. Donna says he works for Uncle Nunzio, and he's there to let her know the family is keeping an eye on her. Anthony knows better than to put the tail directly on her."

"Son of a bitch," Sean mutters. He gets out of bed and calls in the information, adding the partial license plate number that I retained. "I'll drive you to work tomorrow," he says as he returns to my side. "I bet this Ray-Ray has a rap sheet a mile long. There'll be something we can haul him in for even if it's just to hassle him for a day or two."

I snuggle against Sean's broad chest and feel his heart thumping under my ear. Do I want to drive up that slow and regular beat? Not really, but we're not going to see much of each other in the next few days. I need to tell him about Dr. Stein. "I had a doctor's appointment today."

I feel him tense up. "You never mentioned you haven't been feeling well. What's wrong?"

"I'm not sick. I, I went to see a fertility specialist—the best guy in Palmyrton. Natalie got me in on a cancellation."

"Is that necessary?" He pulls far enough away that he can see my face. "We haven't been trying that long."

"Natalie says it's best to find out if I have problems sooner rather than later." I fill Sean in on what the doctor said, and he listens patiently. And then I drop the bombshell about his part in the process.

Sean sits up and turns on the bedside lamp. "Wait, wait—you're telling me I have to go into the doctor's office and jerk off into a cup? And then walk out into a room full of women who all know what I've been doing behind that door?"

"Uhm.... Yeah, that's the way it works. The doctor said the sperm sample has to be...er... fresh, you know." I reach out for his hands. "Please, Sean—I know it's awful, but that's the standard process the doctor follows. He says he has to rule out any problems on your end."

Sean slides back under the covers and pulls me close. "I'm willing to do my part, Audrey, but I think you're jumping the gun. I'm sure neither one of us has a problem. Relax."

"If the tests show there's nothing wrong with us, then I *will* be able to relax. I need to set my mind at ease. Please."

Sean smooths the hair back from my face. His big, hard hands are amazingly gentle. "That's my girl—so sure science and math have the answers to all life's problems. Have some faith."

I pull away. "Don't say it. Don't give me that, 'it'll all work out…. God has a plan' stuff." I don't believe in fate. I believe in taking charge of my own life."

We glare at each other for a moment until Sean starts to laugh. "This is why I married you—because you're nothing like my mother. Send me the contact info and I'll make the appointment." He rolls over. "Now, let's get some sleep."

I feel the weight of worry dissolve knowing that Sean is willing to tackle this baby conception issue head-on.

The concern about Sophia still nags me. Did the funeral really reveal something to her about Trevor's murder, or is she just a teenage drama queen? But Sean is right. We need some sleep. That problem will have to wait until tomorrow.

Chapter 23

Sean drops me off at work on Thursday morning with a promise that he'll call me as soon as he finds out anything about Sophia's interview with the cops. I haven't received any texts from her overnight, and of course, the text I sent her at eight AM has gone unanswered.

I enter the AMT office to find Donna staring at the Chaco's Auto Body calendar on the wall. Given that the picture still shows March's Easter bunny, it's unlikely she's looking for a date. Her eyes are puffy with dark circles underneath, and she's not wearing a lick of makeup. As my friend Maura is fond of saying, she looks like she's been dragged through the trash backwards. Only one person could be responsible for making her look this bad. I don't want to ask, but I have to. "Did you talk to Anthony last night?"

Donna shakes her head. Then collapses onto the desk and lets out a howl. There's really no other word for it. She sounds like a raccoon protesting the arrival of the sanitation crew.

"Oh my God, Audrey! I don't know what I'm going to do. I have to quit my job."

I feel a surge of anger. "Over my dead body will I let Anthony force you to quit your job! Why do you listen to him?"

Donna rolls her head from left to right but doesn't lift it from the desk. Is that a no? She makes some sort of unintelligible sound. I put my hands on her shoulders "Donna honey, lift your head and talk to me. What happened?"

Donna keeps her head buried under her arms. Straining my ears, I still can't understand the words emerging from this lump.

"Oh, Audrey, Uhdunna a tubbla."

"What? Just tell me what's going on."

"Eee—tiiiii."

I feel like I'm listening to a foreign language radio station. "Even time...? In town...?"

Finally Donna lifts her tear-stained face. "It's Ty," she shouts. "I've made a terrible mistake with Ty."

A tingle of anxiety rolls down my spine. What could this mean? As far as I'm concerned, Ty and Donna are the perfect players on my team. They balance each other in temperament and skills. What could've gone wrong? "What kind of mistake? You said something that hurt his feelings? Ty doesn't hold a grudge."

Donna's gaze meets mine. She sits perfectly still and simply stares at me. Her breath goes in and out in raspy bursts and somehow that draws my attention to her chest. Her firm, round breasts move up and down under her tight knit top. The kind of top she always wears.

The kind of top I've noticed Ty noticing.

I feel queasy. "What did you two do?"

"It's all my fault." Her voice quavers. "I was upset about Anthony setting Ray-Ray to watch the office and I told Ty the latest, and when I started crying, he put his arm around me, and I put my head on his shoulder and then, and then...."

I raise my hand for her to stop. I don't want the gory details. "Where did all this happen?"

"At the Freidrich house. Yesterday. Don't worry—I washed the sheets."

Count on Donna to clean up the physical mess. The emotional mess she saves for me. "How did you leave things with Ty?"

Donna shrugs. "He had to go to his night class. I haven't seen him or talked to him since. He texted me late yesterday to say goodnight. I don't...." Donna's lip trembles. "Oh, Audrey! I got carried away because I hadn't been with anyone but Anthony for years. I don't want to hurt Ty. He's been so good to me. He's been my rock, willing to defend me from Anthony. But I'm too old for him. This will never work."

What makes Donna think Ty is looking to get involved? As long as I've known him, he's always juggled a couple different girls—never serious about any of them. But surely, he'd know better than to start a casual hook-up with a woman he has to work with every day. "What exactly did he say to you before he left for class?"

"He said, 'I'll always be here for you. I'll never let anyone hurt you.' Oh, ga-a-awd! I, I can't do this right now. I can't get involved with another man."

Hmm. That simply sounds like Ty being his loyal self. He's spoken words to that effect to me many times. "That's all he said?"

Donna blushes furiously.

Oh, geez—Ty's always been very successful with the ladies. I don't want to know what he says to make the magic happen.

"He said stuff that made me think that he wanted to do it again. And I can't. I don't want him to think that I'm rejecting him because of who he is. But I can't date him, Audrey."

Who he is? A black man? An ex-con? A poor kid raised by his grandmother? "You'd be embarrassed to be with him?" My voice has an accusatory tone, which is ludicrous because I certainly don't think Ty and Donna should get involved romantically.

"Of course not! But, my family—it's not that they're racist, but.... Oh, who am I kidding? They're racist! Audrey, they'd *freak* if I came home with a black man. My Uncle Mario! My grandmother!" Donna rocks back and forth. "It's not right, and I know I should stand up to them, but I can't right now. I need my family to get me through this divorce. I can't start a fight with them."

I'd like to point out that Donna's family are the ones who encouraged her to marry Anthony in the first place and to stick with him for far too long, but that's not what she needs to hear right now. She's taken the hardest step in leaving her abuser. She deserves all the support I can give. Besides, even though my heart wants to scream that Donna would be lucky to have Ty, my rational mind, which always rules, knows that these two would be a disaster together in the long run. Donna wants kids, and Ty is nowhere near ready for that. And both of them are very close to their families. I can't picture Grandma Betty and Uncle Mario ever sitting around the same Thanksgiving table.

My mind keeps coming back to the same question. What was Ty thinking? What did he want from this encounter?

"What do you want to happen?" I ask Donna.

"I need to be on my own for a while, be my own person without any guy in my life."

"I agree."

Donna chews the edge of her thumbnail. "Yeah, but Ty and I have to see each other every day. This is so awkward!"

Somehow, I've got to straighten this up or risk losing the two best assistants I've ever had. I glance at the Tyrolian cuckoo clock ticking loudly in the corner. "Ty will be here soon. Why don't you go stock up on your favorite cleaning supplies and let me see what kind of mood he's in?"

Donna's eyes widen in alarm. "You're not going to tell him that I told you—"

"Of course not." I nudge her out the door. "But I think it's best you don't encounter him just yet."

No sooner does Donna leave than a text arrives from Ty.

Hey. Whattup?

Donna went off to Target to buy supplies. When will you be in?

No answer.

Not two minutes later, Ty strolls through the door. He must've been watching the office from across the street. He glances around the room as if he thinks Donna might yet leap out from under a desk.

"Sorry I'm late," Ty mutters. But instead of sitting at his desk and getting to work, he paces around like a caged tiger periodically checking his phone.

"Something wrong?" I enquire, keeping my eyes focused on my Excel spreadsheet. Will he confess to me? The more I think about what happened, the more I'm irritated at Ty. He should've known better than to respond to Donna's overtures when she's in such a vulnerable state. But when do men ever think with their brains when another organ will give them the answer they want?

"Nah. All good." He looks at his phone for the tenth time. "Yo, I gotta go see this guy who wants to buy the master bedroom furniture at the Freidrichs' house. Donna's not planning on going over there today, is she? 'Cause I got it all under control."

I bet you do.

I keep my voice bland. "You go ahead and handle it. And line up your friend Zeke to help Donna with the sale this weekend. Donna has work to do on the website today. I'll come pick you up at your house tomorrow when it's time to leave for Sea Chapel."

A big grin splits his face, and Ty shoots out of the office. That reaction tells me he's as regretful about yesterday's liaison as Donna is. I'll talk to him about it tomorrow when we're in the car together and he can't escape. By Monday when we're all back together, things will have cooled off and we can all get back to normal.

I hope.

No sooner do I settle myself down from the Ty/Donna calamity than Sean calls and reports that Sophia left the police station at 4PM under her own steam. He hasn't been able to find out what the Ocean County cops talked to her about, but at least we know she wasn't arrested. He also says that a patrolman arrested Ray-Ray for a string of unpaid parking tickets. Sean will talk to him about his other activities. But Ray-Ray will be out of commission for at least a few days. I begin to relax and settle into my accounting when my phone rings.

"Audrey? It's Jane Peterman. Did Sophia spend the night at your place last night?" Her voice is thick and languid, as if these are the first words she's spoken today.

"What? No! You mean she never came home?" My relief that Sophia wasn't arrested is replaced by worry that her melodramatic threat might have been taken very seriously by someone in the church yesterday. Would Trevor's killer go after Sophia?

"Well, apparently not. I went to bed early with a *crushing* headache and now that I'm up, I see that the dog pooped by the back door, which means Sophia never let him out last night. Of course, she's not answering my calls or texts. She never does."

Paco's elimination accidents don't seem to me to be the most reliable indicator of Sophia's presence. "Did you check to see if her bed had been slept in?"

"Well, who can tell? That bed hasn't been made in weeks."

"Jane," I bark. "Do you know what happened at Trevor's funeral yesterday? Do you know that your daughter spent two hours alone talking to the police?"

She sighs. "My phone does seem to have blown up with messages, but I can't deal with all that so early in the morning."

God, Jane could star in one of those bad parenting reality shows. Just when I thought I could stop worrying about Sophia, Jane makes me feel like worrying about the kid should be my full time job. I give Jane a quick summary of the scene at the funeral.

"Ugh," she groans. "Sophia just isn't happy unless she's the center of attention. This is what I get for choosing an actor to be her father."

"What if Trevor's killer really was at the funeral. What if he was spooked by what Sophia said? Your daughter could be in danger." How can someone with an Ivy league degree be so dense?

"You don't know my daughter like I do. This is all a ploy for attention. And no one we know *murdered* Trevor." She says this as if she thinks the coroner is just as prone to exaggeration as her daughter.

"Well, someone crushed his throat and threw his body in the ocean. He didn't do it to himself."

Jane sighs as if I'm pestering her with tiresome details. "Maybe he sold some of his meds to an unsavory character who killed him."

Arguing with Jane about whether Sophia is in a murderer's sights is pointless. We just need to find the girl. "Have you called her friends?"

"Friends? Now that school is back in session, all she does is complain about how she has no one here to hang out with."

"How about that boy who works at Elmo's?" I suggest.

"I don't have *his* number." Jane says "his" as if a dishwasher's ten digits would contaminate her iPhone. "I suppose I could call the restaurant. Do you think they're open yet?"

"I'm sure there's someone in the kitchen by now. Try that."

I hang up with her and tap my pencil on the desk. If Sophia never returned to Sea Chapel at all, could she be with Fly, another lost teenage soul? How can I find out his real name and track him down?

I know! Palmyrton High School has a full-time resource officer, and Sean knows the guy. Fly seems like the kind of kid who'd be well known to the cop who patrols the halls of the school. I trade messages with my husband, and within ten minutes I'm talking to the high school cop.

"Ah, my man, Fly. What's he done now?"

"Nothing. I met him yesterday at the funeral of his friend, Trevor Finlayson, and I'm just wondering if he's seen another girl who was at the church."

"I saw on the attendance report that he skipped school yesterday. Glad to hear he was in church, not hanging out behind the Burger King."

I know from Sean that the weed-choked empty lot behind the fast food restaurant is the first place the cops go when they're looking for drifters, runaways, or drug dealers. I feel my stomach curdle at the idea that Fly might have taken Sophia there. "He didn't strike me as a bad kid...just a little lost."

The cop's gruff tone softens. "Frankie's all right. He needs a goal. And an old man to kick him toward it. I haven't got today's attendance yet. I'll go find out if he's here and get back to you."

Suddenly, the office feels oppressive to me. Ty, Donna, Sophia, Ray-Ray, Fly—they feel like they're all crowded around my desk, staring at my spreadsheets and scrolling through my emails. I don't have my car since Sean drove me to the office, so I decide to walk a few blocks to Caffeine Planet for lunch. I can sit at one of their outdoor tables and use their free wi-fi to do anything I'd be doing here.

Even though I know Ray-Ray is at the Palmyrton police station, I keep a sharp eye on my surroundings. But my street is quiet, and no one pays attention to my journey. Cool breeze, warm sun, a cascade of falling leaves—my spirits begin to lift as I stroll toward the center of town.

I reach Caffeine Planet by twelve-fifteen, just as the lunch rush has begun. Taking my salad and iced tea outside, I nab the last sidewalk table. Sitting there, I encounter a parade of people I know in Palmyrton: Joan, the librarian; Mr. Swenson, my lawyer; two former clients; Beverly Masterson from the Rosa Parks Center; and Bill, my father's favorite chess partner. In addition to all the people passing by, a steady stream of customers enters and leaves Caffeine Planet through the door right beside my table. Maybe this wasn't the best place to get serious work done, but I pull out my iPad and try to at least send some emails.

I've fired off invitations to the Sea Chapel sale to several of my best customers when I hear the extra chair at my table being dragged out. I glance up to let the person know they're welcome to move it to another table and see yet another person I recognize: Trevor Finlayson's mother, Jeanine.

I smile and make a "feel free" gesture toward the chair, assuming she won't recognize me.

I'm wrong.

She sits down at the table. "You were at my son's funeral with Sophia Peterman, weren't you?"

"Uhm...ye-e-es."

"Who are you? Why did you let Sophia create that scene?" Her hands grip the edge of the tiny table and she leans so close I can see the clumps in her mascara. "Hasn't my family suffered enough?"

I hold my hands up in surrender. "Look, I'm sorry. I had no idea Sophia was going to do that. I barely know the girl. She asked me to come along for moral support because she'd never been to a funeral before."

"But who are you? Someone told me you were in Sea Chapel when Trevor's body was recovered."

I explain my presence and how I got to know Sophia. "She says that Trevor was terrified before he died. She seemed to think it had something to do with a group of kids from Bumford-Stanley."

Jeanine tosses her head in exasperation. "And you believe that? Do you know why Sophia was expelled from Bumford-Stanley?"

"Expelled? I thought she just left for more academic freedom."

Jeanine picks up my spoon and taps the table for emphasis. "Sophia boo-by-trapped a girl's locker with a firecracker. It exploded in her face. The poor child needed eye surgery, but Jane acted like it was a silly prank. The girl's parents wanted Sophia arrested. The headmaster got both sides to settle on expulsion. After that, I told Trevor to stay away from Sophia. That's why she's cooking up these crazy stories."

I'm appalled by Jeanine's story. Certainly, Sophia never struck me as mean-spirited or vindictive. But as Sean points out, I'm not always the best judge of character. "Still, I think Sophia genuinely cared about Trevor."

Jeanine's lips press together in a tight line. She takes a deep breath to steel herself to keep talking to me. "Sophia was drawn to Trevor's craziness. So was that boy, Fly." Jeanine rakes her fingers through her hair. "I loved my son, but I'll tell you this—he was different from the moment he was born. He cried for hours on end as an infant. He pitched terrifying tantrums over the smallest disturbance in his surroundings. His father and I were taking him to psychiatrists by the time he was three. So many different diagnoses! Schizoaffective disorder, bipolar disorder, oppositional defiant disorder. No one knew what was wrong with him or how to make him better. And after Trevor's father died, his grandfather, that spiteful old man, refused to help me pay for Trevor's treatments. He thought I should send him to military academy or boot camp. A child!"

Jeanine leans back in her chair. "I'm shot, drained. I can barely force myself out of bed in the morning. And just when I think things can't get any worse, they do. I cried a river of tears when I thought Trevor had killed himself. But it didn't really surprise me that he'd commit suicide."

Jeanine's voice gets louder, more agitated. "Then the police say no, someone murdered your son. And they come to my house and question us as if my husband Ken had something to do with it! And now that showboating little bitch Sophia is trying to make trouble for our friends by telling the police lies about the kids Trevor went to school with. I'm in a nightmare I can't wake up from."

"I'm sorry for your troubles," I say softly. "The police have to follow up every lead. But whatever Sophia told them, they won't believe it unless there's solid evidence to back it up."

Jeanine studies me through narrowed eyes. "You said your husband's a cop?"

"Yes, but here in Palmyrton. Not with the Ocean County Sherriff's department that's got Trevor's case."

She's thinking. I can practically see the wheels turning under her tousled, wavy hair.

"Someone did kill Trevor." I speak softly. "Who do you think it was?"

Jeanine falls silent and studies her folded hands. She has a theory, I can tell. Will she share it with me?

I wait.

"Trevor's grandfather. He was the last person to see Trevor alive." She speaks so softly I have to lean forward to catch her words. "When he turned eighteen, Trevor was due to inherit money from his father's estate. It was supposed to be used for his college education, but who knows if Trevor would have been well enough to go to college? Trevor's grandfather was ashamed of him. He kept saying no one in the Finlayson family has ever had mental health issues. Ha!" Jeanine bangs the table with her fist. "That's only if you don't count being mean as a snake as a mental illness. Anyway, Arthur Finlayson had already started contacting lawyers to keep Trevor from getting the money on his birthday, but he wasn't having much success."

"Whoa—you think Trevor's own grandfather killed him for money? I thought the old man was already rich."

Jeanine picks at the cuticles of her bitten nail. "I told you—Trevor embarrassed him. And it's not that Arthur wants the money for himself. He just wants to keep us from having it. That's how spiteful he is."

"Who is *us*?"

"The trust says that in the event of Trevor's death the money would go to his siblings, and if he had no siblings, would revert to his grandfather. But the daughter I have with my husband Ken is Trevor's half-sister."

"But Grandpa Finlayson doesn't see it that way?"

"He says Roxie isn't a Finlayson. He's afraid his precious money will go outside the family. The trust was set up at Trevor's birth." Jeanine turns her palms to the sky. "Who could have foreseen that Trevor's father would die just a few years later? I got remarried—I was only thirty-two."

Jeanine bangs the table with her clenched hand. "The money should go to Roxie, Trevor's sister. For years we spent money we didn't have to get Trevor the best treatment possible. We sent him to Bumford-Stanley while Ken's kids went to public school. We took things away from the others because we felt Trevor needed the resources more. That inheritance is a way to pay the other kids back."

"But that's why the cops suspected your husband. Have you told them your theory about Arthur Finlayson?"

"Yes, but they don't think the old man was strong enough to kill Trevor." Jeanine's eyes dart from side to side. Her voice contains a frantic urgency. "But he could have paid someone to help him. And he has so much influence and power in Ocean County—it's no wonder the police are ignoring him as a suspect and focusing on Ken and me. He's poisoned their minds against us." She falls back in her chair, exhausted.

Jeanine is unraveling right in front of my eyes. I'm not sure what to do for her. Luckily, two women emerge from Caffeine Planet and come over to our table. One of them looks familiar from the funeral. She puts a hand on her friend's shoulder. "Come on, Jeanine—we'd better get you home."

The other woman makes eye contact with me. "Jeanine saw you out here and wanted to talk to you. We'll let you get back to your work now."

"Tell your husband what I said," Jeanine says to me as she rises from the table. "See if he can help us."

The friend nudges Jeanine toward the sidewalk, then looks over her shoulder at me. "Sorry," she mouths.

Chapter 24

G eez! That was some encounter.

I wonder if the Ocean County Sherriff's department is taking Jeanine's theory seriously despite what she says about the cops? After all, she's not the only person in Sea Chapel who thinks Mr. Finalyson is ruthless. The old codger used his influence to get his way in the dune construction debate, but that doesn't mean he has a goon squad at his disposal. Sophia didn't seem to think Grandpa Finlayson was dangerous even if he was disapproving. I really wish I knew what she told those cops.

Stop it, Audrey! I give myself a virtual slap upside the head. I need to focus on my work, not my never-ending curiosity.

When I pick up my iPad and try to resume my tasks, I see I've missed a text from the school resource officer. *Fly showed up late for school today. I told him the woman who was with Sophia at the funeral was worried about her, and he says she went back to Sea Chapel this morning. But he also says he wants to talk to you. Can you drop by the high school?*

I clear my table with a sigh. The day's already shot to hell. What's one more distraction? Maybe if I finally get to the bottom of Sophia's motivations, I can set my mind at ease and stage the Gardner sale with no further complications.

Still carless, I start the five-block walk to my alma mater, Palmyrton High School. As I walk, a huge Lexus SUV slows beside me and the passenger window powers down.

Immediately, I step away. Could this be Ray-Ray in a new vehicle?

But a woman's voice calls out to me. "Hey!"

I peer into the SUV. It's one of Jeanine's friends from Caffeine Planet.

"Did you tell Jeanine that you're organizing a sale at Brielle's house?" Her face is scrunched in doubt.

"Yes, that's what I do. Another Man's Treasure Estate Sales." I pass my business card through the SUV window.

She studies it like it's a scroll of ancient hieroglyphics. "Like the kind of sale where people come and walk through the house and buy stuff?"

"That'd be it."

"*Brielle*? Is going to let *strangers*? Walk through her *house*?" The woman shakes herself like Ethel after she's gotten caught in the sprinkler. "Brielle never even lets people she knows come inside her house! What day is the sale going to be?"

"October 1 and 2."

"Wow, I'm marking my calendar. I'll drive down to Sea Chapel just to see that!"

She floors her powerful SUV and zooms into traffic.

I don't encounter anyone else I know on the final couple blocks of my walk. I turn the corner, and there it is: Palmyrton High School.

The school has changed very little since the days I last haunted its halls seventeen years ago. The same big pile of dirty yellow brick, the same beaten down grass, the same double glass doors. Except, of course, today the doors are locked, and I have to be buzzed in by a security guard. Once I'm inside, the smell—sweat, floor wax, French fries—takes me right back to those four years of academic success and social misery. A shiver passes through me. Thank God I can't be dragged back!

The school resource officer meets me in the lobby and leads me to his small office. "Send Frankie Kelso down to me, please," he says into his phone. We sit and wait for the boy to arrive. The cop is young enough and buff enough to impress teenagers, but old enough and tough enough to lend some gravitas to his role. I suspect he's very good at keeping the peace and steering wayward teenagers away from a life of crime. We chat amiably as we wait.

And wait.

A look of annoyance passes over the resource officer's face. "Maybe the teacher didn't release him right away." He picks up the phone and calls the classroom again. He doesn't like what he hears.

"Wait here," he tells me, and strides out into the lobby. He's gone for a good ten minutes.

When he returns, his face is dark with annoyance. "The little weasel sneaked out the gym door. I found it on the security camera footage. What the hell is he playing at, telling me he needed to talk to you and then running off?"

What indeed? What could have changed in the forty-five minutes between Fly's expressing his desire to talk and my arrival? While the cop is angry, I'm worried.

"Where do you think he went?"

The cop holds out his hand and begins ticking off possibilities on fingers large enough to break Fly's neck: the fountain in the green, the duckpond in Weston Park, the train station, and the ever-popular Burger King parking lot.

I'm not spending the rest of my day searching for the kid, and neither is the school resource officer. We agree that he'll call me when Fly returns to school.

"Leaving school in the middle of the day without permission—Frankie is looking at a good week of after-school detention for this stunt," the cop grumbles.

His words make me think of Sophia. "What would happen to a kid at Palmyrton High School who put a firecracker in a locker and injured another student?"

The cop's eyes widen in shock. "These days, anything even remotely resembling a bomb is a huge deal. Some kids were suspended for a week for planting alarm clocks around the school that rang at different times as a senior prank. Something that actually exploded would get a kid arrested and sent to juvie." He squints at me. "Why do you ask?"

"Just curious." I thank him and leave his office thinking about how different Sophia and Austin's world is from Fly's. She did something that would've got her locked up in public school, and she was punished, or maybe I should say rewarded, by getting to spend her senior year at home drawing pictures and pretending to study physics.

And between the two extremes stood Trevor, a kid with a foot in each camp.

The big clock above the main door reads two o'clock as I leave the school building. I've managed to squander half the day. I vow to go directly to the office and work straight through until it's time to meet Dad and Natalie for the Gregory Halpern performance tonight.

My phone chirps. Sophia.

I'm home now. Nothing to worry about. Can I still work at the sale this weekend? I really want to ☺

I stare at my phone screen and feel my heart rate accelerate in aggravation. I can spend the next hour in pointless texting and unanswered phone calls seeking an explanation, or I can do my job.

Fine. See you Friday.

Chapter 25

The Drew University auditorium is packed to the gills.

In an impressive burst of afternoon efficiency, I managed to send out enticing emails to my customer list promoting both the Freidrich and the Gardner sales, while finding an early buyer for Brielle's creamy leather sofa. I'm ready for a guilt-free evening of entertainment with Dad and Natalie.

The audience surrounding us is a testament to the breadth of Gregory Halpern's appeal: college students rub shoulders with people my parents' age, and Jersey City hipsters mingle with staid suburban couples. There's not an empty seat in the house.

Soon the lights dim, the crowd hushes, and a single spotlight illuminates a wooden, straight-backed chair on the otherwise empty stage. As the theme music from *The World in a Week* plays, a tall, lean man with a mop of wavy dark hair lopes across the stage and into the beam of light.

"Isn't he handsome?" Natalie whispers to me.

It cracks me up to see my dignified stepmother gushing like a middle-schooler at a boy-band concert. I wouldn't say Gregory Halpern is handsome in the conventional sense. He's too lanky and his nose is kind of beaky, but he certainly projects an aura that grabs our attention, even from ten rows back.

For the next hour, Halpern holds us in thrall. He tells about his narrow escape from marauding Boko Haram extremists in Nigeria and his encounter with an isolated tribe who'd never seen a person in western clothes in the jungles of Borneo. Sometimes he perches on the edge of the chair; sometimes he spins it or crouches behind it. When he talks about eating locusts, I feel like I'm crunching them in my own teeth. When he describes a slum in Mumbai, I can smell the filth. His long-fingered hands are so expressive. He stretches them wide and gazes up at the ceiling when he wants us to ponder the diversity of the universe. He steeples them under his chin when he wants us to focus on a small point.

Halpern ends with a quiet story about a 101-year-old woman in a Vietnamese rice paddy. The spotlight goes out. The theatre plunges into darkness.

When the house lights come up, the stage is empty. I feel unwillingly jolted back to reality. The colorful market stalls and frigid icebergs and lush jungles fall away, and I've crashed-landed back into a scratchy tweed lecture hall seat in New Jersey. The audience sits in stunned silence. Then a man leaps up and begins applauding. Soon the entire audience is on their feet, clapping, cheering, hollering.

"Encore!" someone shouts. But Gregory Halpern knows how to maintain his magic. The only person who comes on stage is an employee of the university who thanks us for coming and directs us to the exits.

"Wow! That was amazing." I follow Dad and Natalie out of our row. "Thanks for inviting me." I had considered taking two cars to the event because I didn't want to get stuck at the afterparty, but now, I have to admit, I'm keen to go and meet the star of the show.

"The party is in a reception room on the second floor of this building," Natalie tells us. "I think we have to take the stairs on the far side of the lobby."

We mosey along with the departing crowd, then break free when the masses head out the main door as the select few head upstairs. At the door of the reception room, we join a queue waiting to show their VIP passes to a university employee who checks names off a list. Dad, Natalie, and I chat as the line shuffles forward until a commotion at the head of the line halts all conversation.

"This is bullshit," a young man shouts. "I paid fifty bucks for my ticket, and I pay a ridiculous amount of tuition here, and I deserve to get in."

"I'm sorry." The woman at the door maintains a polite, patient tone. "As I explained, this is a private party. Admission is by invitation only."

"I left my invitation at home."

"Young man, your name is not on the guest list."

"That is such elitist crap! I need to meet Gregory Halpern. I have something important to tell him." In his agitation, the kid knocks his backpack into the lady behind him. His Adam's apple jumps up and down in his long neck.

A burly security guard shows up beside the door monitor. "Step out of the line, son. Let's talk about it over here."

The kid follows the guard into a corner, gesticulating and arguing every step of the way. My father shakes his head. "Students today have such an air of entitlement. That's one thing I don't miss about teaching."

After the incident, the line moves quickly and we're soon inside. Gregory Halpern stands surrounded by a gaggle of admirers. They push their programs at him and beg for autographs. This is what I dreaded. I'm certainly not going to elbow my way through that crowd just to gush at him.

"There's Gregory's mother, Lorraine." Natalie waves and moves purposefully to the opposite side of the room toward a tall, slender woman her own age. Dad and I follow, and we're soon chatting with the star's mother and father. "Gregory gave a fabulous performance." Natalie kisses her friend. "You must be so proud."

Lorraine beams. "Every time he does a show in New York or New Jersey, his father and I go. I'm always a nervous wreck when he walks on stage. I feel like I used to when he played for the high school baseball team. I'm praying he won't strike out!" Her laugh peals out. "And at every show, I simply fall under his spell and forget he's my son. I say to him all the time, 'How in God's name did you learn to do that?' Right, Stuart?"

Mr. Halpern, who's got the same beaky nose as his son, shakes his head. "The kid spoke about ten words total in four years of high school. Maybe twenty in college. We don't know where this comes from. I just pray it lasts." He rolls his eyes. "Podcasting! It's a fad."

Lorraine shoots her husband a dirty look. "Let's celebrate our son's success, Stuart, instead of waiting for him to fail."

I suppress a smile. Given that Gregory Halpern is in his mid-forties, this parental argument must have been going on for decades. Their son is a late bloomer, and the father hasn't accepted that his son's success will last. "Is this performance part of a tour?" I ask to change the subject.

"A short tour." Stuart takes a slug of wine. "Gregory has three weeks of podcasts recorded, then he has to go on the road again. Next stop is Nepal."

"Nepal! How exotic!" Natalie's eyes open wide in wonder.

"They have terrible earthquakes there." Lorraine gazes across the room, where Gregory is listening intently to a pretty young woman. "If only he'd meet a nice girl and settle down."

Given that the secret to his success hinges on traveling to a new location every week, this seems highly unlikely. Parents' dreams so often are out of alignment with the dreams of their kids. It took my father a decade to accept that I'll never give up Another Man's Treasure to get a PhD in math.

"Ha! Don't count on grandchildren from Gregory," Stuart says. "By the time he gets around to it, we'll be cold in our graves."

Man, Mr. Halpern is a real ray of sunshine!

"I wish he could stay home longer." Lorraine bites her lower lip. "He'll be here in New Jersey for a week, with shows at Princeton, Monmouth University, and Villa Nova."

Natalie pats her friend's arm. "Enjoy him while you can."

Lorraine cranes her neck to catch sight of her son again. The crowd around him is thinning, and he breaks away to come over to us. He hugs his mom and kisses her cheek, slaps his dad on the back, shakes hands all around. "Thanks for coming tonight." His smile is warm and genuine.

My father dips his head. "We're happy to be here. We enjoyed the show very much."

Gregory won't realize it, but that right there is a twelve on Roger Nealon's one-to-ten scale of effusiveness.

"Your show seems so spontaneous," I say. "Is it different every time you perform it?"

"Yes, I have a general idea of what stories I'll tell, but each crowd has its own vibe. I read the room and change up the show as I go."

"Fascinating," my father says. "I understand your next stop is Nepal."

"Yes, Nepal to interview the Sherpas who lead trips up Mt. Everest, then on to Yemen."

"Yemen! Oh, Gregory, surely not." Lorraine's face constricts in alarm.

I have to agree with Lorraine. Terrorists, civil war, and famine—Yemen's a real trifecta of danger. Gregory must enjoy skating close to the edge.

Unwilling to listen to Lorraine's pleas to scratch Yemen, I sidle away from the parents and set off to see if I can score a glass of wine and a few nibbles. When I get near the bar, I spot a familiar head of beautifully styled hair: Brielle Gardner is here. Somehow, I wouldn't have pegged her as the brainy/geeky podcast type. Her gaze meets mine, and she smiles and heads right over.

"How nice to see you here." Brielle pecks the air near my left ear. "Are you flying solo tonight like I am?"

"I'm here with my parents." I nod vaguely in their direction. "They're big fans of Gregory's."

"Gregory and I are old friends." She sips from her wine glass. "We went to Princeton together."

That surprises me. As perfectly groomed as Brielle is, she seems older than Gregory. From behind, with her great figure and perfect hair, Brielle could pass for twenty-five. But face-to-face, her age shows in tiredness around her eyes and tension in her mouth. I suppose Gregory's lifestyle gives him the aura of a perpetual teenager. "He leads a fascinating life."

Brielle offers an indulgent smile. "He's quite the rolling stone, our Gregory. If I didn't try to connect with him at one of his shows, I'd never see him at all." She turns her gaze away from me and follows Gregory as he moves on to another clutch of fans.

"His parents seem torn between being proud of his success and sad that his career takes him so far away from them."

"Their plan was that Gregory should go to law school, join his father's law firm, and buy a house across the street from theirs. Gregory got as far as attending an Ivy League college, then he ditched his parents' plan." Brielle smoothes her already perfect hair. "He's always been a free spirit."

"The parents are always last to know." I intend this as a light-hearted comeback, but Brielle's face darkens.

"Yes, parents have an endless capacity to deceive themselves."

Someone calls Brielle's name and waves from across the room. Her face lights into its socially appropriate expression, and Brielle turns away from me. Before she leaves, she makes one more remark. "I'm *so* glad you found a good home for my seascape."

Then she strides into the crowd. "Darling! It's been too long!"

I join the queue at the bar thinking about what Brielle said. How did she know I found a buyer for the painting? I didn't tell her, or anyone else for that matter.

Except Jane. I mentioned it to Jane when she came over looking for Sophia.

Clearly, she reported back to Brielle.

What else does Jane tell her friend? How many hours I work? How I priced her steak knives?

I give myself a little shake. I'm being paranoid. The painting must've come up in casual conversation between Brielle and Jane.

As I wait for my drink, I notice the servers, who all appear to be Drew students, going in and out of a door behind the bar that apparently leads to a service area. Finally, I get my wine, and as I step away, I notice one of the servers hold that door open. A tall young man, not dressed in black pants and a white shirt like the other servers, slips through.

It's the kid who was trying to crash the party and got turned away at the door. I have to chuckle at such determination in a fan! Clearly, security is meaningless here if you have a friend on the inside.

I watch as the kid scopes out the room looking for Gregory. The crowd has thinned a bit, and Gregory is no longer swarmed by admirers. When the kid spots his idol, he strides across the room with determination.

No one else pays any attention. Although most of the guests are older, no one is particularly dressed up, so the kid doesn't stand out. The boy reaches his target just as Gregory has turned away from another fan. The boy plants himself in Gregory's path and says something.

I watch in fascination as Gregory's face undergoes a transformation: friendly...startled...appalled. Gregory jerks his head in the direction of the hallway, then grabs the boy's elbow and marches him there.

Interesting. When the kid was trying to get past the door monitor, he'd said he had something important to tell Gregory. Apparently, the star wants to hear it.

For an instant, I'm tempted to wander out to the hallway to...say...look for the ladies' room. But I finally got my glass of wine, and the kid's message to Gregory is none of my business.

Not that that's ever stopped me before.

I settle on a compromise: I take the long route back to Dad and Natalie, passing the exit to the hallway as I go. I pause to sip from my glass when I hear muffled voices from just outside the door.

"Look, I'm sorry you're disappointed, but that's not what I signed on for."

"You refuse to even meet with us?" The kid's voice grows squeaky with indignation. "You don't even want to meet the others?"

"No. No, I don't. There's nothing more to discuss."

The kid must have wanted Gregory to address some student group at the university, and he's outraged that Gregory won't drop everything to comply. Dad is right—kids today do have an air of entitlement. I hustle away from the door so that Gregory won't trip over me when he reenters the room. Once I'm back in Dad and Natalie's circle, I glance over my shoulder.

Gregory stands by the door, pale and jittery. Then he flings back his shoulders, dredges up a smile, and plunges back into the scrum of his fans.

Chapter 26

Thursday morning finds me mercifully alone in the office. Ty has classes at Palmer County Community College that will keep him busy all day. Donna is at the Freidrich house, fussing over the first sale she'll be running solo as if she's planning a royal wedding. I have phone calls to make finding buyers for some of Brielle's larger pieces. Some of them are to people I don't know, so naturally procrastination is in order while I work up my introvert's sales pitch.

I scan the top stories in my digital edition of the *New York Times*. Nothing but doom and gloom. I scroll past the big news and click on an article about the sudden resurgence in popularity of Paul McCobb furniture. Once I finish that, the next article in the Style section pops up:

Hiraku Maki to Close Design Atelier

Prominent interior designer Hiraku Maki announced yesterday that he would close his design practice as he fights pancreatic cancer. Mr. Maki, who is noted for working without assistants, had been declining new projects in recent months. Rumors swirled about his mental health as he had a reputation for volatile outbursts. However, friends and associates were stunned to hear of the cancer diagnosis. "This is a tremendous loss to the design community," said Klaus von Reimer....

My attention drifts away from the expressions of support and encouragement. What does this mean for the sale? Clearly, Hiraku Maki will not be redecorating Brielle's house. But the article's claim that Maki had been declining new projects for months makes me wonder if my friend Tim was right all along—maybe Hiraku Maki had never been scheduled to work on Brielle's house. Why would she lie about such a thing?

I'm two days away from what promises to be a hugely profitable sale. There's a cancellation clause in my contract, but my kill fee won't be anywhere near what I stand to make if I sell the contents of the Gardners' house.

Calling Brielle and asking her if she wants to go forward with the sale gives her an out that I don't want her to take. Is she even aware of this news about Maki?

While I sit at my desk contemplating my options, I hear footsteps outside my door.

Next, a sharp, authoritative rap.

When I answer the door, a short, pale man with a broad face and pouchy eyes stands before me. He looks familiar, but I can't decide if I actually know him or if he just bears an unfortunate resemblance to one of my favorite characters, Toad in *Wind in the Willows*.

"Everett Gardner," he intones as he offers a hand that I half expect to be webbed.

"Oh, Mr. Gardner—come in. I don't think we've ever met. I'm Audrey Nealon."

He nods his large head, causing his starched shirt color to cut into his fleshy neck. I watch him glance around the office. Although he remains expressionless, I cringe at my clutter. I wasn't expecting a client visit, but let's face it—no amount of straightening would make this place acceptable to a man who married the meticulous Brielle. Did she send her husband—the man Tim called a real bastard—here to deliver the news that the sale is cancelled? How cowardly!

He chooses the chair we've nicknamed "the throne" which only serves to emphasize his small stature. He must be a head shorter than his wife, and maybe ten years older. She has beauty; he has money—a perfect match, I guess.

"So," he begins. "I understand this weekend you'll be selling off all the furniture and artwork that Brielle bought for Sea Chapel five years ago. How much do you think you'll get for it?"

Hmmm. This doesn't sound like the preamble to cancellation, but he may be coming at it from a different angle. He's probably a ferocious negotiator. "Uhm—it's hard to estimate." Of course, I've made my own estimate, but I'm always reluctant to be tied down to a projection of what a sale will bring in. It invariably leads to client disappointment or arguments. "Your home is lovely, but—"

He interrupts me with a raised hand. "I know—furniture and decorations are like cars—they lose half their value the moment they leave the showroom. Believe me, I'm not expecting much," he squints at me, "but will the transactions extend over the next month or more?"

"Oh, no—everything will be sold and paid for by Sunday. Your wife did insist that she wants the house entirely emptied by October second...." I take a gamble "...for the decorator."

His heavy-lidded eyes blink, the full extent of his reaction. "Yes, I don't care about that, but Brielle never remembers that her actions have tax implications. I've been asking her all week to get me a preliminary estimate. I finally decided to come here and get it myself. The way my accountant handles the revenue from the sale impacts the timing of some other investment decisions."

"No problem." I feel the knot in my shoulders unwind. I should have known that Mr. Gardner doesn't give a rat's ass about Hiraku Maki or even about the actual amount of revenue from the sale. All he wants is projections so he can accurately juggle his money to make even more money. I slide into my desk chair and flip open my laptop. He wants projections? I'll give him spreadsheets out the wazoo.

While I'm tapping away, I keep up a line of chatter with Mr. Gardner. "Your beach house has a spectacular view. I've really enjoyed working there."

He's studying his phone and doesn't look up. "Mmm. I suppose. I'm rarely there. I don't care for the sun."

I suppress a giggle. He probably prefers a lily pad in a cool pond. "But your son must love it. Does he surf or sail?"

Suddenly, I have his attention. Gardner's face softens. "Yes, Austin surfs. Beautiful to watch—he makes it look so effortless. And he has a small sailboat—a Sea Ray. Spent a few summers at sailing camp. He's always been a natural athlete."

I don't know anything about sailboats, but I'm guessing Austin's boat isn't like a Sunfish that you just drag out into the waves. "Is it docked down near Elmo's? That's a cute little restaurant."

"Yes, we keep it there. Brielle's after me to get him a bigger boat." Mr. Gardner grows more animated. I seem to have hit upon a topic he likes discussing—his son. "I told her once he's accepted at Princeton, we'd talk about it."

Given his smile of paternal indulgence, I'm pretty sure Princeton is already in the bag. Bring on the 30-foot schooner. I hit "print" and my sales projection spreadsheet begins grinding out of my low-tech printer. "Does Austin know what he'd like to study at Princeton?" I ask to distract Mr. Gardner from his wait.

"He's a science man. Not interested in finance at all." The father beams. "Last summer he did an internship with a geneticist at MIT—Wolfgang Eck. Gene editing to cure hereditary diseases. I told him, 'You find the cure. I'll get you the financial backing to bring it to market.'"

What could a sixteen-year-old boy possibly do to assist an MIT geneticist? But kids like Austin Gardner don't spend their summers scooping ice cream or sitting in the life guard chair at the Palmyrton town pool. No siree, they're busy burnishing that resume to pave the path to the Ivy League and beyond. Austin might be interested in science now, but his father will make sure he doesn't spend his life clattering among the test tubes in some research lab. No profit in that!

After I hand the spreadsheet to Mr. Gardner, he scans it and gives a brisk nod of approval. "Just what I needed. Very efficient. How soon after the sale can I expect the check?"

"I'll need to do an accounting after the sale. So probably Tuesday or Wednesday."

"Make it Tuesday. Bring it to my wife's store."

And without further ado, he's gone. I feel like I've gotten off easy in my encounter with this wizard of Wall Street. Standing at the side of the office window, I peek through the crack in the shade as he gets into his large, black Mercedes.

What must it be like to never doubt that your life and your child's life will always go according to plan?

Chapter 27

On Friday morning at breakfast, Sean chuckles as he stares at his laptop screen.

"What's so funny?"

"Colleen got an email from my mother in Ireland and she forwarded it to the rest of us."

"An email from your mother? She never emails."

"She emails from Ireland—you know she's too damn cheap to make an international phone call. She befriended a more tech-savvy Royal Hibernian and the lady showed my mother how to use the free wi-fi at the hotel in Dublin. So my mother sent this blow-by-blow description of every single thing they've seen."

"That's nice. So they're having fun?"

"They're having a blast. But here's the funny thing. They're meeting all these relatives that Colleen tracked down with her family tree research. Mom told her she missed one of the cousins on Granda's side—the most distinguished, most successful man in the whole family. A true paragon of all the best O'Shea virtues."

Sean grins. "But Colleen says her research shows there's not a drop of O'Shea blood in this man. According to her, this cousin must've been born on the wrong side 'o the sheets, as they say in the old country."

I stop what I'm doing. "Surely Colleen didn't tell your mom that?""

"Hell, no. But we're all getting a laugh out of it. Mom and Granda are always going on and on about what 'true' O'Sheas do and don't do. And how sinners always receive justice from an angry God. Looks like this guy's mother pulled off a fifty-year lie with no repercussions. And whoever her baby's father was, he seems to have polished the O'Shea family name to a high shine."

AFTER BREAKFAST, I pack my bag for my final weekend in Sea Chapel and head over to pick up Ty. He likes driving more than I do, so I toss him the keys and fiddle with the radio as Ty drives us south on the Parkway. Since I refuse to listen to hip-hop and he hates rock, we have to listen to jazz or the news. As I bounce through the channels, I pause on the weather report.

"A big storm is headed toward New York and New Jersey Friday night into Saturday morning. Gale force winds and heavy rains are expected in the city and northern New Jersey, with less intense winds further south."

"Shit! That doesn't sound good. I hope it doesn't affect our sales."

"Weatherman said it won't be as bad at the shore. You know a little bit of rain isn't bad for our business. Keeps people from wantin' to spend their day out in their yards."

"True. But gale force winds in Palmyrton sounds ominous."

"Well, nuthin' we can do about it. Besides, half the time, the weatherman is wrong."

Next up on the radio is a weekend arts update.

"....and Sunday afternoon at four, Gregory Halpern, host of The World in a Week will appear at Monmouth University. Limited tickets are still available."

"I really enjoyed his show at Drew," I tell Ty. "I'd go see him again except we'll probably still be wrapping up on Sunday afternoon."

Ty makes a face.

"Don't worry. I'm not going to make you sit through a lecture by a podcaster."

"I do enough sittin' and listenin' at school," Ty grumbles. He keeps his eyes laser focused on the road ahead and speaks again. "I might need to take some time off."

"Sure, if you need some extra time to study. Is there a course you're struggling with?"

"No-o-o." He hesitates. "Or maybe just quit."

My head jerks around. "What? You call that nothing wrong?"

Ty squirms in the driver's seat. "I made a big mistake. I gotta lay low for a while." He realizes how that sounds and straightens his spine. "Nuthin' illegal! This is personal."

"Want to tell me about it?"

"Can't."

Ah, here comes the Donna confession. "What kind of personal problem would be solved by quitting Another Man's Treasure?" I keep my voice non-committal.

Ty swallows hard. "I don't wanna quit, Audge. It's just...."

"Is this about Donna?"

Ty narrows his eyes. "How you know that?"

"You've been avoiding her. Yesterday, you waited until you were sure she'd be out for a while before you came in. Then you found some errand to run. Tell me what's wrong."

Ty clearly is dying to unburden himself but must feel some sense of honor not to talk about his involvement with a woman. How can we get around this without my admitting I already know? "Did you and Donna fight? You and Jill used to argue all the time, but it never made you want to quit."

"Not a fight," Ty mutters.

"The opposite of a fight?" I keep my voice light.

Ty bows his head toward the steering wheel in an uncanny mirroring of Donna's reaction. "I shoulda known better. It was my duty not to cave in. But she was hanging on me, wrappin' her arms around me. She just wanted some sympathy. I shouldn't a done her like that."

No, he shouldn't. But when are twenty-four-year-old men good at resisting needy women? "Well, that ship has sailed. Now what?"

"She's gonna want me to be her man. I can't do it, Audge. I'm not ready to settle down. I got too much still to do for me. Besides, Charmaine and Grams would kill me if I came home with a white girl. They're always tryin' to set me up with sistas."

I hadn't thought of that. It's true that the older ladies at the Parks Center are always checking Ty out, asking about his availability, eager to match their daughters and granddaughters with a handsome, hardworking man like Ty.

So it looks like neither Ty nor Donna wants to continue their moment of madness. But how can I let each one know that without revealing that they both blabbed to me? "What makes you think Donna wants a relationship with you? Seems to me she hasn't decided what to do about Anthony. And if she does divorce him, she'll probably want to take a break from all men for a while."

"Hmph. She sure wasn't takin' no break on Wednesday!"

"I meant an emotional break. Maybe now that she got the passion out of her system, she'll want to pretend it never happened."

Ty steals a glance at me. "She told you something."

So much for trying to maintain discretion. "I came in yesterday morning, and I could see Donna had been crying. I asked a few questions and—" I raise my palms. "You know me—people are always telling me their secrets."

"What'd she say?" Ty is so interested in my report, he lets the car slow down and a big truck barrels past us on the right.

I can tell that Ty's curiosity is greater than his outrage. "She said she got carried away. She said she didn't want to hurt you but that she's too old for you and a relationship would never work out."

Ty's face brightens. "Really? Well, can you tell her—"

"No! We're not all in middle school." I pick up my phone. "I'll text her that you're not mad and don't want to be in a relationship either. You have the weekend apart from each other. After that, you two need to talk and work it out. I've cleared the way."

Ty grins. "Thanks, Audge. You the best!"

<hr>

WE PULL INTO 43 DUNE Vista drive half an hour later. I've watched Ty's reaction when he enters a client's house many times, and it's pretty easy to read his emotions: amazement, revulsion, awe, surprise, pity. But this is the first time I've seen this particular emotion.

Envy.

"*Damn*. This is one fine crib." He tiptoes across the living room, skimming his long fingers across the back of Brielle's pale blue sofa. "This my kinda house. So open. So fresh. So clean." He gets to the window and takes in the view. "Yes. I could really kick back here."

"It's all yours...for the weekend."

"We've worked in some nice houses, but I never felt like I wanted to live in any of them. Too stiff. Too straight." Ty grins. "But I'd like to live here."

He spins around. "How much you think this place goes for?"

"Three million? Four?"

Ty whistles. "I've never really cared about being rich. Money don't buy happiness and all that. But man, I think living in a house like this would make me pretty damn trippy."

I smile but don't answer.

"I know what you thinkin', Audge. This house hasn't made the Gardners so happy, or why would they be tossin' out all this really fine stuff?" Ty drops into the easy chair that faces the view. "You think there's something about havin' lots of cash that makes people miserable? 'Cause I can tell you this—ain't no picnic bein' poor."

I sit in the chair beside his and watch a bird circle then dive into the water. "I think there's a tipping point. People who don't have enough money to feed their kids or pay the electric bill get desperate. But people who have more than enough get desperate, too. Desperate to maintain their position. Desperate to impress others. What strikes me about Brielle and Jane next door is they both seem exhausted by their lives."

"Humpf. They think they're exhausted, they oughta try a double shift in Housekeeping at the hospital like my grams used to work."

I don't reply. After a while, Ty speaks again, softer. "I know what you sayin'. There's different kinds of wore-out. These rich people get stretched about to snap with all the effort of tryin' to always be the main man. I sure don't need that."

I reach over and lay my hand on Ty's arm. We sit like that for a while. Then he grins and leaps up. "C'mon, Audge—we got work to do."

While I pick up where I left off pricing in the family room, Ty makes several trips back and forth to the van to unload the supplies we'll need for the sale. The sliders to the pool are open, and I hear his voice from the driveway. "Yo, no early birds. Sale starts tomorrow morning."

A low voice murmurs something in return. The next thing I hear is "Audge! Hey, Audge, c'mere."

I know the difference between, "Come look at this cool thing," and "Get your ass over here—we got trouble," and this is the latter. I drop my marking pen and run outside.

A tall, strong man with close-cropped hair strides toward me. He looks vaguely familiar. Ty trails behind him in an uncharacteristically meek way.

"May I help you?"

"Detective Larry Croft. Ocean County Sheriff's Department. I just need a moment to look around."

One of the cops who talked to Sophia after the funeral. He doesn't seem to recognize me. At the funeral, I was wearing make-up and slacks. Today, my hair is yanked back, my face scrubbed, and I'm sporting the faded UVA sweatshirt I've owned since graduation. I stand blocking the sliding door. "You can't enter this home without the owner's permission."

He smiles, trying for "aw shucks" innocence and missing the mark by a mile. "You're not the owner, so there's no need to worry about it." He takes another step toward the door. "I won't get in your way."

I plant my hands on my hips. "I'm the owner's agent. I'm responsible for the property in her absence. Do you have a warrant?"

"Heh, heh, heh—a warrant? You've been watching too much TV. Tomorrow, you're going to have hundreds of people in here looking around. What's the harm in me doing it a little early?"

I hold my ground, steadfast as a Texas Ranger at the Alamo. Obviously, he's fishing—he doesn't have probable cause for a search warrant. So why would this detective want to poke around in Brielle's house? I remember that odd encounter outside the church when Brielle ran after one of the other mourners. What is this tight-knit little circle of families trying to hide? Still, this cop should be doing his job according to procedure. I have a duty to protect my client's property. And unlike Ty, I have no qualms about crossing swords with the police. "You're welcome to come tomorrow as a customer. Maybe you'll find something to brighten up your office. Now, if you'll excuse us, we have work to do."

As I turn away, he grabs my elbow. "Hey, weren't you with Sophia Peterman at Trevor Finlayson's funeral?"

"Yes." Never lie, but never offer more information than you're asked for.

"How well do you know the kid?"

Both of us look over at the Peterman house. It's quiet—doors and windows all closed. I've been expecting Sophia to pop over, but she and her mother must not be home.

"Not well at all. I met her last week when she came over to help me organize the sale."

"And Trevor and his family—you know them?"

"No."

"But you went to the funeral? And you offered Sophia advice about getting a lawyer before she talked to us? And now you're guarding the Gardners' house like a pit bull?"

With every question, his voice carries a greater inflection of suspicion. I can't blame him. My actions do seem a little odd when they're laid out so starkly. I don't owe him any explanations, but I want to get information out of him as much as he wants to get it from me.

So I try to do as Grandma Betty always recommends: catch some flies with honey instead of my customary vinegar. "Have a seat." I smile and gesture him toward Brielle's sleek patio furniture. Ty still watches me from a distance. I nod at him and he shrugs and goes back to work.

Sitting across from Detective Croft at the umbrella table, I smile and lean in. "You know, my husband is a detective on the Palmyrton police force. He and I were staying here on the night Trevor's body washed up on the beach. So we have a personal connection to the case."

Detective Croft squints at me with deeper interest. "Your husband was the one with the local guys...kept them from tramping all over the crime scene?"

Once I nod, I sense a subtle change in his demeanor. I'm okay, he thinks. I'm on his side. He knows how to handle a cop's wife.

But knowledge cuts two ways: I know how to handle a cop.

"How long's your husband been on the force?"

"Fifteen years. But we're newlyweds." I try to mimic that Princess Diana demure look: chin down, eyes gazing up through the lashes. "Last weekend we were combining work with pleasure. Sean came down here with me while I was organizing Mrs. Gardner's house sale."

I keep chatting, friendly as a spouse at a backyard barbeque. "And the next day we met Sophia and her mother. After my husband returned to Palmyrton, Sophia helped me do some sorting and pricing to get ready for the sale. She's a sweet kid, but a little...high strung. So when she drove up to Palmyrton to go to the funeral, I agreed to go with her for moral support." A dead leaf has the audacity to land on Brielle's table. I brush it away. "I certainly didn't expect her to make that declaration from the pulpit."

"Why didn't you want her to talk to us?"

I glance at the gold band on his left hand. "You have kids?"

He nods.

"You wouldn't let one of your kids who was barely eighteen talk to the police alone, would you?"

He opens his mouth, and I can practically see the party line about how the innocent never have anything to fear forming on his lips. Then he catches my steady gaze and thinks better of it. He shifts in his seat and mutters, "I guess not."

"We were worried when Sophia disappeared after talking to you."

He holds up his hands in protest. "We told her to go straight home and lay low for a while. Can't help it she didn't follow our advice."

Hmm. So whatever Sophia told the cops, it was concerning enough that they advised her to watch her back. I glance over at the Peterman's house again. "I haven't seen any sign of Sophia today, but she says she's going to help out at the sale tomorrow."

Detective Croft extends his large body back in the patio chair and drums his fingers on the table. "So tell me about this sale. Are the Gardners getting ready to move out of the house?"

"No, Mrs. Gardner plans to redecorate. The designer wants a clean slate."

He peers at the open sliding door. "I checked out your website. You usually do sales for people who've died or are moving. You ever encountered a situation like this before?"

"No. But if I've learned one thing in my business, it's that the rich are different from you and me."

"Mmm. What I've learned in my line of work is that the rich have more to lose, so they're more likely to go to extremes."

He's got a point. I think of my previous clients, the Finnerans and the Eskews. "You think she's selling off the contents of her house to cover something up? Something associated with Trevor's death?"

Croft remains silent.

"Look, I can assure you there are no large blood stains on the rugs or bullet holes in the walls. It's the cleanest house I've ever worked in." I stand up. "I can't give you access today, but everything that's in the house now will still be here tomorrow morning. Come back then if you want to look around."

He rises too and reaches out to shake my hand. "Fine. I'll be here. You gonna get on the horn and tell Mrs. Gardner I came by?"

Am I? I've followed the letter of the law in my contract with her. Truth is, I don't like her and her son and her husband much. And I feel no need to protect them—they've got enough money to hire a platoon of lawyers to do that job.

I shake Croft's hand firmly. "My client doesn't like to be disturbed."

Chapter 28

Ty and I have finished the set-up for the sale and are eating a pizza when Sophia turns up at the back door. She strolls in like she owns the place, perches on a stool, and nabs the last slice, which I know Ty would've polished off. "Hi, I'm Sophia," she tells him. "I'm going to help you with the sale tomorrow."

"That so?"

Sophia doesn't seem to notice Ty's lack of enthusiasm. "Have you been here all day? My mom and I were shopping in Rumson."

"Yes. We got here at ten and we just finished all the set-up. The sale will open at nine tomorrow morning. I'll need you here at eight."

"I'll be ready." Sophia finishes her slice and hops off the stool. "I'm going to look around at everything."

I think about how Jane reported back to Brielle about the sale of the big painting. Did Jane send her daughter over here to spy on my work? "I'll come with you and explain how the sale will operate tomorrow."

I follow her into the dining area explaining how we've grouped all the small items together on the table where we can keep an eye on them. Of course, Brielle doesn't have jewelry in the sale, and there are very few small knick-knacks, so shoplifting shouldn't be a big concern.

Once we head upstairs, I launch into the topic I really want to discuss with Sophia—the funeral and its aftermath.

"You know I was worried about you after Trevor's funeral, especially when your mom called and said you hadn't come home."

Sophia dismisses this with a wave. "I told her before I left that I would probably stay over with a friend in Palmyrton, so I didn't have to drive home in the dark. She never remembers a thing I say."

That could be true, or it could be revisionist history. Who can be sure with Sophia and Jane? "How did it go when you talked to the cops?"

"Fine." Sophia stares at the price tag attached to the slipper chair in the guest bedroom. "They said I wasn't supposed to tell anyone what we talked about."

I'm sure they did, but when has Sophia ever listened to adults' advice? Still, I won't stoop to egging her on to break her word.

"Isn't Brielle's stuff nice?" Sophia asks as she runs her fingertips over the folded duvet at the foot of the bed. "I've never been in this room."

"Yes, I think everything will sell." I put my hand on her shoulder as she moves to leave the guest room. "Sophia, that was quite a dramatic statement you made at the funeral. It seemed like you were threatening someone there. What did you mean by that?"

She glides away from me and darts across the hall into Austin's room. "Threaten?" she says with her back to me. "How could I threaten anyone? Hey, look at this—Austin's BSS sweatshirts priced at fifty cents apiece. I hope some Mexican landscaper dude buys them. Wouldn't that make the alumni association crazy!"

Clearly, Sophia's not going to tell me a thing about the aftermath of Trevor's funeral. But she certainly seems to be in good spirits, so I have to assume there hasn't been any fallout for her personally. "Well, you've seen all we have to sell." I nudge her toward the stairs. "You'll be working in the dining room tomorrow." I tug at her ratty T-shirt. "Dress code is business casual."

"Okay, I can do that." She trots downstairs and heads for the back door. "I'll see you in the morning, Audrey."

After she leaves, I put on my jacket and go out on the deck to enjoy the ocean breeze and the sound of the waves. From the lower level, the sounds of *Sports Center* drift up as Ty relaxes in front of the huge TV before we sell it. From next door, I hear Sophia's excited voice through her own open kitchen window. ".... The sale's going to be awesome, Mom. I bet everyone in Sea Chapel will be there. Are you coming?"

"No, Sophia. I'm not going to buy my best friend's cast-offs."

The light in the Peterman's kitchen goes off, and the two of them move to a part of the house where I can no longer hear them.

Interesting that Jane considers Brielle her best friend.

I wonder if the feeling is mutual?

Back inside, I say goodnight to Ty and settle myself in the guestroom.

I brought a book to read, but my thoughts keep returning to Jane and Sophia. How does a woman as scattered and unfocused as Jane run a business so profitable that she can afford a house almost as grand as Brielle's?

I'm a lot more organized but a lot less rich.

Who is Jane Peterman anyway? Given what Sophia told me about her estranged grandparents, it doesn't seem like Jane inherited her money. When I Google her, the first thing that comes up is her own website: Peterman Consulting, LLC. The "about us" section says the firm is a boutique consultancy laser focused on outside-the-box marketing initiatives. Whatever. The photo of Jane is so flattering as to be unrecognizable. She's thinner, with perfectly coiffed hair, a snappy suit to prove she's serious, and a rakish scarf to indicate she's got imagination and flair.

The page headlined "What clients say about Jane" contains quotes from high-level executives at Fortune 500 companies.

"Jane gets results!"

"Her insights are extraordinary. We saw a 200% increase in return business after implementing her strategies."

"Jane cuts through the BS to get the job done."

Impressive. Her bio says she spent eight years at Quantum Consulting before leaving to start her own firm three years ago. Quantum is a huge firm with branches all around the world. The firm recruited heavily among all of us math majors at UVA, so I happen to have a college friend who works there. When I text her to ask if she knows Jane Peterman, she immediately answers, *Do I ever! She's legendary at Quantum.*

Legendary in a good way?

Seconds later my phone is ringing. As a fellow math major, Kelly and I were in a lot of the same classes, but she is an irrepressible extrovert who was born to go into consulting. She also loves a good gossip.

"I haven't heard from you since your wedding, Audrey. And then you text out of nowhere asking about Jane Peterman, of all people! What gives, girl?"

Immediately, I feel guilty about only calling when I want information. So I spend a few minutes catching up on news and end by telling Kelly about my current sale and how it's brought me into contact with Jane.

"Wow, so she used her payout to buy a big, fancy beach house, eh?"

I sit up and tune in. "Payout? What payout?"

"When Jane was working for Quantum, she spent long hours on a high-profile project with a female client about her own age. They got to be friends, but then the client said Jane wouldn't leave her alone. She accused Jane of stalking her. Jane's boss pulled her off that project and put her on a much less prestigious project. At Quantum, getting yanked from a project like that is a career-killer. Well, Jane fought back, and said she was a victim of mental health discrimination. She accused Quantum's human resources department of violating her privacy by scrutinizing her health insurance claims to see what kind of doctors she consulted and what meds she took."

"Whatever they were, she's still taking them," I add. "Her kitchen windowsill looks like CVS."

"So Jane hired a big-name lawyer, and I guess her case must've been pretty convincing because Quantum struck a settlement deal. Quantum offered her a big payout if she would leave voluntarily. Both sides signed nondisclosure agreements, but the office grapevine was on fire for weeks when it happened. People claimed she got a million bucks."

"Are people at your office pro-Jane or anti-Jane?"

"Jane was a high-flyer at Quantum before the incident. She's super smart and had a reputation for coming up with innovative ideas. But she also had a reputation for being volatile. Everyone who ever worked with Jane knew she was a nut, but we had to admire how she played her cards. It was a ballsy move to threaten that lawsuit. She walked away with a pile of cash and a letter of recommendation that paved the way for her to start her own boutique firm."

"What about the woman who said Jane was stalking her?"

"I don't know. Rumor had it that she applied for a transfer and moved to the Midwest."

Did she move to further her career, or to get away from Jane? I guess we'll never know.

I thank Kelly for her help, and we make a plan to get together next month. After I hang up with her, Sean calls to say goodnight from Granda's house. "You okay down there? It's raining and blowing like crazy here."

The guest room curtains billow in the breeze. "It's gusty here, but the weatherman said we wouldn't get as much rain and wind this far south."

I hear a boom of thunder over the phone. "Shit, the lights flickered," Sean says. "I wonder where Granda keeps the candles?"

"You'd better go. Goodnight, Sean."

"Hey—one more thing. I made an appointment with Dr. Stein. I go next week."

My heart swells with love for my husband. I know he really doesn't want to see this doctor. He's doing it for me. "Thank you, darling."

Another boom of thunder.

"The old man's calling me. Goodnight, baby. Good luck tomorrow."

Chapter 29

Sophia shows up at the deck door at 8:00 AM, just as we agreed. But she's wearing ripped cut-off shorts and a vintage David Bowie *Aladdin Sane* T-shirt—not the customer-facing wardrobe I had in mind for the sale.

She appears both excited and anxious. I didn't realize working the small items table at this event meant so much to her.

"Audrey, listen—I can't help at the sale today after all. I'm really sorry, but my mom has finally agreed to drive to Maine so I can visit Bowdoin College. And then we'll stop at Bennington on the way back. I've been begging her for months, but she kept saying she was too busy. Today she just woke up and said, "Let's go!" So I gotta roll with this because who knows when I'll get another chance." Sophia's brow furrows and she looks down at her purple painted toenails. "Are you mad?"

Am I mad? You bet I am. But not at Sophia, at Jane. She knew her daughter made a commitment to work with me today, yet she dangled something the kid's been longing for to lure her away. What's that all about?

I pull Sophia into a hug. The poor kid's got enough trouble having Jane for a mother without getting grief from me. "Don't worry about it. We'll manage. Have fun on the college visit."

"Thanks, Audrey. You're the best!"

Half an hour later, I see Jane's BMW glide out of the garage and head north.

No sooner does Sophia leave than my phone buzzes. "Audrey, we have an emergency."

Donna's breathless voice causes my heart to miss a beat. "What's the matter? Are you in danger?"

"No, I'm fine. It's the Freidrich sale. In the storm last night, a huge oak tree got hit by lightning and fell right across the cul de sac. It brought down the power lines and broke off a fire hydrant. There's water everywhere and live electrical wires and no electricity and no one can get into or out of the street. What should I do?"

It's eight-thirty. Clearly, live power lines in a flooded street aren't going to be resolved any time soon. And from what Ty has heard from his grandmother, there are trees down all over Palmyrton. No one's going be up for exploring estate sales today. "Cancel the sale. Send out an email to our customer list. Announce it on the website."

"Who's going to tell the Freidrichs? Won't they be mad that we're canceling the sale?"

"It's an act of God. There's a clause in all our contracts for that. I'll call them and get it rescheduled."

"Oh...okay." Donna sounds like a kid whose trip to Disneyworld has just been called off.

"What's the matter? You've got the weekend off."

"I don't *want* time off," she wails. "I was looking forward to running the sale. Now I'll be sitting here all alone dwelling on my problems."

"Well, get in your car and drive down to Sea Chapel. We can use the help here. People are already lining up, and the kid who was supposed to help out has cancelled."

"What about Ty?"

"What about him? He's here. You two need to deal."

Long silence.

"Okay," Donna squeaks. "See you in two hours."

Ty looks like a provoked porcupine when I tell him Donna will be joining us. "But you said—" he sputters.

"I said you had two days to get your shit together. Now you have two hours. Deal."

Ty glowers at me and stomps upstairs muttering under his breath. "You kiss your grandmother with that mouth?" I shout after him.

Knowing that Ty will get over his snit, I do the last-minute tasks on the main floor. Because all the big windows in this house face the ocean, I have to go into the powder room to peek outside and check on the crowd.

Cars line Dune Vista Drive, and people have begun to queue up on the front walk and the driveway.

The very first person in line is Detective Croft.

I'm glad Jane and Sophia aren't here to see him and report to Brielle.

When the clock strikes nine, I take a deep breath and open the door.

Croft nods at me and heads directly for the stairs to the lower level. Other buyers surge past, asking questions as they walk.

"Tools?"

"Antiques?"

"Records?"

No, no, and no. Those are the hard-core estate sale junkies of the Jersey Shore. They found me; I didn't have to find them. They may be disappointed by how new everything here is.

Next come the gawkers.

"Oh my gawd, Gloria—can you believe how gorgeous this house is? Didn't I tell ya?"

"I've walked past this house on the beach a million times. I've always wanted to look inside."

Finally, come the friends and neighbors.

"I haven't been here since the housewarming party."

"Be grateful you were invited to that."

"Are those red wine goblets? Surely Brielle never served Cabernet to people sitting on her white chairs."

"I want that bowl."

"So, buy it."

"Everyone who comes to my house will know where it came from!"

The ladies collapse in giggles.

I get behind the sales desk and within minutes, start taking money. I'd love to know what Detective Croft is up to, but I can't leave my post.

By the time Donna arrives shortly after ten, Ty and I are so busy with customers that there's no opportunity for any awkwardness. Donna jumps into my spot behind the sales desk, giving me a chance to patrol the house looking for problems and answering questions. I stop a four-year-old from flying his toy plane near the glassware, decline to cut the price of a fabulous end table, and finally make my way to the lower level.

There I find Croft on his hands and knees in front of the sofa, looking under the cushions.

"Find any loose change?"

He stands, utterly unembarrassed. Evidence collection envelopes peep from his shirt pocket. Some customers out on the pool deck debate the merits of the lounge chairs, but no one is near us.

"You vacuum this furniture to prep for the sale?" Croft asks.

"Didn't have to. It was that clean when I got here. Mrs. Gardner's house cleaners come every week even when the family isn't using the place."

"Any signs that her kid used this as a party room?"

I spread my arms like Vanna White displaying prizes: the cream sofa, the bleached oak floor, the polished teak bar. "This look like a good place to play beer pong and flip cup?"

I finally get a laugh from the poker-faced Croft. "Still, the kid must've had his friends over some time." His voice rises as if this is a question I should know the answer to.

"You know how it is with teenagers. Some houses are the hang-out houses; some aren't." Certainly, the library-quiet house I shared with my father was never a gathering place for my small circle of high school friends.

Croft makes a face and takes one more panoramic survey of the room. Then he lifts his hand in farewell, and exits through the pool area.

Chapter 30

Relieved to see the back of the detective, I head upstairs just in time to glimpse an elderly couple toddle into the kitchen. The old woman holds a cane in one hand and clings to her husband's arm with the other. The old man faces the world with ram-rod posture and a stern profile. I recognize them from Trevor's funeral: Grandma and Grandpa Finlayson.

Surely, they didn't come here to pick up some stylish serving utensils.

I draw back into the alcove at the head of the lower level stairs and watch. The old man scans the room with hawk-eyed attention. He runs an appraising hand over the gleaming granite countertop and squints at the huge fridge. Then he steps up to the window to take in the view, his frail wife trailing behind him. When he turns around, she stays at the window. The old man sees me.

"Are you the person running this event?"

Certainly, that's a question I've been asked many times in my professional life, but it's never sounded so disapproving. "Yes. May I help you with something?"

"Why are the Gardners allowing all these...people—" he glares at a woman in Crocs as if he would've preferred to say "riff-raff"—"to prowl through their house? Very out of character. Are they moving?"

"Not that I know of." I'm getting tired of telling the redecorating story.

"Good. My father and Everett's grandfather worked together at J.P. Morgan before the war." He scowls at a very large man who pushes past him to get to the barbeque implements. "They're a fine addition to the Sea Chapel community. Need more like them."

Then we're both distracted by a sound, almost a mew. Could a cat have gotten in here with all the coming and going?

Mr. Finlayson hustles toward his wife, and I realize the sound came from her. Her thin shoulders tremble as she continues to stare out the window at the beach.

The beach where her grandson's body was found.

"Hush, Emily. Why are you carrying on here in front of all these strangers?" The old man doesn't embrace his grieving wife. He just turns her around like he's placing a doll in a dollhouse. "I told you not to come."

"This is where he died," she whimpers. "You shouldn't have let him go out that night. You should have known. That boy was not a friend to him."

Known what? Which boy? I'm watching this drama unfold with open curiosity. Could this haughty old man have participated in his grandson's death? When I was listening to Trevor's mother, the idea seemed far-fetched. Now that I'm watching the old man in action, Jeanine's theory seems more plausible.

"There's no point crying about it. What's done is done." He places her hand on his arm and steps forward. "We must maintain our dignity."

Mrs. Finlayson allows herself to be propelled out of the kitchen. A customer with a question gives me a reason to follow the couple at a discreet distance. While I'm demonstrating the dimmer switch on a halogen lamp, I see my last view of the Finlaysons.

The old lady stands at the front door and looks back over her shoulder. "I never cared for this house. It's cold. Just like her."

NOON COMES AND GOES with sales so brisk there's no possibility of breaking for a meal. I take two protein bars upstairs to Ty. Patience for ridiculous customer requests is the first thing to go when that man gets hungry.

I find Ty in Austin's bedroom having an increasingly animated discussion with a thin woman dressed in tennis whites. "I'll take the dresser and one of the night tables, but I don't want the chest of drawers. I'll give you five hundred for them."

"It's too early to break up the set. I'll have a hard time selling the other pieces. If it's still here tomorrow, you can have that deal." Ty folds his arms across his chest.

Mrs. Tennis sniffs. "I'll need to speak to your supervisor."

Ty catches my eye over the woman's head. "You in luck. She's right there."

I glide into the dispute. "Hi, I'm Audrey Nealon." I shake the woman's hand and smile sweetly. Ty turns away, but not before I note the eye-roll. "I'm afraid my assistant is correct. It's too early in the sale to break up this set. I'm sure you understand; I have to do what's best for my client."

"Humpf!" The woman slings her Louis Vuitton bag over her shoulder. "Like Brielle needs the money!"

Like you need to bargain at an estate sale. I continue to speak as if I didn't hear that crack. "If you'd like to leave your name and number, I can call you tomorrow at this time if the pieces are still available."

"Regina Mosby," she says as she scrawls her number on a scrap of paper from her bag. "My daughter Ava is a friend of Austin's. I've known Brielle for years. Maybe I'll just call her directly about these pieces."

"That's a great idea." I'm as placid as the Mona Lisa. "She can text me if she agrees to your terms."

Given the twist of her mouth, I'm guessing ol' Regina is not quite as tight with Brielle as she claims. "Well, I don't want to bother her. She's been a little tense lately." With a toss of her hair, she turns toward the door, waving at a woman she spots in the hall. It's one of the ladies who was with Trevor's mother at Caffeine Planet.

"Hi, Regina," the other woman trills. "Look at me—I finally got all the way into Brielle's house. Never made it past the pool deck before."

Regina links arms with her friend. The last words I hear her say are, "I don't know *what's* going on here. I feel like Ava knows something, but of course she won't tell me a thing."

Chapter 31

At four, we shoo the last of the customers from the house, promising them mark-downs tomorrow.

"Whew!" Ty sits on the stairs since all the living room furniture has been sold. "I haven't worked this hard since the Eskew sale."

"We sold so-o-o much," Donna marvels. "There's not that much left to sell tomorrow."

While Donna sweeps and straightens the house for tomorrow's on-slaught, I do a quick tally in my head. A grin spreads over my face. "Guys, let's go out to dinner. You choose the place—my treat."

An hour later, Ty's lust for red meat and Donna's skill with Yelp have led us to a highly rated steak and barbeque restaurant in Atlantic Highlands. The hostess has seated us at a window table with a panoramic view of the minia-ture golf course next door.

"I love miniature golf," Donna gushes. "I used to play all summer long with my cousins. But Anthony takes it too seriously. He broke a club over the windmill one time when the blade knocked his ball sideways."

"Have you heard from Anthony today?" I ask.

"Lots of texts, but I was too busy to answer. I'm so glad I drove down here to help with the Gardner sale."

Ty says nothing, keeping his eyes glued to the menu. On the way over here, he grabbed my car keys so he could drive, and I'd be forced to sit up front, leaving Donna alone in the back seat.

This tension is killing me.

But there's nothing I can do to resolve it other than gamely keep up a line of chit-chat about the sale and hope they'll each chime in. So we talk about the day's craziest customers until the food arrives. Then our hunger drives us to focus on the food and forget about conversation.

Only after the plates are cleared and we're sipping decaf cappuccino does our attention turn again to the view out the window. Lights have come on to illuminate the eighteen holes of tricks and traps. This late in the year there are only a few players making the rounds. A dad with two tantrum-throwing kids. A couple clearly on their first date. And two young men.

They talk intently walking from the seventeenth hole to the eighteenth.

I hitch my chair closer to the window as they prepare to play directly in front of us.

It's an uphill obstacle. Hit too gently and your ball will roll right back to the tee; hit too hard, and it will ricochet off a statue of Snow White who smiles angelically at the hole.

The taller young man sinks to one knee to size up the lay of the hole. Then he takes one careful swing and sinks a hole-in-one.

"Nice!" Ty approves.

The other guy steps up to the tee, lifts his arm for the swing, and whacks the ball. It hits Snow White in the head and bounces into the shrubbery.

They turn to walk off the course.

The taller guy is Austin Gardner.

The other is the young man who pursued Gregory Halpern at the party.

AT NINE PM, I FALL into bed, too exhausted to read the novel I brought along, but too wound up to sleep. Ty, Donna and I talked all the way home about why Austin Gardner would be in Sea Chapel this weekend of all weekends. Did Brielle send him to spy on us since Sophia is away? But none of us saw any sign of him or his friend these last two days.

And the friend. He must be a year older than Austin since I heard him say he's a student at Drew. If he's the same kid. But I'm certain he's the one who was having the argument with Gregory Halpern, who also happens to be in the area this weekend.

These people! I need to unwind.

I lie propped up with the last of the unsold pillows, idly scrolling through Facebook.

Pictures from my friend Maura's vacation in Italy....scenes from our niece's first middle school field hockey game....cat videos....an ad for Ancestry.com.... dog videos.... snarky commentary on politics....an ad for 23 and Me.

Why am I suddenly getting all these ads for genealogy websites and DNA testing in my Facebook feed?

Then I remember—Colleen did family tree research to track down all the O'Sheas and Coughlins in County Cork. She submitted DNA from Sean's parents and herself, but not Sean and me. But she must've plugged me into the tree, and now I'm getting solicitations to do my own research. Creepy that Facebook knows this!

There's nothing of interest in my newsfeed, yet I addictively keep scrolling. Another ad: *Spend Less. Learn More. Let American Genetic Solutions connect you with your family. Take a DNA test for as low as $50.* The picture shows two smiling, middle-aged women embracing. The green and blue logo of the company looks familiar, but I'm pretty sure Colleen used 23 & Me. I close my eyes to summon up where I've seen that logo before.

The image swims into focus. The logo is on a white background. In a corner.

My eyes snap open. This is the logo on the envelope I found under the mattress in Austin's room. The envelope he drove down here to get in the middle of the night.

The envelope with names written on the back of it.

I squinch my eyes shut again trying to remember the names on the list. I'm better at recalling numbers than words. All the names were young, trendy names. Agnes or Gladys or Clyde—names likely to be long-ago ancestors—were conspicuously absent. And they were all first names. If Austin was doing a family tree, wouldn't there be last names too?

I concentrate on picturing the list in my mind's eye. Mason was definitely one of the names. So was Trevor. And Ava—didn't Regina Mosby say her daughter was named Ava?

Sean speculated that the list of names were kids Austin was selling drugs to. Was it just a coincidence that he wrote the names on an envelope from a DNA testing company?

If Austin were doing legitimate research, why hide the information he got from American Genetic Solutions? Why get so agitated asking me if I'd read the contents of the envelope?

I slap my laptop shut.

This is *not* relaxing.

Chapter 32

The second day of the Gardner sale flies by.

Sunday crowds are always less intense. People arrive later, browse longer, haggle with the confidence that I'll cave to their demands.

Ty gleefully sells the entire set of furniture from Austin's room to a customer who's not Regina Mosby.

Donna convinces a woman she really does need twelve scallop shell napkin rings.

And I find a home for a dramatic abstract statue with a nameplate that says it's Poseidon.

At four, Ty does a slow pirouette with his hands on his hips. "Man, that was some sale. We sold everything. Every. Single. Thing. That ain't never happened before."

"That's 'cause there was no junk," Donna says. "No family heirlooms. No ugly gifts that the client never had the courage to get rid of. The only things in this house were items that Brielle selected, and that woman has never made a mistake when she bought anything."

I laugh thinking of the soap dispenser I selected for our hall bathroom. Every time I go in there, I'm filled with buyer's remorse. But Donna is right. Brielle's impeccable taste has resulted in a total sell-out.

Donna sweeps up the last of the sand that all those shoppers tracked into the house. "Empty houses look so sad," she sighs. "Even a gorgeous one like this looks forlorn when there's nothing left but the bare walls and floors." She walks onto the deck and tosses the dustpan of sand over the railing since Ty has already tied up the trash bag and packed that and the last of the supplies into the AMT van.

When Donna returns, she takes one last look around. "I guess in a few months this house will look totally different. I'd love to come back and see what the new decorator does with it."

I sling my tote bag over my shoulder and usher Donna through the front door. "Not gonna happen, girl. We'll never be guests here again."

———————⊙———————

TY DRIVES THE VAN TOWARD Palmyrton, while Donna follows in her own car.

We spend the first fifteen minutes of the trip chatting about comical customers at the sale and items that brought in much more or much less than we expected. Then the traffic gets heavier, and I let Ty concentrate on driving. I reach for my tote bag so I can use my iPad to pass the time with some preliminary profit calculations.

I can't find it by touch, so I pull my overstuffed bag onto my lap and start digging. Not in the center compartment, not in the side pocket.

It's got to be in here somewhere. I dig some more, and my fingers close around the sticky wrapper of a protein bar. The wrapper unlocks a scene in my mind's eye. Right before we left, I dug through my bag looking for that snack. I took my iPad out and laid it on the counter so I could get to the bottom of my bag. Then I ate the damn bar, put the garbage I created in my bag, and left my silver-covered iPad on the stainless-steel work surface in Brielle's kitchen.

"Shit! I left my iPad at the house. I have to go back and get it."

Ty's face creases in concern as he glances at the dashboard clock. "I promised your man Tim Ruane I'd deliver that table to him by seven tonight, Audge. He said he wouldn't take it unless I could get it to him by then."

"Right. I remember. And that table is bringing us a cool five grand." I get a brainstorm. "Donna is behind us. I'll tell her to meet us at the next rest area. You can drive her home in the van while I turn around and go back to Sea Chapel in her car."

Ty grimaces. I guess he's not relishing forty-five minutes alone in the van with Donna. But he does what I ask, and soon we've regrouped.

Ty slams the passenger door after Donna gets in. "You sure you gonna be a'ight going back there alone?"

"I'll be fine." I wave as I start Donna's car.

"Text me when you get back to P-town, you hear?" Ty shouts after me.

I toot my horn and head to the shore.

When I get to the front door of 43 Dune Vista Drive, the security system light next to the front door is blinking green. That means the system has been deactivated.

I'm positive I set the system to activated before I left.

Didn't I?

Well, I thought I had all my possessions with me when I left, and clearly that wasn't true.

I enter the empty house. All the lamps have been sold, but the recessed lights that illuminate the shelves beside the fireplace still work. I turn them on and head for the kitchen.

There sits my iPad in its new silver-gray case, blending into the stainless-steel prep area. I grab it, but before I can turn to go, I hear noises downstairs.

I stop breathing and listen, every nerve tuned to the sounds beneath me.

A faint murmur, sometimes sharper, sometimes lower. Someone is definitely talking down there, but the soundproofing installed in the ceiling of the home theatre area is doing its job to muffle the noises.

Heart pounding, I creep to the top of the stairs leading to the walk-out lower level.

Here the voices are clearer. Male and female, but they all sound young.

"Stop all talking at once. We'll take turns saying what we need to say to him."

That sounds like Austin. Did he invite his friends down here for one last party now that the house is empty, and it doesn't matter if they make a mess? But why tell partiers not to all talk at once?

"Mason, you go first." Austin's voice again. "Tell Gregory what you need him to understand."

Gregory? Gregory Halpern? And isn't Mason one of the names on the envelope? What's going on down there? I creep down three steps to the landing. By crouching in the corner, I can see part of the room, and sure enough, Gregory Halpern stands facing a half-circle of teenagers in the empty room. His face projects bewilderment and curiosity, the way it must when he encounters some odd custom in a remote foreign land.

I prepare to eavesdrop unashamedly.

Mason stands up. It's definitely the kid from the party. "Look at us."

"Look. At. Us." He puts his hands on either side of Gregory's head and forces him to look at the group of teenagers.

"We are your children. Every single one of us shares your DNA. You made us, and then you abandoned us."

What? A piece of information clicks into place in my brain. The envelope from AGS with the list of names. Austin's internship studying genetics. The kids in this room were all fathered by Gregory? Whoa! He must've been awfully busy in his younger days.

Gregory pulls out of Mason's grasp, but he still doesn't seem concerned. "I didn't abandon you. I never agreed to be anyone's father. I was doing a service, helping infertile couples create the families they desperately wanted."

A sperm donor. Wait...that means Austin was conceived by sperm donation. And Trevor, too?

"I call bull shit!" Mason's voice rises. "You weren't a donor out of the goodness of your heart. You got paid big money, over and over again. Because everyone wanted some of your high class, 1600 SAT, blue-eyed, Ivy League baby batter."

Mason shoves Gregory. "Didn't they?"

Ah, I see. Gregory was broke for years before he found success with his podcast. Sperm donation must've helped make ends meet. I wonder how much he earned?

"Yes, I was compensated, but..."

Now Gregory seems distinctly uncomfortable. What's going on here? Should I sneak back upstairs and call 9-1-1? What would I tell the operator when she asks, 'what's your emergency?'

A kid who lives here has a bunch of other kids here and apparently they're all related and they're talking to their biological father.

And she'd ask if they're drinking, taking drugs, fighting, displaying weapons.

No, no, no, and no.

I stay in my position and keep listening.

"Look how many of us there are," Mason continues, his face twisted with fury. "Twenty-three right in Palmer County. Seventy-five in the whole state of New Jersey. One hundred and eighty-four across the US, and the matches are still coming in. Every day we could wake up to a new brother or sister.

You have over two hundred children. We all have more than two hundred half-siblings."

"Look, I was barely older than you guys are right now." Gregory attempts a reassuring smile. He's a man accustomed to talking himself out of tight spots. The man has eluded terrorists! "I was broke. My parents wouldn't support me unless I agreed to go to law school."

"You could've gotten a real job." A tall, slender girl tosses her wavy hair. "Like, where you work for eight hours and get paid."

"But it was easier to jack off into a cup and make babies everywhere," another boy says. "How did Central Repro Systems recruit you back in the day? An ad in the Princeton student newspaper? A flyer on a bulletin board in some dive bar?"

Gregory turns on Austin. "So, you haven't told them how this all got started?"

Austin's face twitches in suspicion. "What do you mean? When I showed my mother the results of my DNA test...that I was related to tons of kids my age, some of them right in my own school...she admitted I was conceived through a sperm donor. I tracked you down by tracing distant relatives registered on AGS and Ancestry and 23 and Me. I've studied genetics. It wasn't hard."

Mason doesn't look entirely convinced. He squints at Austin. "Sounds like you left something out of the story."

For once, Austin's air of supreme self-confidence slips. "No, no I didn't." He turns to Gregory. "What did you mean?"

Gregory hesitates, but continues. "Your mother is the one who got me into this. She and I dated in college. She got pregnant and had an abortion. Later, when she couldn't get pregnant with your father, she knew the problem had to be with him. She persuaded me to donate sperm to make the baby she never got to have when we were twenty."

Gregory shrugs. "So the first time, I did it as a favor to an old friend. But the clinic paid me anyway and asked if I would donate some more. They had invested in me by testing to make sure I didn't have any genetic diseases, so they wanted to earn back their investment by having me donate a lot. I didn't realize my donations would be used so often and so, er, successfully," Gregory stammers.

Mason grabs another girl's arm. "Ava and I were dating. And then I discovered she's my sister. Any girl I see I ask myself, am I related to her? What am I supposed to do—get a DNA test before I hook up with anyone?"

Gregory extends his hands in appeasement. "I understand that was upsetting, but it was a fluke. It won't happen again."

"Did you hear what we told you? You have two hundred kids, and the tally is still rising. We keep finding more on this website called Donor Sibling Registry. Your offspring are everywhere. Especially here in New Jersey." Mason extends his arms to include the group. "We're freaks. Freaks of nature."

"I didn't know they'd use my sperm with so many different women in the same community," Gregory protests. "Aren't there rules about that?"

"Nope." Austin says. "There are regulations requiring testing for diseases like HIV and genetic disorders, but there are no rules for how many times a given donor's sperm can be used."

Gregory lifts his hands to heaven. "So then why are you so mad at me?"

"You could have asked some *questions*—like 'where is all this juice going, man?'"

Gregory sighs. "Alright, I didn't inquire enough. I see that now. But I was young."

The girl who Mason dated steps forward. "We're young," she taps her chest with her thumb, "and we know that every single sperm and egg has the potential to grown into a real, live human being. Are you telling me you were clueless of how babies are made when you were what, twenty-five?"

"The sperm bank is the organization who acted in bad faith." Gregory spreads his hands wide. "Why don't you complain to them about how they overused my donations in the same community?"

"The doctor who ran the place eighteen years ago is long dead," Austin says. "The current management is more careful. We checked."

Gregory massages his temples. "Look, what's done is done. Why did you bring me here? What do you want me to do about this mess?"

"We want you to acknowledge what you did to the world," a girl who hadn't spoken previously says.

"Publicly? I can't do that! I have a reputation. I have fans."

"Exactly," Austin says. He spreads his hands in a gesture that's uncannily similar to Gregory's. "You have a platform. You could do a podcast on sperm donation. Spread the word that other people born through sperm donation should have their DNA tested so they don't end up screwing their sister. So other couples know they should ask a lot of questions before they do this."

Gregory lowers his voice and speaks like a man trying to settle a panicked horse. "I'm sure that seems like a great idea to you. But I have advertisers who won't want to be associated with a scandal. This involves more than just me and all of you."

"Oh, *advertisers*—you hear that, Mason? Dad doesn't want to upset his *advertisers*," Clark sneers.

"Don't call me that!" Gregory's eyes shoot daggers. Gone is the man who charms his audience. "I have a right to make a living. I finally found a job I adore and now you want to take it away from me. For what? What's to be gained?"

Another boy steps forward. "Look, you're getting off easy. Some of us were hoping you'd be happy to gain a family. We talked about asking you to claim us as your children. But others didn't want to go public. So you could do the show without admitting that you've done sperm donation. Right guys? That's what we compromised on."

There's a low grumble from the circle of half-siblings. Some nod, but some shake their heads.

Gregory takes a deep breath to regroup. It seems he regrets his outburst. "I'm glad I met you. Happy to stay in touch. But you have to understand something. There's a reason I never married, never had children that I planned for. I know I'm not cut out to be a good dad. I have no desire for a house and a yard and a two-week vacation to Disneyworld. Kids need stuff like that. And I'm not the man to provide it."

Gregory spreads his hands to the group. "You all have fathers. Good men who love you and want to raise you. Why would you want to hurt them?"

A kid snorts. "My parents have been lying to me for seventeen years. I want them to realize the same thing that they always say to me—actions have consequences."

Another laughs out loud. Of all the kids, this one bears the most striking physical resemblance to Gregory: same beaky nose, same wavy hair, same bright blue eyes. "My mom is gay. I have two mothers. I love them both, but a dad would be nice. Even though they think it doesn't matter."

Now Mason steps forward. "After my parents had me with your sperm, my mom got pregnant again—the old-fashioned way. My little brother looks just like our dad, has the same high forehead, the same smile, they even walk the same. They're both fast runners and love soccer and they're both allergic to strawberries and neither one can carry a tune but both of them can build anything with Legos." He stands next to Gregory. "What notes are these?" Mason sings three notes.

"C sharp, G, A."

"Perfect pitch, just like me." Mason takes a step closer. "And what instrument do I play?"

"How should I know?" Gregory backs away from the boy's urgent presence.

"Oh, you know. You do. Say it. SAY IT."

Gregory takes a shuddering breath. "Cello."

"Mason..." Austin tries to calm the other boy, but Mason ignores him.

"And what's my best subject in school?" he demands of Gregory.

Gregory purses his lips and refuses to answer.

"History! Sociology! You and I have all the same interests." He points to Gregory and then himself. "I've read every article about you, every interview. But I'm like a freak in my own family. I have nothing in common with my father and brother. From the moment my brother picked up a soccer ball and pushed away the toy piano, my father favored him. He knows who his real son is. And it's not me."

"Mason, back off." Austin speaks with the authority his upbringing has embedded in him. "We discussed how this would go."

So the kids planned this encounter. Did Gregory have a choice about participating?

Gregory extends his long, expressive fingers. "Look, Mason, I'm sorry you feel that way. But my father and I don't have anything in common even though we share the same DNA. He's cautious and conservative and detail-oriented. He's everything I'm not, and I've always been a disappointment to him. Even now. He thinks a travel podcast is a ridiculous way to earn a living." Gregory reaches out to put a hand on Mason's shoulder. "Believe me, being raised by your biological father is no guarantee of happiness."

Mason jerks away from Gregory's touch. "You're a fish," he screams. "A freakin' fish. You sprayed your sperm everywhere and then you swam away."

And then I see Mason's right arm draw backward.

Chapter 33

"Watch out!" the warning escapes my lips instinctively. Of course it's too late. The punch has landed, and Gregory lies sprawled on the floor, blood pouring from his nose onto the pale bleached oak floor.

The room explodes into pandemonium. Half the kids look up to see who shouted the warning. Two pounce on Mason to pull him away from Gregory.

Austin sinks to his knees beside the fallen man, his eyes wide with alarm. "You idiot! Look what you've done! You've destroyed everything."

At the same time, the kid named Clark dashes up the stairs toward me. I scramble off the landing, hoping to barricade myself in the first-floor powder room and call 9-1-1.

Now, I definitely have an emergency.

But Clark is young, tall, and athletic. He grabs my arm just before I reach the door and jerks me around.

"What are you doing here? Why were you spying on us?"

"I wasn't spying. I came back to the house because I left my iPad here." I hold up my tote bag as proof. "When I came into the kitchen, I heard voices downstairs. I was just coming down to see who was here when I saw that kid ready to punch that man." I fudge the truth. There's no need for them to know how long I was listening.

Clark drags me toward the stairs. "Come down here until we can decide what to do."

I pull back. "No. It's none of my business. Just let me go home."

"Who's up there?" Austin shouts.

"That chick from the sale."

Austin curses and delivers his command. "Haul her ass down here."

Clark's hand tightens on my biceps, and he drags me toward the stairs.

He's bigger and stronger than I am, but he's not a criminal. He's just a confused teenager. I use the self-defense skills Sean has taught me: go for his weakest points.

With my free hand, I bend back his little finger while twisting around to kick him in the groin.

In a split second, Clark has me pinned on the ground. "I'm a state champion wrestler, bitch. Don't mess with me."

Clearly, I underestimated my opponent.

He marches me down to the lower level.

Downstairs, I size up my new reality.

A dazed Gregory sits propped against the wall holding a T-shirt against his face to stanch the blood.

Austin stands next to him, bare-chested, contemplating the bright red splatter on the pale floor. His hands clench and unclench. His teeth gnaw on his lower lip.

Mason paces on the other side of the room, attended by Ava.

The other kids shift their gazes from me to Gregory to Austin to Mason, baffled by what to do next.

I'm the uninjured adult in the room, so I feel like I should try to take charge of the situation.

But I'm not sure what to suggest. "Let's all go home and pretend this never happened," doesn't seem like it will fly.

Of all of them, only Austin appears terrified. His gaze hasn't left the blood on the floor, not even when Clark marched me into the room.

Why is he so scared? It's not like Gregory is mortally wounded. Given the circumstances, it's unlikely he'd even complain about being punched.

I try to recall exactly what Austin shouted when Gregory fell. *You've destroyed everything.*

What has Mason destroyed? These half-siblings had a plan. Trevor was one of their group, but now he's dead. Could Austin's fear be related Trevor's murder? But the others don't seem afraid, only confused.

If I had time to sit quietly and ponder these questions, I might come up with a theory, but that's not happening.

I have to move cautiously, not dig myself in deeper.

Get out, then figure out what's going on. Luckily, I've got my tote bag with my keys and phone still with me. Maybe I can find an opportunity to dash through the sliders and out to my car in the driveway.

Austin raises his eyes from the mess on the floor. When his gaze meets mine, it sends a tremor down my spine. Those aren't the eyes of a confused, reckless teenager. I see a cold, determined calculation there that unnerves me.

Before, I was worried. Now, I'm scared.

"You—get over there next to him." Austin tilts his head from me to Gregory. Gregory staggers to his feet as I approach him.

"We need a crowbar, some claw hammers," Austin continues. "I need two of you to go into old man Finlayson's garage and find some. Sienna, Clark—go."

Sienna, a delicate, feminine girl, tosses her long hair. "Are you crazy? I'm not breaking into someone's garage."

"A crowbar? For what?" Clark asks.

Austin looks like an exasperated teacher confronting a dozing slacker. "To pry up those floorboards, moron. We're going to have to dump the stained boards in the ocean, but the whole floor has to come up, so we can say it was part of the remodeling project."

"This is crazy." Sienna buttons her jean jacket and heads for the sliding door. "I'm outta here."

Austin grabs her arm as she passes and yanks her so hard, she plops down on her ass. "You're not going anywhere until we're done. We're all in this together." He points at the blood. "His blood contains DNA. DNA he shares with all of us. DNA he shared with Trevor. The police *cannot* find that in this house. How do you not understand that?"

The third girl steps forward. "I'll clean it up."

"You can't clean it!" Austin's voice rises toward hysteria. "The blood has soaked into the wood. The cops can find the traces. Haven't you ever watched a crime show on TV?"

He's right. No amount of scrubbing will get rid of the residual traces that show up with Luminol. Now, a piece of the puzzle clicks into place. This sale to get rid of every item in the house...the tight deadline...the lie about the decorator—it was all about finding a plausible way to scour this house of any trace of DNA linking these kids to one another and to Gregory.

And to Trevor.

No wonder Austin is panicked. Obviously, his mother was in on this plan. But does she know he planned one more gathering of the half-siblings in this house?

A gathering that's gone horribly off the rails.

Gregory has finally pulled himself together. He steps forward with his hands outstretched. "Kids, come on. None of this is necessary. I'm not calling the police on you. I need to be on a plane to Nepal two days from now."

This makes me suspect Gregory doesn't know he had one more child.

A child who was murdered.

Did it happen in this house? Did one of these kids put his hands around Trevor's neck and squeeze the life from him?

Austin whirls around to face his father. "Shut up! This isn't about you."

The boy paces anxiously. The rest of the kids watch him—some nervously, some seeking leadership. Finally, Clark speaks. "All right. I'll go find the tools. Mason can come with me."

Clark puts his hand on his half-brother's shoulder, but Mason jerks away. "What do you mean it's not about him? It's *all* about him. Gregory has to commit to doing the podcast on sperm donation. That's what we all agreed to."

Gregory's nose has swollen to a grotesque blob, and he has dried blood caked around his nostrils and chin. Nevertheless, he's regained some of his usual confidence. "I am *not* doing a podcast on sperm donation. You can put that idea right out of your head. I'm leaving now." He steps toward the sliding doors.

Mason lunges for Gregory, Austin blocks him, and in a flash, all three of them are rolling on the floor.

A noise at the sliding door makes everyone freeze.

A man stands on the threshold. His massive biceps look about to split the fabric of his polo shirt. A gold chain with a crucifix nestles in the dark mat of chest hair showing at his neckline.

He points a gun at my chest.

"Where's my wife?"

Chapter 34

Anthony!

Sienna screams. Ava clings to Mason's arm. Gregory, Austin, and Mason untangle themselves.

Anthony scans the room. "Where's Donna?"

"She's back in Palmyrton. She—"

"Don't lie to me! Her car's in the driveway. Tell her to get her ass down here now." He keeps the gun pointed at me and moves to the foot of the stairs. "Do-o-n-n-a!"

Anthony's arrival has shifted the dynamic in the room. All eyes are on the stranger with the gun.

But Anthony doesn't care about the kids or Gregory. He's only interested in finding his wife via me. In the corner of my field of vision, I notice Sienna edging behind one of the basement's support columns. It's the only place in the empty room that provides a little cover. Her hands move inside her jacket pocket. Is she using her phone to dial 9-1-1?

If she is, I want to keep Anthony's attention focused elsewhere. "I borrowed Donna's car. She went back to Palmyrton in the van," I explain.

"Liar! She can't drive that big van. She told me it's too much for her." Again, he bellows up the stairs. "D-o-n-n-a!"

"Go on up and look for her," I encourage him.

He waves the gun at me. "Fine. You lead the way."

Shit! That's not what I want. "I'll call Donna. I'll put her on speakerphone and ask her if she made it home okay."

"Don't touch your phone! I'll blow your head off!"

If Sienna managed to get an open line to 9-1-1, I sure hope they heard that. "Donna spent the day working here at the Gardners' house," I say loud and clear. "Then she went back to Palmyrton."

Anthony's eyes grow wide with fury. "She's with that jig who works for you!" He grabs my arm and drags me toward the sliding door. "You're coming with me. You're taking me to where those two are holed up together."

There's no way I'm getting in a car and driving anywhere with Anthony Frascatelli. Sean has lectured me many times: if someone tries to carjack you, your best chance of survival is to run even if they're pointing a gun at you. Because their intention is not to murder you on the spot; it's to get what they want from you, and then dispose of you.

"Okay," I say. "But it's a long drive. I have to use the bathroom before we leave. There's one out here beside the pool."

He jerks me toward the driveway, not the poolside cabana. "Too bad. Hold your water."

"I have my period. I have to change my tampon. You don't want me to ruin your upholstery, do you?"

Anthony wrinkles his nose in disgust and changes direction. I've guessed correctly that he's a man who highly values the condition of his car. "Get what you need outta your bag and leave it with me when you go in there."

For once, I'm very glad I'm not pregnant because I do indeed have tampons in my bag. I take one out and leave the bag at Anthony's feet as he paces beside the pool. Inside the spacious cabana, I start the water running, then head for the window that faces the ocean. Like everything in Brielle's house, it's a generous size. I slide it open, climb out, and run toward the ocean, remembering to zig-zag back and forth to make myself a hard target to hit. My feet barely make a sound on the soft sand. By the time Anthony starts shouting for me, I'm halfway to Elmo's.

Up on the road, I hear the howl of sirens.

Chapter 35

The hours after the police arrive at 43 Dune Vista Drive pass in a blur of activity.

By the time I turn around and go back to the house, Anthony has screeched off in his Caddy, but the state police soon pull him over on the Parkway.

Some of the kids have scattered, but Austin knows running is pointless, so he sits on the stairs refusing to talk while he waits for his parents' lawyer to arrive.

Sienna maintains she's done nothing wrong and stands outside talking to two cops.

Gregory walks a fine line between cooperating and stonewalling. He requests medical attention for his nose, which, I presume, will buy him some time to talk to Brielle and try to find a way to tell his story that's not too damaging.

And I, as usual, find myself with lots of explaining to do.

The local police have contacted Detective Croft. I have just enough time to call Sean and Ty before I join Croft for a talk in his car.

"Tell me everything that happened from the time I left here this morning," he says.

Now that I'm sure someone in the circle of half-siblings murdered poor Trevor, I'm eager to unload everything I know on the police. So I present a recap of the final hours of the sale, my departure and return, my eavesdropping on the kids and Gregory, and finally, the significance of Anthony's arrival.

Naturally, it's what I learned from eavesdropping that interests him the most.

"So you're telling me that all those kids are biological half-siblings and Gregory Halpern fathered them all through sperm donation."

"Yes, and Trevor Finlayson was also one of them."

"How do you know that?"

"When I was setting up the sale, I found an envelope from a company called AG Solutions pushed under the mattress in Austin's room. It had a list of names written on the back. Trevor was one of them. So were Mason, Sienna, Clark, Ava and a couple other kids who were here tonight. The night after I found the envelope, Austin came to the house in the middle of the night to get it back."

"You talked to him about it?"

"No. I heard him walking around, and after he left, the envelope was gone. I never looked inside the envelope—I didn't realize what kind of company AG Solutions was at the time. Recently, I learned that Austin did a summer internship with a geneticist. So I think he must've decided to send off his own DNA for testing and persuaded a couple school friends to do the same just out of curiosity. Needless to say, he was stunned to learn he had half-siblings right in his own school."

Croft writes furiously in his notebook. "We'll have to compare Trevor's DNA with Gregory's, but it sounds like you're right. But how did Austin get all those kids to test their DNA? And how did he figure out Gregory Halpern was his father?"

"I suspect he persuaded only a couple to participate in his experiment. But as soon as Austin realized he had any half-siblings, he asked his mother about it. And she must've told him the truth: she couldn't conceive with her husband, so she turned to sperm donation without telling her husband."

Croft scratches his head. "So she told Austin that Gregory was his father?"

"No. She told her son she used an anonymous donor, not sperm from her brilliant friend. What Brielle didn't realize at the time was that Gregory kept making sperm donations for payment. And the clinic unethically allowed over one hundred couples in New Jersey to use the same sperm."

Croft whistles. "Why did they all want his juice?"

"Tall, thin, blue eyes, 1600 SAT scores, Princeton grad."

"Ah—designer babies. So I guess an overweight, brown-eyed, graduate of the police academy wouldn't be in such demand, eh." He shakes his head. "But I gotta tell ya, I've produced two pretty spectacular kids."

"I'm sure you have. And I bet neither one of them is a murderer."

"So you think these kids turned and killed their own half-brother?"

"The group was arguing about what they wanted from Gregory. They all wanted to meet one another and meet him. But some wanted him to claim them as his children, while others were ashamed of how they were born and wanted to keep it quiet. Brielle never told her husband that he wasn't Austin's biological father."

Croft scratches his head. "And I bet Jeanine never told her first husband that he wasn't Trevor's biological father. Or if she did, neither one told old man Finlayson. The grandfather's all about blood ties, and the Finlayson family name being carried down through the generations."

"Sophia told me that Trevor kept going to parties with a group of kids from Bumford-Stanley that he didn't even like. She said he was afraid of them, but he wouldn't stop going out with them, and she was never included." I gaze over at the Peterman's dark house. I'm glad Sophia is off in Maine on her college visit, but I'm curious about how much she knows and what she told Croft. "At the time, I thought she might just be jealous of Trevor and mad that she was excluded from the cool kids' group. I take it she didn't tell you about the half-siblings?"

Croft gives an almost imperceptible shake of his head. Although I can see he's grateful for all the information I'm giving him, his natural impulse is to not share anything in return.

"Half-siblings and sperm donation were not part of our conversation," he says. But he looks perplexed, as if something Sophia told him doesn't jibe with what he's learning now.

Croft's reticence doesn't deter me from sharing my theories. "Well, now I think those so-called parties Sophia wasn't invited to were actually Trevor meeting with the half-siblings. And I suspect he got on the wrong side of their plans."

"So they killed him. Or one of them did." Croft shifts his large body and looks toward Brielle's house where we can just make out Austin sitting alone on the steps. "It doesn't matter that Austin won't talk to us. With a group of kids this large, you can bet one of them will crack and start ratting on the others."

We both look at Sienna earnestly talking to two other cops.

"Yep, we'll have the Finlayson murder case wrapped up by tomorrow."

Chapter 36

A s it happens, Detective Croft's prediction was overly optimistic. By Monday, all the kids, with the exception of Sienna, have lawyered up.

And when six rich families hire six different high-profile lawyers, even getting a straight answer to, "What color is the sky?" becomes problematic.

"Everything is a negotiation," Sean reports to me on Monday evening after touching base with Detective Croft at the end of his work day. My husband has recovered remarkably well from the news of my antics last night, especially since he knows Anthony is locked up in the Ocean County jail with no likelihood of bail.

We're prepping a dinner of grilled mahi-mahi and roasted broccoli which Sean has pulled together effortlessly. After a very stressful weekend apart, and a Monday spent catching up at our respective offices, we're relieved and grateful to be together at home.

"So far, they've only pieced together a few details about Trevor's last days from what you and Sienna told them," Sean says as he pours me a glass of Sauvignon Blanc. "Apparently, the kids *persuaded*—he makes air quotes around the word— "Gregory to come back to the house with them after his matinee performance at Monmouth University. When you saw Austin and Mason at the miniature golf course, they must've been making their plan. Croft thinks the boys probably jumped Gregory and dragged him into their car, which would be kidnapping, or at least unlawful restraint, but Gregory insists he went willingly, so no charges there."

"Gregory can't deny that Mason punched him." I toss Ethel a cracker smeared with brie as I set the table.

"No, but he refuses to press charges against his son. I once socked my brother Terry in the jaw and knocked his tooth out. No one arrested me."

Sean goes out on the deck to tend the fish on the grill. I watch him through the kitchen window as he adjusts the heat and sprinkles the seasonings. Whatever he does, he does with total concentration.

My heart swells with love.

Did Donna used to feel this way about Anthony? Where did their love go so horribly wrong? How did Anthony change from warm and affectionate to jealous and possessive? Did Donna see it coming, or did it just creep up on her?

At the office this morning, I told her what Anthony did last night. Not surprisingly, she collapsed in a heap of tears and apologies. But when I told her not to worry because Anthony had been arrested and was being held without bail at the Ocean County Jail, she cried even harder.

Love doesn't die easily.

Sean looks up from his grilling and smiles at me through the window. I remember I'm supposed to be watching the broccoli in the oven, and snap to attention.

Once we get our food arranged on the table, I return to the topic of what Detective Croft has learned from Sienna. "What does Sienna say about the night Trevor died?"

Sean spears a broccoli floret and uses it as a pointer. "She admits the siblings had a meeting that night. Unfortunately, she couldn't go because she had to be at her great aunt's wake."

"And there are multiple witnesses to alibi her," I interrupt before he can confirm the fact. "But didn't any of the others tell her what happened that night? Six kids can't be that good at keeping a secret."

"Sienna says Ava told her the kids met at Brielle's house and argued about planning an encounter with Gregory, and Trevor ran off. And that's the last they saw of him. Later, when his grandfather found the note and raised the alarm, all the kids believed Trevor had killed himself."

"What about that note? Are the police positive Trevor wrote it?

"The paper had his fingerprints and his grandfather's prints. A handwriting expert confirmed it's Trevor's writing."

"But that's just an expert opinion, not confirmed fact. Could the old man have forged it, or forced Trevor to write it?"

"You still think the old man was involved in the murder?" Sean asks. "But if the news came out that Trevor wasn't a biological Finlayson, the old man might've had a better shot at preventing the trust fund from going to Roxie—she really isn't Trevor's half-sister."

"Hmmm. Maybe that ambiguous note is just an incredibly lucky break for the killer. It helped everyone believe Trevor committed suicide."

"Until the body washed up and the police said it was murder." Ethel has been circling the table for the past five minutes, and I finally slip her a singed edge of fish when Sean isn't looking. "What does Sienna say was the kids' reaction to that news?"

"According to Croft, Sienna says that's when the group started splintering. She said it was all too much drama for her, and she refused to talk to some of them. But Ava persuaded her to come to one last meeting."

"Which turned out to be Sunday night." I swirl the wine in my glass. "Does Croft think Sienna is lying to protect the others?"

"He says no. Sienna's parents have been totally cooperative. They've always been honest with her about how she was conceived. She never wanted to hurt them by going public, and she didn't really care about connecting with Gregory."

"I believe that. She was the least confrontational of the kids that night. So why did she go to the meetings at all?"

"Sienna's an only child." Sean strokes my hand as it rests on the table. "She told Croft that she was intrigued by the idea that she had siblings."

"Wow—I totally get that. When I was trying to find out what happened to my mother, there was a short period of time that I thought she might have run off because she was pregnant, and that I might have a sibling. I hafta say, letting go of that fantasy was tough."

Sean frowns. "Well, Sienna's *Walton's* fantasy of a big, happy family has imploded. One of her siblings is a murderer."

"One of her brothers, surely. A girl wouldn't be strong enough to strangle Trevor, would she?"

"Trevor wasn't a big kid, but it's unlikely a girl could pull the murder off single-handedly. It takes time to kill someone that way—a good seven minutes of sustained pressure."

My delicious dinner churns in my gut as I picture Mason or Clark or Austin crouching over Trevor. "How could anyone squeeze a person's throat for that long and watch him struggle and turn blue? They all seem like normal teenagers, not psychos."

Sean makes a face as he knocks back the last of his wine. "A person doesn't have to be a psycho to commit murder, Audrey. You know that. He or she just needs to want something desperately."

"But strangling someone is so *personal*." I push my plate away, all appetite extinguished. "With a gun, it's one squeeze of the finger and a life has ended."

"Yep. That's why having a gun in the house is dangerous for everyone in the family. Too easy to pop off a shot when you're mad. But Trevor's killer didn't necessarily kill him with his bare hands. He could have caught him from behind and strangled him with a belt or a rope. Given the condition of the body, the medical examiner couldn't tell if a ligature had been used."

"Ugh." I lean back in my chair and stare at the ceiling. "Where does the investigation stand now?"

"The long and short of it is Sienna has told the police all she knows." Sean stands up and clears my plate. "But it's not enough to make an arrest. The kids maintain the last they saw of Trevor, he was alive. And Croft has no way to prove he wasn't."

Chapter 37

Tuesday morning finds Donna, Ty, and me all together at the office with, mercifully, no drama whatsoever.

Ty and Donna have fallen back into their old relaxed banter, and Donna has come to terms with Anthony's arrest and confinement.

"Uncle Nunzio is furious with Anthony," Donna tells us as she pursues cobwebs with her DustBuster. "He says if Anthony had stayed put in South Carolina, none of this would've happened. And when my mother heard that Anthony threatened you with a gun, Audrey, she finally agreed that there's no hope for our marriage and we hafta get divorced. So I'm moving forward with the filing." She guns the DustBuster at some dry leaves Ty has tracked in. "No more procrastination."

"Good. Now all three of us can work on the Freidrich sale this weekend." Ty lifts his feet for Donna's vacuum. "The power company finally got the lights back on in that neighborhood last night. Imma go over there later and see if there's branches on the walk and driveway that need to be cleared away."

"I already updated our website, Facebook, and Twitter with the new sale dates and sent out an email to all our regulars," Donna reports.

"Great work, guys." There's no doubt my staff is on top of this sale. Still, I have a powerful urge to go over to the Freidrich house myself just to double-check that everything's been done correctly.

But that would be insulting.

Wouldn't it?

When I was preoccupied with the much bigger Gardner sale, I was willing to let this smaller sale slide a bit. But now that I'm done with the Gardners, the Freidrich sale is back on my front burner.

"Last week, I told Mr. Gardner I'd take the check with the proceeds of the sale to Brielle's store as soon as I finished the accounting. I've got it all done, so I think I'll swing by there now. You'll hold down the office until I get back?"

"Yeah." Ty frowns at a big vase of Brielle's that I sold via photograph to a customer in upstate New York. "I gotta figure out how to ship this. Gonna take a crap ton of bubble wrap."

Great. I'll take the check to Brielle's store, then slip over to the Friedrich house for a quick look. No one will be the wiser.

On the quick drive to Elle's Choices, I speculate on whether I'll find Brielle there or not.

I'm hoping she'll be too preoccupied with Austin's issues to manage her retail hobby because I can't quite imagine how we'll deal with talking about what went down at her house on Sunday. The check in my tote bag represents a fraction of the value of all the lovely items she carefully selected for her home, all now dispersed to other houses across New Jersey and New York.

Now I understand that she never really wanted to get rid of her possessions; she did it to protect her son and her marriage. Worse yet, her elaborately planned ruse was all for naught. The arrival of the police at the Gardners' home means that her husband now knows the truth about his son's parentage.

But maybe emptying the house wasn't pointless.

If Trevor's murder really did happen at the Gardners' house, the police will have a hell of a time finding any forensic evidence to prove it.

Regardless, it's hard to imagine Brielle will be in the mood for polite chitchat. Will she find some way to blame me for what her son did? It sure isn't my fault that Austin planned one final meeting of the siblings with their biological father, but if my presence there hadn't attracted Anthony, Austin might've gotten away with his plan to rip up the floorboards.

And if I hadn't eavesdropped on the confrontation between the kids and Gregory, no outsiders would have known about their true relationship.

I'm not sure why I hadn't thought this through before, but now I'm really nervous about encountering Brielle.

However, Everett Gardner seemed pretty adamant about having the check today, and it's not like the Gardners' mood is likely to improve any time soon.

I may as well suck it up, so I can put the whole crazy incident behind me, the sooner, the better.

I find a parking spot on the pretty side street where Elle's Choices nestles in the middle of the block. On this side street, signs of the destruction wrought by the weekend storm are everywhere. A branch hangs limply from a curbside tree and the storm drains are blocked with heaps of leaves, twigs, and flotsam. I pass a store that sells mother-of-the bride dresses and formal wear for ladies who travel the charity fundraiser circuit, and a small wool shop where women sit around a table, knitting. Across the way, an indie bookshop promotes book signings by authors I've never heard of and a Friday night poetry slam.

Seems like no one here is hellbent on crass commercialism.

I pause in front of Brielle's display window before I enter the shop. No surprise—it's arranged invitingly, with artful placements of pottery and candles and table linens and three droll little sandpiper statuettes. A semi-sheer scarf in shades of aquamarine and sea foam floats above it all.

Ah, Brielle—what an eye!

I take a deep breath and push open the door. A little bell announces my arrival, and a lovely scent of lavender and citrus envelops me.

The shop appears empty. I creep around like a home-invader looking for priceless gems. I spot an item I've seen before: a tall, narrow, green ceramic vase. Did I sell it at the sale?

No. Now I remember. Jane Peterman has that vase in her kitchen. It looks different here because at Jane's house, it was filled with dead flowers.

I continue browsing. There's nothing in this shop that anyone needs—not the polished driftwood candelabra, not the delicate blue and gold glass salad plates—but everything is so pretty, it's hard not to feel like I want it all.

Maybe that's the secret to Brielle's success: imbuing customers with envy.

Acquire my stuff and you'll acquire my life.

Luckily, I know enough not to want her life.

I tune my ear to a low voice coming from the back room. "Yes....yes. I told you, I'm fine.... I don't know. Nothing's been decided yet.... Look, I have to go. There's a customer in the shop. Have a safe trip."

Brielle emerges from the back room with a customer-greeting smile affixed to her face. It disappears when she sees me.

I hold up the envelope. "I brought you the check for the proceeds of the sale. There's a detailed accounting included."

She stands frozen. I think reaching out for the envelope would cause her to shatter as surely as an icicle falling from the eaves of a house.

I place the envelope on the elegant table holding the modified iPad Brielle uses to accept credit card payments. Nothing so gauche as a cash register here. Maybe I can just back out of the store...and her life...and never see her again.

Brielle regards the envelope like a roach that's crawled out of the woodwork. Her eyes narrow. "So, you spied on my son. I hope you're satisfied with what you learned."

Should I attempt to explain that I was simply in the right place at the wrong time for Austin? Brielle is an influential person in Palmyrton. Still, no amount of rationalizing from me is likely to make her give Another Man's Treasure a glowing recommendation.

Should I offer one of those "sorry, not sorry" apologies? I'm sorry if my actions revealed the web of lies you've been living for two decades. I'm sorry if my employee's deranged husband upset the plans of your unhinged son. I'm sorry if I disrupted your scheme to perfectly control the police, your husband, and your son.

I settle on, "I'm sorry for the unfortunate...er...confluence of events."

"Ha, ha, ha!" Brielle's laugh threatens to careen into hysteria. "*A Series of Unfortunate Events*—my son used to read those books when he was a child. He loved trying to figure out the crazy plot twists. Austin is relentlessly curious. I suppose he gets that from Gregory. I won't say 'his father.' Everett is Austin's father. He's devastated by all this. Devastated."

I'm sure she doesn't want advice from me. But I wish I could tell her that keeping secrets is corrosive. She and her husband should have faced their infertility problem head- on twenty years ago and decided together how to handle it. Maybe they'll all be better off now that the secret is out in the open. I know my father and I are better off now that we're not keeping secrets.

Much better.

Brielle's hands tremble. Her eyes look beyond me to something only she can see. "The family I had is gone. I don't know what will happen next. I don't know."

The bell above the door tinkles again and a large woman with bright pink lipstick enters. "Bri-el-elle?? I've come to get a shower gift for Linda Thornton's daughter."

Brielle snaps back into character. "Maureen! Of course—I have just the thing."

I take the opportunity to escape. Out on the sidewalk, I take one last look at the display window.

That chiffon scarf would make a great birthday gift for Natalie.

A shame. I won't be shopping here again.

WITH THAT ONEROUS TASK off my back, the day is looking a whole lot brighter. I'll drive by the Freidrich house to make sure everything is set up perfectly then head back to the office.

The route to the Freidrichs' neighborhood takes me toward Palmyrton High School. It's lunch time, and clusters of kids pass me on the sidewalk because seniors are allowed to leave campus and walk into town for pizza or fast food. I stop at the corner to let a horde of them cross the street, and that's when I spot him.

All alone.

Head down. Hands jammed in pockets.

I wait until he reaches the middle of the block and glide up beside him, lowering my car window as I stop. "Hey, Fly," I call.

He stops and peers at my car, then recognizes me.

Will he run?

Nope. He trots around and hops into the passenger seat just as the car behind me lays on the horn.

"How's it going?" I ask.

"'K."

"Looks like you were headed into town for lunch. Can I buy you a slice?"

He shrugs. I take that to mean, "Yes, please. That would be lovely."

Fifteen minutes later we're sitting side by side on a bench in Palmyrton town green, balancing paper plates of hot pizza on our knees.

He hasn't said one word other than "no pepperoni" since he got into my car. I can see he'd sit in silence until sunset, so I get the ball rolling. "You wanted to talk to me last week, but then you took off when I got to the high school."

"My bad."

"So what did you want to tell me?"

"It doesn't matter."

I'm not sure where I'm finding these reserves of patience. "Go ahead and tell me anyway."

Fly shoves half a slice into his mouth, chews interminably, and finally speaks. "That kid Austin told Trevor something about Sophia's father."

"Something that upset her?" I keep my tone light. How much does Fly know? I'm not yet willing to tell the boy what I learned this weekend. Even though the police, Gregory Halpern, and Everett Gardner now know about the half-siblings, it's not down to me to spread the word to the general public. Maybe the families who want to keep the connection quiet can still manage to do so.

"Austin told *Trevor*. Trevor never told Sophia." He peels a wad of melted mozzarella off his paper plate and contemplates it with the level of attention usually given to nuclear fission experiments. "I remembered it after Sophia left. I thought maybe I should tell you, not her."

"Did Sophia spend the night at your house after Trevor's funeral?"

Fly squints at me like I've lost my mind. Of course, I should have known she wouldn't have a sleepover at the home of a boy she barely knows. She and Fly are both awkward kids. She and Jane only recently moved to Sea Chapel full time. Sophia must have a few friends in town.

I want to ask Fly why he feels he should tell me, not Sophia, what he knows, but I'm pretty sure I'll just get a shrug. Asking teenage boys about emotions or intentions is an exercise in futility. I vow to keep focused on facts. "What did Trevor tell you about Austin and Sophia?"

Fly squirms. He looks about ready to cram another half-slice into his mouth, so I lay a restraining hand on his arm. Reluctantly, he speaks. "Trev always said that him and me and Sophia could be our own crew 'cause none of us knew our fathers. But then he started talking crazy and saying he would know his father soon. And that was whack 'cause his father was dead."

Not so whack.

"And then Trevor said Austin could find Sophia's father and he was going to make him do it. And that maybe Austin could help me if I wanted him to. But I didn't. I know my old man's a piece of shit."

Fly turns to face me, his sneakered foot tapping, his right eyelid twitching. "Then Trev said he wasn't going to give Austin what Austin wanted until Austin gave him what he wanted. And I thought it was all just Trev's crazy talk.

"But that was the last time I saw him before, you know...."

He was murdered.

Chapter 38

I spend the next fifteen minutes impressing upon Fly the importance of talking to Detective Croft about this. He whines that that's why he told me, so I could tell Sophia or Croft or whoever should know.

Finally, he springs off the park bench calling over his shoulder that he has to get back to school for a test.

Like he cares about his grades.

Fine. I'll tell Croft and leave it to him to manage a face-to-face with Fly.

Before I call the detective, I sit and think about the implications of what Fly has told me. Neither Jane nor Sophia has made a secret of how Sophia was conceived. But who is Sophia's father? Does Jane even know the man's name? Or was he just some actor she hooked up with for the night? Does Sophia want to know who her father is?

Does Jane want Sophia to know?

Austin clearly has specialized research talents. Did he and Trevor argue about how they'd be used? Would Austin have killed Trevor in such a brutal way over that argument?

I keep coming back to the way Trevor died. It wasn't the result of an impulsive act, a teenage tussle that resulted in a fractured skull.

And Austin isn't an impulsive kid. He's a planner.

So are his parents.

I can relate to that.

But Austin clearly undertook some of his plans without his parents' knowledge or support.

I have no doubt Brielle Gardner will do everything in her power to protect her son.

How much power does she really have now that Everett knows Austin isn't his biological son?

194

DETECTIVE CROFT DOESN'T answer my call, so I leave a message and finally get going to the Freidrich house.

The neighborhood is on the far west side of Palmyrton, where the houses are widely spaced. I see signs of the big storm's destruction in toppled trees and fallen limbs at many houses. The buzz of chain saws never ceases. The tree that blocked the Freidrichs' street has been cut into segments and stacked on the curb. Ty was right to worry about access to the house. A large branch from a maple tree lies across the front walk. I try to drag it away, but it's much heavier than I expected. I'll have to leave it for Ty. I clamber around it, and use my copy of the keys to enter through the front door.

In the foyer, Donna has set up the sales desk for maximum efficiency. In the dining room, Ty and Donna have arranged the most desirable items on the table and buffet, with neatly lettered signs warning customers to ask for assistance if they want to examine pieces still inside the china cabinet.

In the kitchen, I double-check the prices of the Cuisinart and the block of German knives. Ty has done his research—priced for a profit with room for negotiation. Every room is the same: perfectly arranged goods, well priced.

I couldn't have done it better myself.

That makes me happy.

I think.

Isn't it a sign of successful parenting when your kids can manage without you?

But isn't it painful when you're no longer needed?

Accepting that I have absolutely nothing to do at the Freidrich house, I finally head back to the office.

"What took you so long?' Ty says as soon as I enter. "I need to get over to UPS."

"Sorry. I ran into someone I know and stopped for a bite to eat in the green." I toss my tote on my desk. "Boy, the streets around Palmyrton sure are a mess. Thank goodness the Freidrichs' street was at the top of the town's clean-up list. You know, you might need your friend Zeke's help to drag that big limb off their front walk."

Ty's eyes narrow. "How d'you know there's a limb on the walk at the Freidrichs' house?"

Shit! That just slipped out. "I, uh, happened to drive by there this morning when I was out."

"You said you just went to Brielle's store to drop off the check and had lunch in the park. The Friedrichs' house is way on the other side of town." Ty cocks his head. "You were checkin' up on us. You didn't think me and Donna could set up the sale right all by ourselves."

I'm caught in my lie. And what makes it worse is the look on Ty's face. He's not angry.

He's hurt.

Hurt that I didn't trust him. Hurt that I didn't think he was competent enough to manage without me.

Why did I have to be such a control freak and go over there? Was setting my mind at ease worth wounding Ty like this?

"I'm sorry, Ty. I shouldn't have gone over there. The house looks great. Everything was set up perfectly. I knew it would be."

"No." Ty points a long finger at me. "You were surprised. Otherwise, why would you go over there? You were expecting that we screwed up."

"No, I wasn't!" I massage my temples. "Look, I've been waiting for the right time to tell you this. But Sean and I are trying to get pregnant. If I have a baby, I'm going to have to turn the business over to you for a few months."

Ty's face softens. "A baby! That's great. You know we gotcha covered, Audge. Why you worried?"

"I know I shouldn't be. I know you're dedicated, and you understand the business totally. It's just...."

Ty starts to chuckle. "You can't let go. You like one o' them helicopter moms. Yesterday, I saw this lady on campus. She gave her son a ride to school, and then she jumped outta the car and chased after him shoutin' about what he needed to do to pass his Psych class."

I cover my head with my arms. "Oh, God—please tell me I'm not that bad."

"You *are* that bad." Ty gives me a hug. "But Imma do what that kid did to his mother." He reaches into his pocket. "Put in my headphones and pretend I don't know you."

Chapter 39

When I leave the office at six, a woman's voice calls out to me. "Audrey, can I have a word?"

I spin around, and in the dusk I can't see anyone on the deserted street. Then out of the shadows, I see a woman approaching me on the sidewalk.

Plump. A little unsteady. A scarf trailing crookedly from one shoulder.

She comes two steps closer. Jane Peterman.

What's she doing in Palmyrton? And on my street?

She looks at the discreet sign on my door. "Let's go into your office."

Let's not. "I'm in a rush to get home. I need to walk my dog."

She shakes her head. "They can always las-s-s longer than you thin'."

Is she drunk? I take a step forward to get under the streetlight. Jane follows me. Her eyes are bloodshot; her pupils big pools of black.

She's definitely on something. I think of the line-up of pill bottles in her kitchen and the rumors surrounding her departure from Quantum Consulting.

"I wanna talk to you 'bout a job. I need you to run a sale at my house. I'm going to sell it."

"Sell it? You just bought it."

Jane gives an exasperated grimace. I feel like one of her clients who refuses to see the wisdom of her guidance. "The kids will be starting college soon. We don't need all the space. Now's the time to move to the city."

"Manhattan?"

"Is there another city? Of course, Manhattan." Jane rakes her fingers through her hair. "I won't need so much furniture there. Sell it. Sell it all."

This seems impulsive, even for Jane. Her staccato delivery makes me uneasy. I'm not that eager for another job at the shore, especially one that involves selling dirty, stained furniture. I want to get away from her before she escalates into full-blown crazy.

"Sure, I'll call you next week to give you an estimate. I have to get going now." I turn and start striding toward my car. My hand closes around the keys in my pocket.

"Next week is too late." Jane runs after me and grabs my arm. Her grip is surprisingly strong. She nearly knocks me off my feet. "I need to sell fast." Her words come in breathless gasps. "I made a plan for us. I can still make this plan work. You have to believe in me."

A plan for *us*? Who's she talking about?

I really want to get away from this woman. I don't care if I'm rude—she's creeping me out.

I press the panic button on my car key fob. The Honda's lights flash, and the horn honks rhythmically. I use the distraction to yank my arm from Jane's grasp, and I sprint to my car.

Jane may be stronger than I am, but she's not faster. I'm in the driver's seat with the door locked as she pounds on the passenger side window.

I put the car in gear and peel away from the curb.

Chapter 40

"Help me go over this."

Sean has barely walked through the door when I wave him into a seat at the kitchen table. In front of me sits a yellow legal pad that I've filled with notes as I awaited my husband's arrival.

The strange encounter with Jane Peterman has scared me in a way that's out of proportion to what took place between us. I'm struggling to understand what just happened, and I need Sean's help to put my scattered impressions into perspective.

Jane grabbed my arm. She chased me to my car.

I'm fine. I'm here at home with my husband and my dog.

Why am I so unnerved? I've written down everything I know about Jane Peterman. Maybe a neutral third party can help me make sense of it.

"I'm just going to read off the facts."

"I'll supply the interpretation." Sean leans back in his chair and waits.

"Jane was forced out of her previous job because she developed an obsession with a female colleague. Now she considers herself Brielle's best friend," I begin.

"... but the feeling doesn't seem to be mutual."

I go to the next item on my list. "When Brielle bought a house in Sea Chapel, Jane followed."

"And it was more than just keeping up with the Joneses," Sean says.

"Jane reports back to Brielle on what happens at the house. And the houses are so close, you can hear conversations in the other house when you're out on the deck and the windows are open."

"...so Jane could've told Brielle about the first meeting the siblings had at the house, and what they argued about." Sean drums his fingers on the table. "Seems to me Croft must've known about that meeting before the sale. That's why he came to search the sofa cushions. He was looking for forensic evidence that Trevor was there that night."

"If Jane heard the meeting going on, Sophia could have too. Maybe that's what she told Croft about." I scratch my head. "Hmmm. But Croft didn't know about the siblings until I told him. I'm sure of that."

Sean rises to pace around the kitchen. He does his best thinking when he's on the move. "Regardless of what Sophia told Croft, Jane must have told Brielle about the first sibling meeting, and Brielle would have panicked. Her son had told all these other kids that Everett Gardner wasn't his biological father. And the kids were arguing about whether to go public about Gregory or keep it quiet."

"But why did that lead to *Trevor* getting killed? He wasn't the only one who wanted to meet Gregory."

Sean shrugs. "Maybe he was the most outspoken?"

I look in the corner at Ethel who is hunkered over her chew toy working on extracting a treat. Something about the way her ears flop over her face reminds me of...Fly. Fly said Trevor wanted Austin to use his skills to find Sophia's father. That he could make Austin give him what he wanted. And suddenly I know why my encounter with Jane chilled me to my core.

I was face-to-face with a murderer.

"Jane wanted to impress her friend by getting rid of the kid most likely to reveal Brielle's family secret. Trevor was the unstable one. The unpredictable one. Not to mention, he'd suddenly taken an interest in identifying Sophia's father, as well."

"*Impress* her friend by committing murder?" Sean objects. "Jane's not a kid in the Bronx auditioning for gang membership."

"Impress is the wrong word. Jane's work as a consultant is to come up with out-of-the-box solutions for her clients' business problems. Killing Trevor was her way of making herself invaluable to Brielle. And at the same time, preventing Trevor from meddling in Sophia's parentage."

I look at my notes again. "The kids say Trevor left the house that night and they never saw him again. I assumed they were lying. That one of them killed Trevor right there in Brielle's house. But maybe the kids are telling the truth. Trevor would have walked alone along the beach to get back to his grandparents' house. The other kids drove to Brielle's house."

"So someone followed him from Brielle's house and strangled him before he reached his grandparents' house."

My hands feel cold and clammy. My throat is dry. "Jane Peterman wears long, silk scarves. And she's probably a good thirty pounds heavier than Trevor was."

Sean nods. "...she came up behind him on the beach, threw the scarf around his neck, and pulled."

I shudder. "For seven long minutes."

"How'd she dump the body?" Sean challenges me.

"Jane has a small sailboat that she keeps docked at Elmo's. One of the guys at the bar told me she just hired him to refinish the deck. She could've brought it around to where she left the body, then headed out into the surf."

"But she didn't go out far enough. So the body washed up on Brielle's beach. Karma's a bitch."

My body feels limp, like my bones have dissolved. "Jane is a mother herself. How could she have killed a child? A kid who was her own daughter's good friend."

"She was desperate to keep Brielle's friendship. Maybe just as desperate to keep her daughter all to herself."

I scan my list of notes. The facts seem solid, and yet there are alternate explanations for some of them. "What if I share this with Detective Croft, and I'm wrong? This is all circumstantial."

"What if you are?" Sean says. "You've caused some inconvenience for a woman you don't like much anyway."

"Defending yourself from a murder accusation is more than an inconvenience."

Sean pushes my phone toward me. "Here's a concept Audrey: Let Croft do his job, and you go back to doing yours."

I dial.

THE NEXT TWO DAYS MOVE as slowly as beach traffic on Memorial Day Weekend.

Detective Croft listened to my theories with only a grunt or two as a response. When I asked if he'd keep me informed on new developments in

Trevor's murder investigation, he told me I could watch the news like everyone else.

But although the news is chock-a-block with violence and tragedy and outrage, there's nothing about an arrest in Trevor Finlayson's murder.

I don't even know if Jane's been questioned, and the only two people who would know—Sophia and Brielle—are off limits to me.

Then one night just as we're getting ready for bed, Sean's phone rings. He looks at the screen, his brow furrows, and he accepts the call.

"Uh-huh." Long silence. "Is that so?" Long silence. "Yeah, right. Well, thanks for calling. Glad we could help."

"What?" I demand.

"Jane Peterman is dead. She killed herself after Croft interrogated her for five hours and had to let her go."

My hand rises to my mouth. "Dear Lord, please don't tell me poor Sophia found the body."

"No, an early morning jogger on the beach saw her. She hung herself from her deck railing." Sean's eyes harden. "She used a long, chiffon scarf."

Chapter 41

J ane's suicide is as close to a confession as Detective Croft will get, and it
concludes the investigation into Trevor Finlayson's murder.

The last few days, the local news has been full of pictures of Trevor, Jane,
and the fabulous houses on Dune Vista Drive. Murder and suicide among
the rich and stylish is infinitely more newsworthy than the same crimes committed in a squalid tenement or a downtrodden trailer park.

I can't stop watching the coverage even though I know more about the
case than the talking-head reporters ever will.

I watch for a glimpse of Sophia, but I never see her mentioned. How
is she holding up? Who is helping her cope? The social workers and school
counselors who would be available for a younger, poorer student aren't there
for an 18-year-old prep school drop-out. Has her distant grandmother
stepped up to the plate? Has Brielle found some reserve of compassion for
the daughter of a friend who killed for her?

In the eyes of the law, Sophia is an adult, but in my mind's eye, she's a
devastated, grief-stricken kid who suddenly has to manage her own life. Has
having a crazy mother prepared her adequately for that?

I'm not sure if Sophia realizes the role I played in her mother's final days.
But I'm positive Jane knew who gave Detective Croft the information he
confronted her with.

And that knowledge weighs on me.

I don't regret helping the police find justice for Trevor and his family.
But I do feel terrible that my actions triggered a chain reaction that ended in
Sophia losing her mother in such a terrible way.

The fall estate sale season is in full swing, and days go by when my frantic
pace drives all thoughts of Sophia from my mind. Then I'll see a kid with
dyed hair or a vintage rock band T-shirt, and Sophia will pop into the part of
my brain reserved for worry.

She crowds right up to my anxiety over Sean's and my upcoming appointment with Dr. Stein, the fertility specialist. Two problems that no amount of worrying will resolve.

Then one day when I'm placing signs downtown advertising my upcoming local sale, killing the hours before our doctor's appointment, I look up and see Austin Gardner walking down the sidewalk toward me. He's reading something he holds in his hand.

Maybe he won't see me. Panicked, I look for something to hide behind. A rock, a car, a garbage can—I'm not picky.

But the sidewalk is wide open. Austin glances up and nods at me.

I offer a half-hearted salute in return and await my doom. Maybe he'll simply mutter a greeting and keep walking like a normal teenager. I busy myself jamming a second sign into the hard ground beneath a sidewalk tree.

"Hey, how's it going?" Austin stops to talk. Of course, he has better social skills than Fly.

"Fine." I straighten up. "And you?"

Austin's eyes scan my face. "I'm good. Really good." He hands me the thing in his hand that he'd been reading—a postcard. On one side, a picture of huge mountains. On the other, a message: *Nepal is fabulous. I hope you make it here someday. Congratulations on getting into Princeton, Gregory.*

Austin takes the card back from me and tosses it into a nearby trash can. "Nice of him to write, but I don't save mail. My father always says to handle everything only once. Make a decision about it and move on."

"Good words to live by."

"They are. My dad is a smart guy."

I watch him stride down the sidewalk, confident as ever.

LATER THAT AFTERNOON, Sean and I sit across the desk from Dr. Stein.

He peers at us through his owlish glasses, upbeat as ever. "So, the tests results are back. You have oligospermia—fewer than 15 million sperm per milliliter of semen."

Sean stares at him in confusion, but I've been doing internet research. I know what the doctor is telling us.

Dr. Stein pats his hands together. "Of course, that decreases the odds that one of your sperm will fertilize your partner's egg, resulting in pregnancy."

Understanding creeps across Sean's face like the shadow of the moon during an eclipse. "Wait. You mean it's me? I'm shootin' blanks?"

"Oh, not blanks—a total absence of sperm in the semen is known as azoospermia. You just have a sperm count that's on the low end of normal. You'll need to see a urologist to perform additional tests. Blood work to check your hormone levels, physical exam to look for abnormalities." He pushes a paper toward Sean. "Fill out this questionnaire and—"

"What if you can't fix it?" Sean demands.

"Far too early to jump to that conclusion. The urologist will determine the underlying cause so we can establish a course of treatment. Although it's not always clear..."

Sean leans toward the doctor. "But what if the treatments don't work?"

The doctor taps his pen on the desk. "There are alternatives. You can choose donor insemination." He pulls a brochure out of a bin on his desk and slides it across the desk to Sean. "Select an Irish donor with red hair and blue eyes. No one needs to know."

Sean's gaze drops to the brochure, which pictures a happy couple with a cute infant. It's the same brochure I picked up from the waiting room weeks ago. I shove it back at the doctor and stand up. "What about my test results?" I whisper.

Dr. Stein beams. "No problems whatsoever. You're in perfect reproductive health."

WE DRIVE HOME IN STUNNED silence. Somehow, I had never allowed for this possibility, so sure was I that my initial fears and doubts about having a child had somehow caused my ovaries to malfunction.

Gingerly, I reach across the car and stroke Sean's hand on the steering wheel. "We'll get through this. Dr. Stein will fix the problem."

Sean jerks his hand away. "This is why I couldn't get Patty pregnant. And then she got pregnant right away with her new husband. I should have known when you weren't getting pregnant either that it was me. My Dad...Brendan...Terry—they produced kids, no problem." He pounds the wheel. "Terry can't even support his son, yet—"

"Sean, stop torturing yourself. And don't compare yourself to your brothers. Now we know what the problem is, so we can work on it. That's the first step."

"If the doctor can't fix me, then we have to get donor sperm," Sean says.

"No!" The word flies out of me with surprising force. "I don't want some other man's baby. If we can't get pregnant together, then we'll adopt."

I notice Sean's shoulders relax. He takes his eyes off the road to shoot me a glance. "Really? Don't you, ya know, want to experience pregnancy and all that?"

"I want to build a family with you. I don't want to have a baby who's biologically mine, but not biologically yours. If we adopt, we'll be on equal footing. Sperm donation might be right for other couples, but it's not what I want for us."

Sean leans back in the driver's seat and takes the next turn without causing me to grab the armrest. "Don't tell my family, okay?"

I kiss his cheek. "I won't tell a soul."

Chapter 42

Thanksgiving ambushed us this year.

One minute I was supplying Deirdre's kids with unsold vintage clothing for their Halloween costumes, and the next I was helping Sean bake pumpkin pies to take to the annual Coughlin turkey day hoedown, this year hosted by Colleen and her husband.

Sean has had his first appointment with the urologist, but the test results haven't come back yet. We made a plan to deflect any and all questions on when we'll be starting a family.

Somehow, we got through the feast maintaining an attitude of gratitude.

After the main event on Thursday, the Coughlin men have settled into a protracted football trance, while the women have started Christmas shopping with a vengeance. Since neither of these pastimes appeals to me, I spend Black Friday at an obscure museum with Dad and Natalie.

Now I'm looking at two more days of enforced relaxation before I can return to the office. So when my phone chirps with a text message—*Wanna come to my house today? There's someone I want you to meet.*—I'm ready to say yes before even registering who sent the message.

Sophia.

I tried calling her after Jane's suicide, but of course, she didn't answer. I finally resorted to sending a condolence text, to which she simply replied, *thanks*.

What could she say to the woman whose evidence revealed her mother killed her best friend?

Now, weeks later, Sophia sends me this message Whom could she want me to meet?

My phone chirps again.

Please. I know it's short notice, but I really want you to come.

Her out-of-the-blue message is odd, but then, Sophia is an odd kid.

And I'm a congenitally curious adult.

So I accept the invitation.

WHEN I ARRIVE ON DUNE Vista Drive, I see a Realtor's sign in front of Number 43. I'm not surprised that Brielle and her husband want to sell a house that holds so many bad memories. Maybe the next owners will manage to find more happiness there.

Sophia has even greater reasons to flee from Sea Chapel, but the Peterman house looks the same as it always has. Maybe Sophia is too overwhelmed by grief and horror to contemplate a move. It can't be healthy for her to be holed up here all alone in the winter. My finger hesitates over the doorbell. What drama am I walking into?

Before I can ring, Sophia flings open the door.

Her face lights up with a big smile, and she spreads her arms wide. "Hi, Audrey!"

The hot pink dye has faded from her hair. Gone are the shapeless clothes—she looks quite nice in skinny jeans and a soft sweater. Without a mother to rebel against, what's the point of dressing ugly?

Sophia and I do a little dance, uncertain if we should hug or not. We settle on an awkward cheek bump and I follow her through the front hall.

"We're in the kitchen. Come on."

I realize I've never been in the front of this house. From what I can see as I walk behind Sophia, the living and dining rooms are very nice although not spectacular like Brielle's. The rugs bear the parallel stripes of a recent vacuuming, and there's no clutter anywhere. Whoever Sophia wants me to meet, she seems to have cleaned up for them.

When I reach the kitchen, I'm so surprised by how clean it is that I don't pay attention to who's in the room. The perpetual mountain of dishes in the sink has disappeared, and the sun shines through pristine windows.

Finally, I focus on the other guests. Two forty-ish men in jeans and sports shirts sit at the island nibbling on snacks and drinking wine. Paco and a big, goofy Labrador-mix lounge at their feet.

"Audrey, this is Dan Knowlton and his husband, Corey."

We shake hands, Corey pours me a glass of wine, and then there's an awkward silence. Why has Sophia brought me down here to meet two unremarkable gay men?

She stands between them, beaming.

And then I see it. Something in the curve of the upper lips, the straight line of the brows.

"Dan is my father." Sophia rests her hand on Dan's shoulder.

Whoa.

Dan reaches up and squeezes her hand. "Reconnected after eighteen long years apart."

"Congratulations," I say. "How did all this come about?"

"You tell her the story, Dan," Sophia says. She hops onto a stool and leans her elbows on the granite island, looking for all the world like a toddler asking for her favorite bedtime story to be retold for the umpteenth time.

Dan is happy to comply. "I met Jane in Manhattan when we were both in our twenties. I was an out-of-work actor—"

"That means waiter," Corey interrupts.

"—and I spent a lot of time at the dance clubs in those days." He gives Corey an apologetic look. "Jane had a responsible job, but she was a girl who liked to have a good time. Every single woman in New York needs at least one gay guy friend, and I was Jane's."

Dan refreshes his wine and delves into his story. "Jane's love life was a disaster and so was mine, so we spent a lot of time commiserating. One night when we were out celebrating her thirtieth birthday, she declared that all straight men were jerks, and she was never getting married. She raised her glass of champagne and asked me to be her baby daddy. I laughed it off because we'd both been drinking, but over the next few months, Jane kept bugging me about it. I had a million reasons not to agree, but Jane kept overcoming my objections. I refused to have sex with her, so she found a doctor willing to do the insemination. I was flat broke and couldn't support a child, so Jane produced a contract drawn up by a lawyer absolving me of all financial responsibility and giving Jane sole custody of the baby. Finally, I gave in and said yes." Dan pauses to make a neat pile of cracker crumbs on the counter. "I relied on Jane a lot in those days, both emotionally and financially, and I couldn't afford to make her angry at me.

"So Jane got pregnant, which put an end to our drinking and dancing. As her pregnancy continued, she got more and more caught up in the baby, and I was so immature that it made me jealous. By the time Sophia was born, Jane and I weren't on such good terms. I came to see her at the hospital, and I held my daughter, but—" Dan shakes his head. "The whole magical connection, love at first sight thing? I wasn't feelin' it."

Sophia pulls a long face, like this is the scary part of a story she knows will eventually have a happy ending. She can't know that's the part of parenthood that terrifies me, too.

"Was I an ugly baby?"

"You were a red, smushy lump like all babies." Dan pats her hand and continues. "Then Jane got a promotion at work and moved to New Jersey. And I met Corey and got my first break as a voice actor. Jane and I had an argument about something stupid that Christmas, and we stopped speaking to each other. Before you know it, ten years went by."

He smiles at his partner. "Over those ten years, I gradually—finally—grew up. I worked steadily. We bought an apartment, we adopted a dog, we built a life. And I kept thinking about Sophia. She was the only child I was ever going to have. Maybe someday, she'd give me grandchildren. I started stalking Jane on social media. I sent a friend request, but she ignored it. I sent an email, and she threatened to sue me. So I backed off. But I never stopped wanting to meet my daughter." He blinks his eyes to hold back the tears.

Sophia takes over the story. "All that time, Mom told me that my father was a broke loser who wanted nothing to do with me. She showed me the document that proved he'd given up his parental rights. She said we had each other and that's all we needed. I thought it was bad enough that my grandparents had rejected me. I didn't need my father to blow me off, too."

So Sophia really never had been looking for her father. She didn't want to risk rejection. It was Trevor's fixation that led him to pressure Austin to do the research.

This part of the story is obviously painful for Dan. "Corey told me to wait until Sophia was twenty-one and try to contact her directly then. So I kept watching from afar. And then last month, the news broke about Jane. I realized Sophia was an orphan, all alone." He takes a deep breath. "I screwed up my courage and wrote her a letter."

"It came on October 22—a personal letter from an address in New York City." Sophia's face lights up. "I remember every second of that day. I tore open that letter. My hands were shaking so bad when I realized my father wanted to meet me."

"And I hope you were glad to know I'm not a loser."

Something about that statement makes the two dogs stand up and wag their tails.

Sophia giggles. "Dan narrates audiobooks—and he's written two novels under a pen name. They're best-sellers!"

"Moderate sellers." Dan blushes. "I write as Lana Del Ray. They're romances."

"Isn't that awesome?" Sophia demands a response from me.

I smile. "It certainly is. Your dad's a novelist, and that's what you want to be."

Dan's expression turns serious. "I told her that's a hard path. She needs a Plan B."

He's only known his daughter a few weeks, and he's already dispensing fatherly wisdom. Maybe it's instinctive.

"You're successful," Sophia reminds him.

"I'm successful, but not famous. That's fine with me."

Sophia approaches Dan and puts her head on his shoulder. "I'm so lucky. This year was the best Thanksgiving ever."

"We're all lucky," Corey says.

The rest of the evening passes with friendly conversation. Dan asks me about my work until a nice lasagna and salad dinner whipped up by Corey and Sophia appears on the table. "I'm a lousy cook," Dan confides, "but a good housekeeper."

"By the way, Sophia, the house looks great," I say.

"Dan helped me hire a professional cleaning company to get it back to normal condition. But I've been doing the upkeep myself. Paco and I don't make much dirt. I start college at Bowdoin in August. Paco's going to live with Dan and Corey in the city, and we can all use this house as a vacation home." Sophia rattles on, excited by her plans.

Maybe over-excited, like a kid wound up on birthday cake and presents. I know beneath this façade of happiness there has to be some grief for her mother. Sophia is a sensitive kid; the pain is there.

But seeing Sophia so happy has certainly lifted a weight of guilt from my shoulders. Still, I wonder why she invited me here. As congenial as our dinner has been, I feel like there's something unsaid hanging in the air between us.

I decline dessert, help clear the table, and announce my intention to get on the road.

Dan and Corey offer farewell hugs, but Sophia follows me to the front door.

We linger in the foyer. I can see Sophia is struggling with something, but I don't attempt to pry it out of her.

I wait.

Finally, she stops studying the floor and lifts her eyes to meet mine. "I know," she whispers. "I know that the information you told the cops is what led to my mother's interrogation."

I nod. I won't deny it. Nor will I apologize.

"But something I told Detective Croft also made a difference. After the funeral, I told him that on the night he died, Trevor had been with a bunch of kids from BSS at Brielle's house."

"You heard them? You knew they were all siblings?"

Sophia shakes her head. "Heard voices, not what they were saying. I recognized Trevor's. My feelings were hurt that he was right next door hanging with them and wouldn't include me. I went up to my room, so I wouldn't have to listen to them all night."

"But your mother went outside so she could hear more. And she didn't like what she heard."

Sophia takes a long, shaky breath and speaks more confidently. "I'm glad the truth came out. Nothing can bring Trev back, but his family deserves to know how and why he died." Her hand grips the doorknob until her knuckles turn white. "I'll never be able to forgive my mother for what she did. I would've met Dan when I was twenty-one anyway. But she didn't know that. She wanted to keep me all to herself. Even though half the time, it seemed like I was just a bother to her."

She kicks at the fringe of the foyer rug. "The terrible thing is, when the police told me what she'd done, I wasn't even surprised. When my mom ran into a problem, she tackled it full speed."

Like her lawsuit against her employer. Like her deal to get Sophia out of trouble at BSS.

Sophia's eyes are glassy with tears, but she doesn't allow them to flow. "My mother was messed up. Trevor was messed up. I'm not going to be like them. I *won't* be like them."

Sophia's voice drops to a whisper. "But I loved them. I loved them both."

———◈———

I HOPE YOU ENJOYED *Treasure Built of Sand*. Please post a review on Amazon or Goodreads to help other readers find this book. I appreciate your support! If you'd like to receive periodic updates on my new releases, sales, and special events, please join my mailing list: http://swhubbard.net/contact.

Read all the Palmyrton Estate Sale Mysteries, available in paperback, Kindle, and audiobook:

Another Man's Treasure
Treasure of Darkness
This Bitter Treasure
Treasure Borrowed and Blue
Treasure in Exile
Treasure Built of Sand

———— ◆ ————

If you've read all the Palmyrton Estate Sale mysteries, it's time to try the Frank Bennett Adirondack Mountain mystery series:

The Lure
Blood Knot
Dead Drift
False Cast
Tailspinner
Frank Bennett Boxed Set (Books 1-3)

About the Author

S.W. Hubbard writes the kinds of mysteries she loves to read: twisty, believable, full of complex characters, and highlighted with sly humor. She is the author of the Palmyrton Estate Sale Mystery Series and the Frank Bennett Adirondack Mountain Mystery Series. Her short stories have also appeared in *Alfred Hitchcock's Mystery Magazine* and the anthologies *Crimes by Moonlight, Adirondack Mysteries,* and *The Mystery Box.* She lives in Morristown, NJ, where she teaches creative writing to enthusiastic teens and adults, and expository writing to reluctant college freshmen. Visit her at http://www.swhubbard.net.

Made in the USA
Las Vegas, NV
07 November 2024

11237605R00122